Ava

By

Lydia Baker

AVA
ISBN: 978-1-913781-26-2
Published by CAAB Publishing Ltd (Reg no 12484492)

C . A . A . B
PUBLISHING

Serenity House, Foxbridge drive, Chichester, UK
www.caabpublishing.co.uk

First Published 2022
1 3 5 7 9 10 8 6 4 2
Printed in the UK
British Library Cataloguing in Publication data available

I would love to dedicate this book to the wonderful people who helped to make this dream a reality. Thank you to my parents for encouraging me from the moment I discovered a love of reading and writing. Thank you to my wonderful husband who puts up with the rollercoaster that is trying to get your novel out there and believed in me all the way through. Thank you to Shirley McLellan without whose help this book could not have got to the point it is now - you were so patient! And lastly, thank you to C.A.A.B Publishing for investing in me and my book.

Chapter 1

I am tough; tough like worn boots on frozen ground, at least that's what I tell myself. Yet the truth is, it's bleak out there, out in the world we live in now, but you wouldn't know it to look at us – there are still men and women walking the streets, shopping, chatting, going to work. Sky-high office blocks full of people in smart suits, carrying briefcases and packed lunches in paper bags, still dominate the business sector – MTech employees, each and every one of them. Shops and cafes still tote their wares; the glass panel doors still ting with the entry of each customer, and the clean-swept roads still buzz with the almost soundless hum of electric cars and the whoosh of buses' brakes and automatic doors. Everyone has something to do and somewhere to be.

We try to be normal, but there are strangers amongst us now: an army of metal soldiers that police our streets and threaten our doorways. They watch us. They are always watching us. You can't miss the large, red MTech logos that adorn every building and every product. It's stamped across anything consumable, anything profitable, anything controllable. They own it all. They own the Mechs, too.

Yet if you step out of the bustling hive of the city, into the quiet, abandoned streets that stretch out towards the edge of this little world of mine, then the desolation and loneliness is earth-shattering. People live here, too, though fewer nowadays. Although we try to ignore the wretchedness of the world we now live in, the lies and the fear that stalk us all, the deserted schools and playgrounds resound with an echo of all we have lost: louder than we can bear to acknowledge. The streets of forlorn houses and broken-down cars, covered in dust, never to reach their destination, always make me shudder. It's a different world out here, outside the inner circle. Yet even here, we are still watched. Still counted. Still subjugated. Still controlled by MTech.

But there is one thing that draws me out. I feel it in every fibre of my body: the outside. If you go far enough, you can hear the hum of the Barrier, feel the electricity in the air. It makes the hairs on the back of my neck stand on end and it cries to me, pulling at my chest. It whispers of a world now forgotten, and I want to know what's left of it. I want to find out if there's anyone out there waiting for me; whether humanity survived the strange things we witnessed before we were locked away from the rest of the world. But no one else cares; no one dares to leave the protective, smothering arms of MTech or stray from the tiny sliver of life that we pretend is normal. I don't really know any different. I just know that I don't want to live like this, not anymore. I've had enough of the lies. I want to be free again. It's been so long since I felt the wind or tasted real rain. So here I am. This is me.

■ ■

Head tilted towards the sun, I close my eyes, trying to remember what it felt like. The real sun, not this lie: replicated, bounced from generators to heat panels, lacking the golden heat of real sun rays. From its clockwork rising to its punctual setting, none of this manufactured sun was real, not anymore. As I stood there, I realised I couldn't remember the blush of a true sunset or the hazy pink of a sunrise, even if I screwed my eyes tight and delved deep into my memories. I'd spent too many years in this artificial greenhouse where we try to cultivate normality.

"Hey," said a voice.

I opened my eyes.

"What are you doing?"

I closed them again. Bloody Cain always knew how to ruin a moment.

"Fourteen years," I told him.

"What?" Cain spat.

He tutted at me under his breath. It was nothing new.

"Since I felt the sun on my face," I said.

It had been fourteen years since the strange, skyward crafts had appeared and the bombs had come, ripping my world apart – since the Barrier appeared, imprisoning us and separating us from whatever was left of the rest of the world.

Even though my eyes were shut, I could picture Cain's face, half his hair scraped back into a 'man bun', the rest shaved close and badly dyed blond. His eyes were narrow, and his face fell in a way that made him look permanently unimpressed. Sulky and exasperated, I could almost hear his eyes rolling back as he tolerated it all. I wondered how much longer he would put up with me. A familiar sinking feeling in my stomach reminded me he was all I had.

He lowered his voice so only I could hear: "Ava!"

I opened my eyes wide. He had my attention. That was not my name, not anymore.

"Shut up!" I hissed through clenched teeth. "What're you playing at?"

"I just wanted you to move, the people behind us are getting pissy."

Glancing over his shoulder, I could see an older couple who were scowling at us and speaking just loudly enough for us to hear them. Moving up in the queue, a step closer to the MTech check-in station, I turned to face Cain again.

"You know this makes me twitchy," I reminded him, fiddling with the cuff of my hoodie.

"Come on, they haven't caught you yet," he said.

"*Us.* They haven't caught *us* yet," I corrected him.

"If they catch you, you won't see me for dust, you're on your own," he laughed.

He gave me a shove forward and I forced a laugh, too. Despite our chafing sibling relationship, I was glad to have someone in this cage who knew me; someone who *really* knew me. The people ahead of me squeezed through the turnstiles to face a row of gleaming silver machines with small, flat screens and scanners – not dissimilar to how I remembered cash machines looking. The open-fronted, pale, stone Credit Assignment Building stood stocky and square in the middle of our estate. Surrounded by concrete-built flats and overcrowded houses with peeling, painted doors, and dusty windows, it was flashy and new, standing out like a sore on pockmarked skin. Unmissable against the stone, I could see the classic, red MTech logo printed on every scanner.

The row of people ahead of me took their turn to be logged, the Mechs' lifeless mechanical eyes cruising over them as they stepped up to the scanners. I smelt fear; it leached out of my own skin, soaking into my clothes and shaking my bones.

There was a shout from behind me, catching the nearest Mech's attention. My stomach lurched as its glance swept over me, but it went beyond, falling on a young woman with fair hair and desperate eyes. She wielded a gun wildly around her head, shouting profanities at the robots before us. I dropped to the ground, eyes down, head covered, just like everyone else. Something pushed past me, and I swallowed hard as I listened to her cries. I knew her frustration: it gripped me like a tight fist around my heart. A shot rang out, loud over the bated breath of those around me. I screwed my eyes shut. As angry as I was, I didn't want to see. I needed to be ignored.

"Just what we need," I heard Cain murmur beside me.

The weight of him next to me allowed me to breathe, his skin surprisingly cool against mine. The ting of a second bullet ricocheting off metal sang through the heavy atmosphere as the crowd trembled on the ground together. Then the click of a Mech's rifle sounded, and the girl's cries fell silent. Cain's hand rested on mine, cold and hard, unlike my sweaty palms.

"Get up!" he said, yanking on my arm. "It's over."

Getting to my feet, I brushed the dirt off my jeans, and shook my arm free.

"I know!"

I didn't look back, no one did. We ignored the blood pooling in the street, turning a blind eye to the Mechs that dragged away her body. The buzz of the Mechs' in-built comms signalled more machines to come and replace the ones that had left, and the credit assignment resumed. I fixed my eyes on the scanners once more, only to find that the pissy couple from earlier were scrambling at one of the terminals. I pushed closer to Cain as the wail of a siren filled the air and the scanners flashed red. Two of the Mechs closed in as the man cowered. He shouted something at the metal monsters, pushing his wife out of the way. She stumbled backwards as he was dragged away;

his heart-wrenching sobs filling the air. The woman stood motionless, her eyes wide and staring, forgotten in the buzz of activity. A Mech stepped forward and ushered her out of the open-fronted building and through a second turnstile back onto the street. There was a moment of heavy silence.

"Wow, two in one morning," murmured Cain as one of the Mechs pressed the buzzer and the turnstiles moved again.

Normality resumed as I shuffled a little closer to the dreaded scanners. My pulse started to race and I let my eyes wander over to the disappearing figure of the abandoned woman instead of the rifles the Mechs carried or the back-up pulse gun I knew was built into every Mech arm. They were unpredictable and unfeeling. Machines show no mercy.

The Mechs were the government's task force created by MTech. They appeared like a plague of cockroaches, emerging from the ashes the moment the Barrier went up: metal soldiers which wandered the streets and infiltrated every aspect of our regimented lives. They were supposed to keep us safe, but they kept us beaten down and afraid. They were stationed everywhere, watching us, checking how much we ate, who we spoke to and where we went – MTech's response to the unrest they knew would ensue after the Barrier appeared; unrest like we had all just witnessed. My mind wandered back to that morning fourteen years ago; to the smell of explosives and ash, the evocative scent of sandal wood - of Dad. Life changed in an instant for so many, yet the Mechs appeared so suddenly that I can only imagine MTech knew that the bombs were coming; the Barrier was no spur-of-the-moment contraption. The programming and creation of such a vast forcefield, designed to separate my world from the outside, must have taken more than a matter of days to be birthed.

The machines stood unflinching and silent despite everything that had just happened, a head taller than us men and women; they made my chest tighten and my eyes drop to the ground every time I saw them. There must have been a new batch of Mechs released recently, upgraded again. These machines looked more like us, moved like us, sounded like us – except for the eyes. They never seemed to be able to get the eyes right; they were blank and lifeless. Dressed in matching grey uniforms, all with the same androgynous human face, their life-likeness was supposed to reassure people. I crossed the street to avoid them; pulled my hood up, kept my eyes down, staring at my phone until they passed. I had to be unnoticeable.

The thought of seeing my face pop up on the little screen on their chests made my stomach clench. If I saw myself there, in the position of guilt, then one of the infamous 'lockdowns' would follow soon. When that happened, no one was free to walk the streets except the Mechs. No doors opened and the microchips in our wrists stopped working. Everyone went to ground and held their breath until whoever the Mechs were after was caught and 'dealt with'.

Another buzz and I moved up a place in the line. My feet shifted as if on hot coals.

"Come on, Dad's tech hasn't failed you yet. No one's noticed you've got a pair of tits instead of balls," Cain grinned.

That was Cain, always vulgar. I scowled, fixing my eyes on the disappearing queue in front of us. Only ten people ahead of us now. Subconsciously, I rubbed the back of my neck and felt the hard lump of the implant that hid my gender. What had once been a painful reminder of the girl I had lost was barely noticeable anymore. Casually, Cain knocked my hand away, urging me forward. The hairs on my skin stood on end and my body went cold; I swallowed hard. This was the only thing that fazed me now: the idea of being caught. There was a buzz, and the next five people entered the turnstiles. Approaching the machines, they placed their wrists under the scanners, which read the microchip buried under their skin. The screens flashed up green with their details before they filed towards the exit and back onto the street.

Moving to the front of the queue, I waited by the turnstile next to Cain. The buzzer sounded abhorrently loud in my ears as the turnstile clunked round, letting me push my way through. One way in, one way out – everyone was accounted for. Gritting my teeth, I approached the scanner, placed my wrist under it, and waited. The Mech's eyes burnt into my skull, as I forced myself to look straight ahead at the screen.

"Come on," I murmured, willing the screen to turn green. But it still displayed the red MTech logo. Cain's scanner had already logged him, and he was making his way towards the exit. He looked over his shoulder at me and shrugged a little. I followed him desperately with my eyes.

"Come on!"

Glancing back at my screen, I expected to see red, flashing and blaring at me. I had been caught; it was my turn to be dragged away – a scenario I had envisioned too many times but was yet to come to fruition. Instead, the usual info flashed up: Alec Scott. Male. 23. Status: green. Credits: 200. Then my screen turned blank, and I was ushered down the row of scanners to the exit. I felt a rush of relief and let out the breath I had been holding. I was safe for one more month.

I pushed my way through the second turnstile, hurrying after Cain. As I caught sight of him, I felt my shoulder catch something hard and unmoving: the shoulder of the woman whose husband had been taken by the Mechs. I spun around to face her. She was still motionless, eyes wide in horror – a look I had seen too many times.

Pausing, I opened my mouth to say something, to urge her on, maybe lead her away. I hesitated. My hand twitched at my side.

"Come on," I murmured.

One of the Mechs clocked us – mechanical eyes evaluating us, calculating our next movements. I couldn't risk them scanning me, not after their upgrade; not until I had made it home to adjust my implant. Stepping back, I knew I had to put myself first. I didn't know her; how could I risk my safety for her?

A small cry escaped her lips and she turned away from the scene, her eyes meeting mine for a moment. Turning around, I hurried to distance myself from her, even though I could feel her eyes searching for mine again, trying to connect.

Spotting Cain lurking in the shadows of a large bin, dark eyes narrowed at me, I made a beeline for him, walking as quickly as I dared, trying not to draw attention to myself. I sidled in next to him, avoiding meeting his gaze. Behind me there was the sound of a body hitting the ground as the woman crumpled to the floor, a messy heap of tears and sobs. Fixing my eyes down, I fought the urge to look over my shoulder, my feet hesitating for a moment, before Cain yanked me closer to him and into the darkness.

"What were you thinking?" he growled.

"Get off, Cain," I told him, twisting in his grip.

He gripped my arm tighter, refusing to let go.

"Are you trying to get caught?" he hissed, his face uncomfortably close to mine.

"No, but I…"

He cut me off, with his hand centimetres from my face. I turned away and out of the corner of my eye I could see people starting to stare at the woman as they passed by. No-one stopped.

"You know you should have just left her. Remember what Dad said, don't stop for anyone. You're too bloody soft, Alec."

At least he was calling me Alec again.

"There had to be a reason they were trying to trick the scanner. That young woman died trying to make a distraction."

Cain shrugged, letting go of me at last and I rubbed my arm.

"And look where that got her."

"There might be a child."

"Don't start this again! Just when I thought you were developing a shell, becoming a real man." His eyes crawled over my body, "No one has kids anymore, don't be stupid. Come on, people are looking!"

With that deafening statement, Cain turned and walked away. I glanced back over my shoulder at the woman who was still cradling her head in her hands, knees pulled up to her chest. There had to be a reason that she

10

was trying to get more than her share of credits, but I was too afraid to ask and too scared of the answer.

Quickly, I closed the gap Cain had put between us, glancing once more at the woman before we rounded the corner. I opened my mouth to speak, ready to fight back, but Cain was in my face again as soon as we were out of sight. There was barely a moment to breathe before he was pushing me hard against the wall, planting his hands either side of my head. The brick was hot from the sun and rough against my back. Taking a deep breath, I prepared myself for his lecture.

"Be more careful, sister," he growled.
His breath was hot and slightly sour. I tried to push him off, but he refused to move, surprisingly solid and strong for his thin frame.

"Do you want to end up like the rest of them?" he pinned me back with his stare.
I looked away. This was just his way of showing he cared, of protecting me and keeping me in check. He was the only person I let speak to me like this.

"You're acting too much like a woman," he continued.

"What, by caring?"
I clenched my hands into fists at my sides. Using my real gender as a weakness, that was a low blow, even for him. Biting my tongue, I avoided eye contact. Better to say nothing more than say something I'd regret later.

"If they find you, they will take you away. You want that?" he asked me, even though he already knew the answer – he helped me hide every day.

I'd seen it, we all had. Women dragged off kicking and screaming. It was brutal and although I had no desire to bring a child into the world, I also didn't want that

11

choice taken away from me. Taking a woman's right to be a mother – there was no humanity in that.

"I understand…all right! Let's just go home," I said, sliding out from between his hands.

Cain looked like he wanted to say something else but instead he turned and fell into step next to me. We walked in silence, following the familiar rat-run of grey streets lined with characterless grey tower blocks, filled with countless blanched faces. I tried not to make eye contact with anyone. The hours after everyone checked in for their credits were always tense. Would your partner come home again? Would you hear the familiar click of the front door as they scanned their way in? Or would you be left alone, wondering where the Mechs had dragged them off to? I had known too many people who hadn't come back. At least once a month a face disappeared from the masses, never to be seen again. I prayed every day that it wouldn't be mine, conscious of the fact that it was only Dad's tech which was still keeping me safe, for now.

As we passed one of the few green spaces in the city, I tried to remember what it had been like before the landscape was filled with buildings and immaculately swept streets. I had a vague recollection that there may have been a play park; the smell of hot rubber and the creak of an un-oiled swing drifted momentarily through my mind before it was snatched away by the heavy, clunking footsteps of a patrolling Mech.

Head down, I walked close to Cain, the familiar thrum of longing to be as far away from the city as I could, solidified in my mind. Life was hard beyond the patrolled roads, but it still called to me; it was one step closer to the Outside. Beyond the city streets the trees were allowed to grow high, and the grass long and wild, but people had abandoned the beauty of nature for MTech's lies and false security. With a growing need to create more farmland, MTech had flattened their houses and given them tiny flats in exchange. People moved, expecting to swap their homes for a full stomach but I've yet to feel full. Instead, they used the land to grow genetically modified crops that produced twice as much as they were supposed to, sucking the earth dry until it was barren and unyielding.

I remembered, as a child, sitting at the window of our flat with Dad, watching as people flooded into the city, emptying out of cars and buses, with bags and belongings on their backs. I can still hear the hammering and grinding of noisy construction work, with its crude builders and the smell of concrete and cement. A lack of living space in the city meant that the buildings had become increasingly taller and more crammed – until the government brought in the Resource Management Programme. It was only two years after the bombs came and the Barrier appeared it started. It was a quiet way of getting rid of those who were no longer adding to the productivity of the city; a way to lure people into a false sense of security, feeding them with one hand and slaughtering their families with the other.

Rounding the corner of the street, we passed a large building, once a nursing home, now repurposed as a Mech upgrade centre.

All those years ago, when the nursing home was still full, I'd often wander past, smiling and waving at the men and women who sat out in the small front garden feeling the false sun on their creased, paper-thin skin. Under the Resource Management Programme, the elderly were the first to go. A lethal strain of influenza swept through the nursing homes, leaving the carers rattling around the empty corridors and twiddling their thumbs.

There was very little outcry, very little anger at the sudden loss of our elderly population. People could see how they were a drain on our limited resources; a group who provided little or no physical contribution to society. I remembered stopping outside that very nursing home and crying at the history we had lost, the memories of who we were, and where we had come from, the generation that knew what life was like before the Barrier, before the bombs. The child I was then had cried at the thought of never seeing my grandparents again, with their wide smiles and open arms.

Then they started on the women and girls, inviting them to store eggs until such time as the hostile world outside the Barrier became safe again and we could reproduce to our hearts' content: bouncing, screaming, puking bundles of joy everywhere. At first, I think some women felt liberated, free from the trappings of unwanted pregnancy, secure in the knowledge that their motherhood was cryogenically frozen. It was all waiting for them, waiting for when they were ready. No one expected to be trapped inside the Barrier for this long.

Then there were those who wanted nothing but to feel their child growing and churning inside of themselves, to hold them in their arms; those were the women who wept silently into their pillows in the depths of the night while their husbands pretended to sleep, unsure how to comfort their wives anymore, knowing they never truly could. Others danced the night away until the morning came, cold, stark and brutal, showing each of us in our true colours: faces tear-stained and make-up running. The feeling of freedom never lasted because that was just the thing we had lost: our freedom – our right to choose motherhood, or not.

14

I decided to hide, along with so many other women. Dad saw it coming before I did. He envisioned the world I would grow up in and made sure he took precautions. The day the chips in our wrists were fitted, he took me to see a man he called a 'friend', with dark skin and broad shoulders. I remembered staring at the tattoos that crept out of his t-shirt sleeves and snaked down his arms. There was a lot of money and a lot of agitated glances in my direction. To me, it seemed we had left with nothing, but Dad knew better. He knew that the tiny chip he had given everything for would save me. He took the tech he was working on and fashioned it for me, teaching me as he went, so I could take care of it myself. A small implant in the back of my neck changed who I was, and who I was to become. From that day on, I became male; I became 'Alec'.

They promised us that the Barrier was temporary, a special measure for our own protection. I haven't seen a baby in years. Dad's foresight had been correct. It wasn't long before sterilisation became law and MTech forced the halting of the human species. There was an outcry but it was too little, too late, and all too quiet. I would watch as women hid their daughters, hear them screaming as they were dragged away, and pray they wouldn't find me. Hair cut short, head down, trembling in some small dark hiding place, pretending to be a boy to keep my ovaries intact – the irony.

As a consolation prize, MTech promised us a generation of perfect children, created from the eggs they had stolen from each woman before she had had her heart torn out by grief. But it was a consolation too small for a people whose future had been ripped from them. It was a future that was government property: a future detached from its past. There would be a generation who would never know their mothers and fathers. Only now do I see how fear can force you to do things you never thought you would.

There wasn't enough food in here for everyone, and no way of knowing what was left outside the Barrier, so MTech reacted. I still think of the empty playgrounds and the silent schools that were torn down once the last child left.

I had to get out. I couldn't live in this place anymore – where human life was so easily disposed of, when it should be held onto at all costs. I couldn't stay in a place where we were dying out and no one seemed willing to do anything about it. Anger boiled inside me as I walked next to Cain. I always wondered if there were women who had avoided sterilisation – created life and hidden it away. The cry of a baby was a sound I struggled to recall, but maybe that woman still knew it: heard it in the depths of the night, eyes half-closed with sleep? Maybe she had links with the outside.

My step faltered - the outside. The very thought of it consumed me. I longed for it, yearned for it. I didn't know what was left of it, but I wanted to see for myself. We were taught to fear the unknown, to be cautious of things unseen and not to question what we didn't understand. MTech wanted us to be meek and subdued: we would just survive until we were told it's safe to live again. But I wasn't afraid. Despite the lies that MTech fed us about the dangers of the outside, I still wanted out.

Cain had stopped and was waiting impatiently. The light was beginning to fade, and I could hardly see his face as the sun set behind him. As I jogged to catch up with him, he turned and carried on walking, yet I hesitated, stopping a couple of paces behind him. I didn't want him to see my face, to enjoy the anger he had fired up in me. He was always annoyingly good at reading me. If only he knew or cared enough to ask. It was all a lie – my very existence – and I was sick of the deception. I was getting out of the Barrier, even if it killed me. Cain had no idea about the people I spoke to, the things we planned or what we were about to do.

Reaching the front of our building, Cain placed his wrist under the scanner built into the wall. There was the usual bleep and his stats appeared on the screen. The door opened with a click. He entered as I took his place at the scanner before following him in. The smell of damp and dirt greeted me and my eyes wandered over to the lift. It had been broken all week, but no one dared call MTech. They would rather walk the twenty flights of stairs than invite the Mechs into the building. Casually pushing the call button as we passed, I lingered for a moment, hoping to see the little blue light flashing, but there was nothing: no light, no movement.

"I could fix that," I said half to myself, half to Cain.

"Don't," he said.

"But…"

"I said, don't! You'll draw attention to yourself," he repeated, without turning around.

There was no point arguing with Cain; yet as stubborn as he was, I was worse. He was just looking out for me, like Dad had asked him to. We looked out for each other.

I ran my hand along the rail as we climbed step after step after step of linoleum-covered stairs. The noises of life drifted out from behind the closed doors of neighbours we hardly ever saw and never spoke to. Life in the crowded building was lonely.

Flat 625 was home: a narrow, grey door registered to Neil Scott, which was now home to Cain and Alec Scott, his 'sons'. One adopted, one biological. Except that now I felt like the adopted son, instead of Cain. It was as if Ava had never existed. Cain scanned open the door and we went inside. I half expected to see Dad there, half-dressed and asleep on the sofa, the smell of booze tainting the air. But the sofa was empty. A picture of the five of us stood on the end table. It was the first thing my eyes were drawn to every time I entered this morbid place: a little splash of colour in the bleakness.

In the days before the Barrier, MTech had gathered all the best minds in the country to the capital, luring them with the promise of awards, grants and conferences. Dad was invited, being ex-military and one of the top minds in his field of Defence Technology. Whenever I asked him what he was working on, he always gave me some vague answer. It was confidential. I had always thought it mysterious and exciting. Dad was my hero. I used to sit on the side of his bed, feet dangling over the side, watching him pack his uniform neatly into a small suitcase. He had seemed so together, so confident of what he was doing. I still wonder if he knew what was going to happen, and then I check myself; had he known, he wouldn't have left the others behind. He would never have left.

That night, Dad had come down with a stomach bug and planned not to take the long train ride into the city. Yet, spurred on by the persistent sulking and whining of his nine-year-old daughter, who was promised a day in the city, he mustered the strength to leave the toilet pan and venture out with Cain and me in tow. Had it not been for my selfishness, then we would all have been together *that* day. We may have been dead but at least we would have been together. The guilt, like a physical pain, made my heart and my very soul restless – knowing the pain I had caused Dad. After that day, with every poison-filled whiskey bottle, he sunk deeper into the darkness, drifted further away from me, lost in dreams of Mum and Anna. I could never reach him, and he didn't want to be found. Dad died of a broken heart and I'm sure I caused it. I didn't send those missiles rocketing into the sky, didn't give the order to destroy millions of lives but I caused their separation. Mum and Anna. Dad, Cain, and me.

"Hey!"

Tearing my eyes away from the picture, I glanced over to where Cain stood, looking at me as if I were an idiot.

"Shut the door!" he barked.

I did as I was told. The scanner screen showed both our names. Log in, log out: they always knew where you were, what you were doing, what you bought, what you ate, who you spent time with. I wouldn't be surprised if they logged every time you flushed the toilet. It was all part of the Resource Management Programme. The Barrier, the thing that was supposed to protect us, was slowly killing us – or MTech would. I played along. The easiest way not to attract attention was to be average, uneventful and boring.

"What's for dinner?" I asked.

Cain shrugged and headed for the kitchen. As I listened to him rummaging through the cupboards, I kicked off my shoes and threw them back at the door. It was credit day, the day everyone had their allotted credits topped up; a day of relief for most, panic for others. I knew what the answer would be. Cain reappeared as I flopped down on the sofa.

"Nothing."

I feigned surprise, "Oh. Pizza then?"

"Sure. You call, I have something I have to do," he muttered, disappearing into the bedroom, phone in hand.

Once a month we treated ourselves to a pizza. The dough was always stretched thinner than I remember it being as a child, the toppings were sparse, and the tomato sauce was bland, yet we still ordered it. Sometimes it meant we didn't eat for the last couple of days of the month, but it was worth it. I wasn't sure how the place stayed open, yet somehow it managed to keep going. Maybe MTech subsidised it in an attempt to make this prison seem normal?

Cain's muffled voice permeated the papery walls as I sat up and swung my legs round, planting my feet back on the thinly carpeted floor. I flicked through the newspapers and books on the coffee table until I found Reggie's Pizza Place. A small boy wielding a steaming hot pizza box grinned up at me. *Lucky kid, he never had to grow up.* Reaching into my pocket, I pulled out my phone and tapped in the number. I listened to the line click through all MTech's check points before ringing at the other end. I'd order Cain his usual, ham and mushroom. Fake ham: it was a poor substitute for the real thing. Honestly, I wasn't sure if I could remember the taste of real meat – the salty crispness of grilled bacon side by side with plump sausages and runny eggs; it was the food of kings. I'd be fat if we weren't rationed.

"Hello, Reggie's!"

The voice at the other end of the phone startled me out of my meat-filled daydream.

"Hi, 625 Foxglove flats," I told the voice.

"Hey, Alec, your usual?"

"Please, Reggie. Thanks."

"I'll send Lucy."

There was a click as Reggie replaced the handset and I chucked the phone onto the sofa next to me. Cain's door was shut and the room behind it quiet, so I swung my legs back onto the sofa and lay down with my hands behind my head; I could feel the springs through the old, sagging cushions. Dad hadn't replaced the sofa when he was alive and we certainly didn't have the money to do it now; plus, I didn't really want to – it felt like a part of Dad, of our history. It was the place where he spent more and more of his time until he had become a part of the furniture itself, melting into the upholstery, increasingly thin and bleached. Until he was gone. I closed my eyes and let my mind wander to the usual places: to Mum, to Dad, to Anna, our old house with its red brick walls and large back garden, and to our silly dog Zumba who followed Anna everywhere – the only one who could tell Anna and I apart.

Chapter 2

Anna. My other half, my womb wrestler, my ten-minute older, won't-let-me-forget-it twin sister: non-identical but almost. The gentle, quiet voice to my loud stubborn one. Anna. I missed her. Anna's face melted into Dad's as I stared. His eyes filled with horror as he pulled me close to his chest, the smell of his aftershave familiar and reassuring.

"Dad!" But he wouldn't answer. "Dad!"

His eyes were fixed on the middle distance. Turning away from his warmth, I looked around. People were gazing up at the sky, silent cries on their lips. I followed their upturned faces to see missiles crossing the sky, leaving trails in the clouds like aeroplanes. There was something else out there, something I didn't recognise. It was the multitude of strange shapes, vast and dark, that scared me more than the missiles. Head still up-turned, earth-shattering explosions shook the ground, breaking the stillness. I covered my ears instinctively, but it was too little, too late. It was like being underwater; all the sound, all the devastation had been sucked from the air. The chaos appeared as if behind glass, close yet distant, disconnected but vivid. More missiles, more explosions of searing-hot fire and ash. Then the screaming started. If it wasn't inside your own head, screeching through the synapses, then it was outside trying to get in.

Then came the darkness. It was more terrifying than the reality: an oppressive unknowing, trembling in the oblivion. The sounds of explosions, of death, were the only constants in the darkness, that and the smell of Dad, his warmth against my cheeks. Tears stung my eyes, running hot down my cheeks. As I reached up to wipe them away,

I realised Dad was gone. My pulse increased and I bit my lip, panic rising in my chest.

"Alec!"

But I'm Ava.

"Alec, man, wake up! You're crying!"

I wrenched open my eyes, to see Cain leering over me. *Damn.* I swallowed hard, pushing the panic back down, hiding again.

"Pizza's here."

Hastily wiping my eyes, I sat up, and glanced quickly over to the door. It was shut.

"Yeah, you missed, Lucy," he said, pushing my legs off the sofa and putting the pizzas down on the coffee table, "she was disappointed to see you snoring your head off."

"Shut up, Cain," I said, opening the top box.

Cain peered over my shoulder. It was his pizza. He grabbed the box from my hands and began tucking in, his feet up on the table. I opened my box to find my usual veggie pizza with extra jalapenos – except it was void of jalapenos, all except a small one in the middle. It looked like a navel. Cain glanced over at my food, swallowing his mouthful.

"Oh, yeah…she said something about them being short of jalapenos, but they had a delivery coming later if you wanted more. What a stupid thing to say. Why on earth would you want jalapenos later?" He shrugged.

Stupid Cain. It was a message; a message just meant for me.

"Bet she doesn't even realise you're not a guy. Man, she'll be disappointed," Cain laughed around a mouthful of pizza.

"It's not like that," I said.

"You might not think that, but I'm not so sure. You're not a bad-looking bloke."

I scowled at him. He was enjoying himself.

"You're better looking now than you ever were as a woman," he said, giving me a nudge.

He had gone too far. Closing the pizza box, I stood up. The heat of the contents warmed the cardboard, grease soaking onto my hand.

"Blow me, Cain!" I shouted.

I turned and walked away quickly; my eyes fixed on my bedroom door. He laughed as I flung the door open and disappeared inside, letting it slam behind me. Sod the neighbours.

"I would if you had a dick!" he called after me, his voice piercing through the plasterboard walls.

Standing inside the bedroom with my back to the door, the pizza still in my hand, I tried to control my breathing. I wanted to scream – but instead I just stood there, motionless and silent. 'Banter' he called it. It would make us seem more like brothers. Like men. But here at home there was no one to see us, and if that was what men were like then I didn't want to be one. I wanted to grow my hair long, put on a bloody pair of heels, and dance until my feet were sore; until someone noticed me, Ava.

I chucked the pizza box at the bin next to my desk. The bitter taste in my mouth from the anger in my stomach made it impossible to eat; any food would taste like ash. I stood for a moment; my mind blank. Cain was an idiot with a cruel mouth and stupid hair, but I knew that; it was just *him*. It didn't stop me from wanting to smack his ridiculous face. Yet for all his shortfalls, he was still my brother and the only one that knew my secret. He watched out for me. He was all I had.

My fingers reached into my pocket for my phone. It wasn't there. I let out a sigh, rolling my head back. I would have to go back out, have to see his arrogant face again. I'd give it half an hour, let my head clear and the anger subside. As I took a step towards the bed, the roar of my stomach echoed around the tiny room. I retrieved the crushed box and sat down on the bed. The toppings were a little skewed, but it was OK – lukewarm but edible. Taking a bite, I caught a glimpse of myself in the wardrobe mirror. Baggy jeans, brown belt, white t-shirt, black zip-up hoodie, black beanie. All big, all loose – easier to hide all the things I wasn't allowed to be. Letting the pizza drop back into the box, I edged closer as if something untoward lurked in my own reflection. My fingers caressed the soft, feminine skin hidden under the illusion of manhood. The gentle chin hidden under a square jaw; a small, round nose under the pretence of a larger, straighter one but the hazel eyes were the same, still Ava. I took off the beanie and ran my hands through my dark hair. I tried to picture myself with long hair, but I couldn't. Short back and sides, long on top and swept to one side, trying to tame its unruly wave – that was my usual order now. At least I looked better than Cain.

I pulled open the wardrobe door: more jeans, more hoodies and more t-shirts. There were a couple of pairs of trainers and a set of red Converse sneakers shoved into the bottom as well. In the drawers below were boxers, neatly paired socks and a couple of belts coiled together like snakes: one black, one brown. I knelt down and reached under the hanging clothes. Crisp and clean, the freshly washed smell engulfed me, reminding me of Mum. I lingered in the scent for a moment, before I emerged clutching an old holdall, with its familiar red and blue stripes, and a broken zip that protected so many secrets.

The zip reluctantly gave way, peeling one side of the bag from the other to reveal the treasures within. My fingers lingered over the top of it, drawing out the excitement of holding the contents before reaching in. The soft fabric that met my fingers whispered of a life I once lived. The first item was a tea dress, short, strappy, and floral. I carefully laid it out on the bed, smoothing out the creases. Next to it I placed a cream cardigan, and then a pair of ballet pumps, which were worn and comfortable.

The clothes were far too small for me now. These were the last things I wore when I was Ava, before I became Alec. I couldn't cry – I had been Alec for so long now it had become second nature. But I still thought about Ava, though often she was disconnected from me. Then, at other times, I was her again. At first, Dad and Cain just called me Alec when we were in public; after a while, I became Alec at home as well. That was when Dad made the implant. No more hoods and hats and creeping in the shadows. The implant changed me physically, like a large dose of testosterone I could turn on and off at the press of a button. It changed my face and voice, attaching itself to the very fibres of my body. It changed me almost down to a DNA level. Almost, but not quite; I had still had to bind my little blossoming breasts. They had arrived before the implant, before Alec, but now they were crushed like the girl I had been. Their growth halted; they were nothing more than mosquito bites now. Though I could turn the implant off the tech never really left my body, it was just dormant. Most important of all, however, it tricked the scanners. I could link them up with the implant in my wrist and fool them into thinking I was Alec – that Ava had never existed. But if I got caught by the Mechs and given a full body scan then the game would be up: my DNA didn't quite tally. But I was careful. Cain was careful, too, and right now they weren't looking for me.

Although it was all Dad's idea, his way of protecting me and saving me from sterilisation, I think he felt like he had lost me. At night sometimes I would hear him creep into my room. I would pretend to be asleep while he sat at the end of my bed, the sound of whiskey sloshing in the bottle and the sharp smell of it filling the quiet, dark, room. He would whisper my name, my real name. Ava. Ava. Ava. Then he would weep ever so softly just for a moment before stroking my hair and leaving just as quietly as he had come in. As soon as I heard the door close, I would sit bolt upright, staring at the space where he had been, feeling the dissipating warmth of him and wishing – longing – for him to call me Ava again. But that was then, when I still fitted the clothes that lay on the bed before me.

"Alec!"

There was a drumming on my bedroom door and my stomach lurched. I gathered the clothes up as quickly as I could and bundled them back into the holdall. Cain opened the door as I slammed the wardrobe shut and spun around to face him. His eyes widened and he shifted his feet uneasily, unable to make eye contact with me. Eventually he looked up, glancing over my shoulder at the wardrobe, then back to me. He cleared his throat.

"Can I help you with something?" I asked, folding my arms across my chest.

"Um, yeah, the news is on, I know you like to watch it," he said.

He glanced over at the wardrobe again; he wasn't good at any emotions other than anger, but I wasn't in the mood to help him out with this one.

"Look," he said quietly, "it doesn't pay to dwell on things, alright?"

I nodded.

"OK. Yeah. Come out when you're ready," he muttered, slowly backing out of the room and closing the door behind him.

I flopped down onto the bed. I didn't feel like joining him. He could stew out there on his own, although I doubted he would give me a second thought once he had plugged into the TV. Often I found him asleep on the sofa, the remote balanced on his gently rising and falling chest, the people on the box talking to an absent audience. I hoped he would go to bed this evening.

Pizza finished, I lay on the bed staring up at the ceiling, waiting for the TV to fall silent and listening for Cain's footsteps in the kitchen or the gurgle of the sink and the flush of the toilet in the bathroom – signs that he was going to bed. Shaking my watch down my wrist, I took note of the time: 9.48. Still a bit early for Cain's usual bedtime, so I got up and crept out of the room. I still needed my phone. I still needed to text Lucy. The front room was dark, lit only by the light of the TV. Cain was lying on the sofa, casually flicking through the TV channels. He didn't move as I approached, just stared at the screen. I started feeling around in the poor light for my phone.

"Looking for this?" Cain said, holding out my phone for me.

I reached out for it, but he didn't let go.

"Look, I'm sorry about earlier, I just get carried away I guess," he said with a shrug.

"Doesn't matter!"

I gave my phone a tug and reluctantly he relinquished it. It felt warm as if he'd had it in his hand for a while. My stomach lurched. What if he had managed to read the messages? The others and I all spoke in code – but still.

"I'm going to bed, got work in the morning," I muttered.

Cain nodded and turned back to the TV. I watched him for a moment. If only he knew where I was going this evening and the things I had planned. I felt the words climb up my throat, loitering on my tongue. Should I tell him? He was my brother after all, and we were so close to finding a way out. The secrets I hid from him churned away inside my stomach but at the same time I quite enjoyed having something that was just mine, something about me he didn't know. Swallowing, the secret slipped back down into the pit of my stomach. Mine.

Heading to the bathroom, I ran the shower as hot as it would go and undressed. The steam rose and fill the room as I stood naked, unbound and uninhibited, enjoying freedom from my bindings. Sweat gathered all over my body, forming cooling beads that trickled down my back, over my face and between my stunted breasts. I sweated in the steam until the room was so thick with it I could barely see my hands in front of my face. I knew it was wasteful, but Cain never washed. I often used up his quota of water as well as my own.

Stepping into the shower, I hung back away from the torrent of water and let all the sweat, along with all the negativity and toxins of the day, leave my body, pooling on the floor at my feet and trickling towards the plug. Taking a deep breath of hot air, I dived under the shower, the scalding water hitting my skin like a thousand needles. I let out a gasp, bearing it as long as I could before it became too painful, then reached for the cold tap. Within a second, the water cooled to a sensible temperature, washing away the saltiness from my glowing, pink skin, and I reached for the bar of unscented soap and lathered it up as much as I could. Climbing out, cleansing ritual complete, I felt warm and clean: renewed – ready for the night's activities.

Grabbing my belongings and wrapping a towel around myself, I opened the door and slipped out into the hall. The cold air hit me hard making my skin prickle as I dashed across the hall into my bedroom. I called out "Night!" to Cain and closed the door behind me. Letting the towel fall to the floor, I shivered in the cool air, letting my mismatched body breathe. The wardrobe door, slightly ajar, caught my eye and I crossed the room to shut it; but as I did, it sprang back towards me, reluctant to close. I spotted the strap of the holdall hanging out. Kneeling down, I pushed it towards the back of the wardrobe, picturing the child-sized clothes once more as I closed the door on my old self.

My thoughts drifted from the child I once was, back to the woman I had left crumpled in a heap on the street and my chest tightened with guilt: I walked away, like everyone else. I was no better than the others, always looking out for number one. Yet I was trying to be so much more, trying to make a difference in the only way I knew how.

The upgrade: I hadn't changed the implant. I grabbed my watch from the heap of clothes on the floor – 10.30 – I just about had time to sort it before I had to meet Lucy. It looked like I wouldn't be getting any sleep tonight. Throwing on a pair of boxers, I sat down at my desk and opened the drawer, hunting for a long cable that plugged into my phone and into a wireless device that communicated with the implant in my neck. It was neatly wound up, a commonplace cable with an extraordinary purpose. It took a moment for the transmitter to connect to the device. A vibration at the base of my neck let me know I was good to go. I scanned my wrist with my phone, waiting for the upgrade to download. Technology was everything nowadays, a blessing and a curse: anyone and everyone could see where you were and what you are doing. No one had secrets anymore. We all knew that MTech watched everything we did; we lived with Big Brother breathing down our necks. But at the same time tech made everything more convenient, more predictable. You could hack a phone line or block a camera. People, on the other hand, were more difficult. Everyone wanted to save their own skin and with the right leverage, everyone talked – they all had a price.

There was another vibration in my neck, and I looked down at the phone. Download complete. Just as I thought, there had been an upgrade to the app that every phone inside the Barrier had pre-programmed onto it. We used it to check rations, credits, and our status. My safety relied on the information I had just downloaded, and the skills Dad had taught me.

I hadn't had much interest in computers or technology beyond social media until we'd been stranded inside the Barrier – until it really mattered. Then I found I had an aptitude for it; in fact, I quite enjoyed it, and Dad had been an enthusiastic teacher. It was then I found out the true nature of Dad's work. I was the first to experience the super-camouflage he was creating. It was the ultimate weapon. A soldier who could disappear into the background, become anyone and go undetected. I marvelled at the technology Dad had created, in awe of his knowledge, not only the physics of it but of every cell in the human body and the part they played in humanity. I watched, speechless, as he explained how he could manipulate skin and bone without a scalpel or knife. Cain would skulk around whilst we worked, often invited to join us but he never did. He preferred to freeload. He let Dad and I worry about the future.

"Take each day as it comes," Cain would say with a shrug.

It was easy for him. He wasn't being hunted down and stripped of his basic human rights. Yet I would see him and his sideway glances at Dad and me. I felt his envy like a wall that pushed us apart; he was jealous of the time I spent with Dad, probably heightened by the resentment he held against me and Anna for being the children Mum and Dad were told they could never have. The fact he was adopted meant nothing to Dad, I knew that. Cain knew that. Dad told me so many times how much he loved us all but now I wonder if he had told Cain enough. He had been so swept up in protecting me that he had almost forgotten his only son, assuming Cain just knew.

Cain's resentment for me had surfaced a couple of months ago when he was angry. He had flung me against the wall and spat into my face all the hate he felt towards me. I had expected to see the Mechs at my door that night but instead I didn't see Cain for a week after that. When he came home he was battered and bruised. I had begun to ask him what had happened but he had shut himself in his room and refused to come out until the following day, when he pretended nothing had happened. It had worried me. He was different after that. I couldn't quite put my finger on why, but there was something about him that didn't quite fit. He was more closed off, his 'banter' nastier, like something bad had happened and it was all my fault. He took to going out at all hours of the night, coming home as it got light, if he came back at all. I caught him once, as I returned from work, leaving my room, face black with anger. I chose to ask no questions in the hope he wouldn't ask me any.

Chapter 3

The artificial moon had replaced the artificial sun in the sky and night was in full swing by the time I was sure Cain had gone to bed and it was safe to leave the flat. Slinging on fresh clothes, I grabbed my phone, MP3 player, and wallet, and headed for the door. My hand hovered over the Land Rover keys, but I left them hanging on the hook and scanned myself out of the flat. My feet barely made a sound as I dashed down the stairs, jumping the last few and swinging the building door wide. I took a deep breath of cool night air and zipped my hoodie up to my chin before pulling the hood over my head. As I did, something in the building above caught my eye. I did a double-take, scanning the windows near my flat but it was still: a trick of the street lamps and car lights. Strolling, head down, earphones in, I ignored the other people who were wandering around at this late hour. Crossing the road, I took a small side street off of the main road, weaving a well-known route through the houses and tower blocks until I reached the bus stop I was after. The number 20, a direct bus into town, was always quiet and the driver was a friend. Sitting on the bench, the coolness of the metal seeped into my thighs. I shivered and hugged myself. It was supposed to be autumn, but the seasons seemed to blur into one continuous mild-weather front, with sporadic rain showers and cool evenings. I never wore shorts – the hair on my legs, like the hair on my face, was poor at best; secretly I was quite pleased.

The smell of body odour and pungent aftershave mixed with thick, grunting voices drifted towards me, cutting through the beats blaring in my headphones.

Glancing up, I caught sight of a group of men talking loudly and crassly. Pulling my hood down a little further and retrieving my phone from my pocket, I engrossed myself in the screen. As I thought about texting Lucy, fingers hovering over her name on the screen, a hand landed on my shoulder. I looked up and groaned.

The guy's mouth moved but I couldn't make out what he was saying, so I took my headphone out of one ear.

"Can I help you?" I asked.

"Yeah, I asked if you were going anywhere nice?" he smiled at me; I knew that smile.

I took a deep breath.

"Just town, I'm waiting for a friend. They'll be here any minute."

The guy laughed and tightened his grip on my shoulder - I flinched a little.

"You sure about that? Looks like you're alone to me."

I didn't say anything, trying to shrug his hand off instead, but he refused to let go.

"Why don't you stay and have some fun with us? Wait, don't we know each other?" he leered down at me, invading my personal space. "Yeah, we do. You're that skinny guy that hangs around with Cain."

He squeezed a little tighter and my jaw clenched. I calmly pushed Lucy's name on the screen and typed, '*Bus stop. Delayed*', then hit send before shoving my phone back in my pocket. As I tried to stand up the guy pushed me back down, and I caught a good look at his face. I didn't recognise him or any of his mates: close haircuts, muscles and not much else. I had heard of gangs like this before, men and women that wandered the immaculate grey streets looking for trouble. They were a law unto themselves and although MTech decreed that anyone caught in these gangs would find themselves at the wrong end of a Mech gun, the threat in itself became the fun of it. Smashing buildings, attacking passers-by and not getting caught was a thrill they repeated over and over again. There were whisperings that people paid them to keep other people quiet. I wondered who I'd pissed off.

"Let go!" I said quietly, gritting my teeth.

"I don't think I want to…you have a pretty face. I like you. I wonder what you taste like." He was so close now I could smell his body odour.

This was going to get messy. Reaching into my hoodie pocket, I turned the MP3 player up as loud as it went, before pushing the earphone back in. The music pounded in my ears, deafeningly loud and I felt my heart rate match it, banging hard against my ribs. With a quick twist and duck, I extracted myself from his grip and floored him with a fist to the side of his head. He lay sprawled on the ground looking confused for a moment before he refocused his stare and scrambled to his feet.

So much for staying inconspicuous. It was moments like these that I was grateful for Dad's insistence on learning how to fight and, to a point, I could see the benefit of Cain's bullying. As they came at me, I remembered the moves Dad had taught me: the upper cuts and left hooks – mementoes of his military past. I had a feeling, however, that this was going to end up being more than self-defence. He threw a fist at me, and I dodged it, much to his amazement. I was faster than him and lighter but if one of his fat fists clocked me, I was in trouble. Taking a swing at him, I caught him hard in the jaw. He reeled for a moment before catching his balance and attempting to drive all his body weight into me. I hung on until he was almost upon me before darting out of the way and, using the bench as a spring board, kicked him as hard as I could in the back of the head. He landed face-first on the floor where he stayed for a moment before slowly getting to his feet. He wiped blood from his mouth with his sleeve and spat on the floor. I turned to run but his friends had encircled me, the laughter gone from their faces. This had gone from a bit of fun to a beat down. I glanced around; there were too many of them to fight my way out. What they lacked in brains they made up for in brawn, and skinny little me had just left their leader kissing the pavement.

The closest two tried to grab me but I managed to fend them off, knocking one to the ground. Yet more were on me, pushing me down and kicking me hard. Boots pounded into my body and my head as I curled up on the ground trying to protect myself. Pain coursed through me with each kick. My ribs cracked. I tasted blood. I prayed it would stop, that Lucy had got my message. Delirious with the pain, I was hauled to my feet. I tried to focus on the guy's face. He ripped the headphones away from me and grabbed my chin roughly.

"There's something appealing about your naivety," he said, "thinking you stood a chance against us."

Locking eyes with him, I spat blood and saliva at him as forcefully as I could. As the glob of phlegm hit his cheek, he dropped my chin and smacked me hard across the face with his fist. The metal rings on his fingers tore into my skin and my head spun even more. As he drew back for a second blow, the pavement drifted in and out of focus. Teeth gritted, I held my breath but the blow never came. There was a loud screech of brakes and the hiss of bus doors opening then heavy footsteps approached, coming to a standstill in front of me. Gingerly, I lifted my head to see who my saviour was.

"Can I help you?" said the guy, holding his fist inches from my bruised face.

"Depends," said a familiar voice.

Bernie! Thank you, God. The men holding me tightened their grip a little, shifting their feet as they waited to see what would happen now a new player had entered the game.

"That's my friend you have there, you see, and I don't like how he looks at the moment. I hope that wasn't you," said Bernie.

Great, big, wonderful, Bernie.

"So what if it was?"

The guy turned on him and squared up. I could smell the testosterone.

"Let's not let this get out of hand now, I think my friend has had his beat down," Bernie told him.

"It's done when I say it's done," snarled the thug.

He took a step towards Bernie, who held his ground.

"It's over," said Bernie calmly, grabbing the man's arm and twisting it behind his back.

I watched his mouth moving next to his ear and the man shift uneasily in Bernie's grasp, his free hand grappling at something between him and Bernie. The man nodded and Bernie shoved him away. I saw the glint of metal as I was flung to the ground; it was over before I really knew what was going on. I stayed where I was, with the rough ground beneath my cheek, just breathing, waiting for my head to stop spinning and the pain to subside.

"Come on, get up, Alec," I felt Bernie's hands under my arms and he hoisted me off the floor. "Get on the bus!"

With Bernie's help, I carefully climbed onto the bus, the bright LED lights blinding me temporarily; I shielded my eyes as he helped me into a seat. The bus smelt a little like feet. It had two other passengers who were huddled at the back looking wide-eyed and terrified. Leaning back gently, I clutched my ribs, closing my eyes as Bernie took his position in the driver's seat. There was the sound of the doors closing and the bus righted itself ready to go. I opened my eyes and shuffled over to the window, leaning my pounding head against the cool glass to watch the streets go by in the darkness. A bump in the road made me draw my breath in through my teeth; I groaned as Bernie's worried face peered at me in the rearview mirror. How was I going to explain this to Cain? I didn't think sleepwalking would cut it.

'Oh, yeah, I sleepwalked into some guy's fist a few times. I didn't know him but he seemed to have some beef with you. Care to explain?'

I visualised the conversation: Cain with his stupid pout and exasperated eye-rolling. Flicking his hair out of his eyes, he would tell me off like a little kid, maybe shove me around a bit and then go to his room. Maybe I could catch him out? He was obviously into something with those guys and they were not the sort of people you wanted to owe a favour to. I closed my eyes again, lulled by the sway of the bus and the passing street lights.

There was a tap on my shoulder and the scent of Dad's aftershave washed over me. As I came round, his name forming on my lips, I let myself half hope, but I was only met with Bernie's concerned face. Dad was gone; I had watched him go, but I had always hoped that somehow Anna had survived, Mum too. Something in my gut, call it twins' intuition, was telling me she was still alive. I really hoped so, otherwise so many of the things I had done, was planning to do, were all for nothing.

If Lucy and the others weren't waiting for me I would have stayed, barely conscious, on that bus and remembered Anna's face; a mirror of mine, hazel eyes, dark hair that never lay flat, but I could hear Bernie shaking me from my daydreams. Focusing on his face and his words, I pulled myself back to my stinking reality.

"Alec, we're here. Last stop," Bernie said.

Nodding, I stood up tentatively, Bernie's strong arms taking my weight. The other passengers had already gone.

"You going to be OK, mate? Want me to take you to Spectrum?" he asked me.

"It's OK, I'll be alright. Thanks, Bernie, for rescuing me back there," I smiled weakly at him and tried to stand up straight whilst my body screamed at me to stop.

Grabbing onto him, I held my ribs with my other arm, and he slowly led me off the bus. As the adrenaline faded, the pain surfaced with a vengeance; the cracked ribs and bruised flesh making itself known.

"Sorry I didn't get there sooner. Looks like you took a beating, mate."

"Yeah, it wasn't the most fun I've ever had. But it would have been a lot worse if you hadn't shown up," I told him.

"Yeah, I did skip a couple of stops when I got Lucy's message," he smiled as sat me down on a nearby bench. "You're onto a winner with that one, Alec."

"You know it's not like that, Bernie," I reminded him.

"I don't see why not, you two clearly like each other," he smiled.

If only he knew. If only Lucy knew. I wondered if they would have my back like they did if they knew I had been lying to them all this time.

"Let it go, Bern," I said quietly, not making eye contact.

"Come on, you'd be great together and you know it."

I grimaced. My lies had repercussions, they had wheedled their way into other people's lives, like all deceit does, but I tried to ignore it, pushing the lies into a tiny box in the back of my mind. Her friendship actually meant something to me; she was the only one I felt was genuine in our circle of friends. To me, she was the sister I had lost. Coming from a guy, I knew how it must have looked to her, and to the others. When she looked at me, the guilt stuck in my throat, a hard lump that was difficult to swallow. Yet my need to get out and to stop living a lie, was greater than her heartbreak. I'd take freedom over Lucy.

I let Bernie's words slide away, falling into the silence, unanswered. I couldn't rock the boat now – we were so close to finding a way out – and if that meant that some of us were emotionally expendable, then so be it.

Bernie held his hands up in surrender and grinned at me again, "Well say hello to Luce for me. You sure you're going to be okay?"

"Yeah, and thanks again," I gave him a little wave.

He turned and walked towards the bus, shaking his head. He took a step onto it, barely fitting through the double doors. The vehicle groaned at the weight of him. As I watched him, I noticed the tell-tale bulge of a gun tucked in the back of his trousers. My heart leapt. No wonder those guys ran – but that wouldn't be the end. There would be repercussions all because of me; a ripple I couldn't stop. I should have run or taken the beating. I shouldn't have texted Lucy. Now Bernie had put himself in the firing line.

"Bern," I called out to him, and he looked up from the driver's seat, his finger hovering over the door button, "just be careful!"

He nodded and gave me a little wave before shutting the door. I sat for a moment, watching the big, red bus disappear round the corner towards the depot. It was late. I should have been at home in bed and then none of this would have happened. I took a deep breath and pain radiated through my chest, but I managed to shuffle down the street, passing a few people on my way to the club. It was the one place MTech left us alone. They scanned us on the way in and on the way out, but inside we were free. They tried to create a sense of normality in this strange way – pumping everyone with alcohol and loud music to numb the lies they force-fed us. Sometimes I envied the drunks, their days forgotten in a whirl of intoxication and cravings, but I couldn't afford to be out of control just in case I let something slip.

Turning the corner onto the pedestrian-only high street, I heard Spectrum before I could see it. The beat of dance music rumbled through the ground, blaring out of the entrance and open windows, the bold lights of the sign illuminating the high street. Grimacing, I pulled myself together and headed for the entrance. *Stand up straight, look normal, breathe.* The Mechs would be waiting outside, standing guard. I couldn't afford to be denied entry or worse, scanned. *Breathe, look normal!*

Gritting my teeth, I took my place at the end of the small queue in front of the grubby club door. Leaning against the wall, I attempted to look casual as I waited my turn, while inside every breath sent shockwaves of agony through my chest. Shuffling closer to the entrance, I listened to the girls ahead of me chattering away about nothing in particular. They were young and must have been sterilised before they knew what was going on: a blessing in disguise, I guessed.

Finally, it was my turn and I pushed myself carefully off the wall trying not to appear drunk. Flashing my wrist under the scanner, the usual stats appeared. I waited for the tall black door to Spectrum to swing open and it admitted me like a gaping mouth. Flicking my hood up, I ventured in. It was dim inside. Lights flashed and strobed over the sweating, heaving clubbers while the deafening music pounded my ears and made my head feel a hundred times worse. The smell of vomit, sweat, and sticky-sweet alcohol accosted me as I reached out for the tacky wall, trailing my hand gingerly along it. I made my way along the familiar route down the stairs, past the cloakroom, and towards the back of the club to the bathroom whilst trying not to bump into anyone. The people on the dance floor swayed together in time to the music, like a writhing animal – I was relieved I didn't have to fight my way across it to reach the toilets. Instead, I could scurry along, hugging the right-hand wall until I saw the door: the familiar little man and woman stood next to each other, signalling a free-for-all inside. My jaw clenched as I prepared myself for the plague of debauchery I knew waited on the other side. As I reached out, it swung open and I nearly toppled head first into the toilets. I bit my lip, stifling a cry as I caught my fragile body hard against the wall. A young couple barreled past, managing to unglue their tongues from each other for long enough to give me an indignant look. Forcing myself to breathe, I ignored them.

Inside, I was faced with a large bank of sinks and mirrors down the centre of a long, brightly lit room; both sides were lined with red cubicles – left for men, right for women. The music was almost as loud in here but I was glad of it. It muffled the noise of people unashamedly screwing in the cubicles.

"Alec!" came a voice to my left.

"Jones."

I headed over to the guy sitting next to a table heavy with sweets, toiletries, and even pepper spray.

"Still selling your wares in this hole I see?" I smiled painfully.

He laughed, showing rows of teeth that looked as if they had all fought to fit inside his mouth, "Yeah and will be for as long as I need to."

"How do you put up with, you know, *that*?" I said, gesturing to the cubicles.

"Don't hear it anymore," he said with a shrug, running a hand through his slicked-back fair hair.

One of the cubicle doors opened with a click and a man emerged, the scent of toilet cleaner following him like a bad aftershave. I quickly pretended to peruse Jones' table of treats until he had left, the sound of the hand drier lingering for a moment after he had gone.

"At least he washed his hands," laughed Jones.
I didn't know how he survived down here in the artificial light, locked away in his black, tiled prison. He got up from his chair and had a quick look under the cubicle doors.

"You know, you look like crap," he said as he peered under the last door.

Walking slowly over to the basin, I peered into the mirror. He was right. My lip was split and a thin trickle of blood had dried down my chin and dripped onto my hoodie; my right eye was turning black already and I was covered in street dirt. Turning the cold tap on, I pushed my hood back before scooping up the cold water and splashing it over my face. It was icy and refreshing on my stinging skin, washing away the dirt and the blood. Leaning forward, I took a swig from the tap, swilling out my mouth. I paused, watching the mixture of blood and saliva wash away before heading back over to Jones' table, where he stood waiting for me.

He looked me up and down as I approached, one eyebrow raised. He shook his head.

"What on earth happened to you?" he asked.

"Doesn't matter. Just life. Come on, let me in, Jones," I said.

"Sure, whatever you say, Alec. Bet it was that pretty face of yours getting you into trouble again," he laughed.

I rolled my eyes at him and caught myself rubbing the back of my neck subconsciously.

"Jones!"

"Yeah alright, alright."

He turned and opened the supply cupboard behind him, turning on the light and bending down to shift a large box, revealing a hatch in the floor. He reached down, lifted it open, and stepped back.

"Here you go," he said, gesturing for me to enter.

The cool breeze of air conditioning units rose from the opening, along with the gentle hum of voices and movement down below. I edged forward and peered down, wondering how I was going to manage the ladder.

"Cheers, Jones, good thing we have you. Hard to know who to trust these days," I told him, delaying the painful journey down.

"I know, I know," he said, but he didn't look at me. The toilet door clicked open and suddenly the cupboard door was shut behind me and Jones was gone. I was left standing in the dim light of a single light bulb, wondering about the best way to attempt the ladder. Pushing my hands into my pocket, I pulled out my phone. There was a large crack in the screen, probably where those men had been kicking me. I felt around in my pockets again. The MP3 player was still there but the headphones were gone. I groaned; I'd have to buy some more when I got the chance. I hated the emptiness without music; often filling the void with it to keep away the sadness.

Slowly, I lowered myself down the ladder into a dark tunnel lined with plumbing for the club's toilets and air conditioners. It was tight, smelling of damp and mould, and I had to stoop as I followed the sporadic lights down the tunnel until I came to another ladder. Climbing slowly down into a small space filled with wires and cabling which were no longer used, I scanned the ground for the slither of light that meant I had found a trapdoor down into the abandoned station below.

Fixing my eyes on the faint, glowing strip ahead of me, I hunched my shoulders and walked carefully over to it. In the darkness I knelt down, feeling for the cold, metal handle. I quickly found what I was looking for and, giving it the hardest shove I could muster, the door swung open, clanging loudly against the brickwork of the tunnel below. I climbed awkwardly and painfully down yet another ladder onto the old tracks, following them for a few minutes, alone except for the odd rat, until I heard familiar voices and appeared in an underground station.

The old place still made me shudder, even though I had been here a lot recently. It made the hairs on the back of my neck stand on end and my skin prickle. The pain in my chest was easing off as I hauled myself off the tracks and onto the platform. I passed the old tube train still waiting for its passengers, covered in graffiti and flyers advertising goods that had long since passed their used-by dates. A pungent smell wafted up out of the darkness beyond the train.

They shut the underground shortly after the Barrier went up. Now that people couldn't travel freely outside of the protected area, the Underground became redundant. It no longer was used enough for the government to spend money altering the routes and creating new tunnels, so they closed it, blocking off its entrances to stop people using it. The government claimed it was now being used for storage. People didn't seem bothered; they were all caught up in their own personal disasters. I only remembered the closure so vividly because the Underground was how we had come to the city. Shutting it had felt to me, as a child, that they had closed my way home. They probably managed to do a lot of things shortly after the bombings that we now think of as normal; they took advantage of us while we were in a state of panic.

I crossed over to the opposite platform and there she was: Lucy, gentle unassuming Luce. She stood at a table, peering at a laptop screen over Chris' shoulder.

"Hey!"

She looked up from the screen with a smile of recognition at the sound of my voice, but her happiness abruptly vanished as her eyes met mine.

47

"Alec!" she cried, running over to me and throwing her arms around my neck.

Unable to stop myself, I let out a yelp of pain and she quickly let go of me. Stepping back, she looked me up and down, hands pressed to her mouth.

"It looks worse than it is," I said with a smile. No need to worry her.

"I got your message, I sent Bernie," she explained.

"Yeah he got it, he came."

"Clearly not soon enough."

"Honestly, Luce, it's OK."

Over her shoulder, I could see Chris, staring hard at the laptop, trying not to look over at us, whilst straining to hear what we were saying. That man needed to grow a pair and ask Lucy out, then maybe he could stop the dagger-eyes he always gave me and the snide comments.

Lucy reached up and gently touched my face, her fingers tracing the cut on my lip. I thought about what Bernie had said earlier and my chest tightened. Reaching for her hand, I quickly pushed it away.

"I'm fine, honest."

Another lie, but what was one more? She frowned and opened her mouth to say something but I spoke over her.

"Where is everyone else?" I asked.

"Oh, yeah, Chris is here and Jennifer is in the back making tea. Josiah said he was coming, something about bringing a friend," Lucy told me.

"A friend?"

My skin prickled. This was the first I had heard of anyone joining our ranks. I was all for people wanting to fight for the cause, but normally we vetted them thoroughly first. There were only five of us, including

48

Jones on the door, and the more people we let in the more chance we had of being caught. Lucy squeezed my fingers gently, sensing my reluctance; she turned to me as we headed over to where Chris was now making notes from the screen.

"He's a tech, helped with the first-generation tech for the Barrier," said Lucy casually.

I caught hold of her arm and stopped her.

"This is big, Luce and you didn't think to start with that?" I clenched my fists.

"Yeah but your face, Alec – you can't come down here looking like that and expect me not to be worried. You text me after all." She placed her hands on her hips, her usual calmness evaporating.

I took a shallow, tight breath.

"Yeah OK, sorry," I swallowed my rage. "When's this guy coming?"

"Josiah should be here soon," she said, backing down, too. She looked down at her watch. "He texted me just after eleven, won't be long."

Nodding, I followed Lucy over to Chris just as Jennifer appeared from the other end of the platform carrying a tray of tea. She nearly dropped it when she saw me.

"Who did you piss off, Alec?" she asked setting the tray down next to Chris.

"No one that matters," I waved a hand at her dismissively. "Apparently waiting for a bus attracts attention. I'm fine."

She nodded and waited for Lucy to look away before mouthing, 'You really OK?' to me behind Lucy's back. I gave her an affirming nod and she rolled her eyes before picking up a tea, adding two spoons of sugar to it, and handing it to me.

"Think you need this more than me," she said.

"Thanks, Jen."

Finding a free chair, I sat down next to Chris, who glanced at me briefly before adjusting his glasses and turning back to the screen. I nursed the hot cup of tea for a moment, letting the warmth of it soak into my hands, preparing me for the conversation I was about to have with Chris.

"So, Chris," I said reluctantly, while he murmured in response but didn't look at me, "where are we at?"

"I think we've got a handle on the blueprints for the generation terminal. I should be able to hack into their systems but there are still a few things that need ironing out," he paused, finally giving me eye contact. "And of course, we still need a man on the ground."

"Yeah, okay, and the Mechs? You found a way of disabling them?" I asked.

"Working on it and the Barrier's back-up system – that's giving me a bit of a headache."

"I thought you were the best hacker around, Chris?" I leaned back in my chair, allowing myself a smile as I insulted him.

"Alec!" exclaimed Lucy.

I regretted my comment as soon as I said it. He turned on me, his chair screeching across the floor as he stood, hands balled into fists. I glanced from Lucy to Chris and back again, then got to my feet. Internally I groaned, my aching limbs crying out at me to stop, to sit back down and shut up. He opened his mouth to speak, the ugly vein on the side of his head bulging. The clatter of footsteps on the platform cut across Chris and we were interrupted by the timely arrival of Josiah. I let out the breath I had been holding.

"Everyone!" he called across the station, cocksure as ever.

Glancing up, he sauntered over to us, an unfamiliar man with him. Jennifer reappeared with more tea and I heard her inhale sharply as she clocked the two men. There was no denying it, the guy Josiah had brought with him was attractive: broad-shouldered and tall with dark skin and soulful eyes. My stomach did a little flip. I thought I recognised him – a sense of misplaced familiarity – from where? I had no idea. Rubbing the implant at the back of my neck subconsciously, I dismissed the thought.

He was dressed in jeans and a black hoodie and wore a grey beanie, which he removed as he approached, revealing a cleanly shaven head. Both Lucy and Chris turned their attention to the newcomer as he reached us. He smelt like aftershave and grit.

"Everyone, this is Jackson Quinn. He's the one I was telling you about, the tech," said Josiah.

Jackson held out his hand. Ignoring it, I grabbed Josiah by the collar of his jacket, struggling to keep a hold of him for a moment before I marched him away from the group and out of ear shot. His eyes darted back at the others as he trip-trapped along after me.

"What are you doing?" I hissed at him.

"Helping us."

"By bringing a stranger down here?"

"He's a tech," protested Josiah, pushing my hands off him and rearranging his jacket. He shrugged his shoulders a few times.

"What do you know about him? Anything?" I was barely able to keep my voice level.

"I did the usual background checks. Alec, you may think you're in charge here but I don't remember voting for you," said Josiah, straightening out his collar again.

Running my hands through my hair, I turned away. He was right. I wasn't technically in charge, but we were a team and every team needed a leader. My stomach clenched.

"We are just so close to getting out, Josiah," I explained.

"I know, Alec, sorry mate, but he can help us. I'll vouch for him."

"Fine, if you think he's OK then I trust you," I said reluctantly. I didn't want to trust him. I couldn't afford to let my guard down with anyone else; I barely trusted any of the people that surrounded me. I called them friends, but none of them had seen the inside of my flat, or even knew where I lived, except Lucy. Not even she had had the opportunity to see the one photo of Ava that still existed.

We walked back to the group, which stood in awkward silence watching us bicker. They pretended not to be staring as we re-joined them. I cleared my throat and held out my hand to Jackson. He looked at me for a moment before shaking it, and I noticed the edge of a tattoo just visible under his jacket sleeve.

"Alec."

"Jackson Quinn."

His voice was deep and quiet but it held an authority that I liked.

"This is Chris, Jennifer, and Lucy. Obviously you know Josiah and I'm guessing you met Jones up top?" I avoided second names – better he didn't know more than he needed to.

He nodded and shook the rest of the outstretched hands.

"So you're a tech?" I asked him.

"Was…before all this," he said gesturing towards the ceiling and looking around.

I knew how he felt. Life was turned upside down that day fourteen years ago, and it hadn't been the same since. Over the years, I've heard so many reasons why the bombs came: weapon trials, arms race, over-population, technical fault, even stupid suggestions like little green men. But all I know is that *they* knew what was happening. The Barrier was premeditated; it was ready when those first bombs hit and those crafts appeared in the sky – a deathly divide that stopped those MTech had chosen from being obliterated, while those outside died painful, fiery deaths. We were told it kept out the radiation that apparently now filled the atmosphere, and it regulated the air, the sun, and the rain. It kept us safe and it kept us trapped. I can only assume other cities and countries built their own Barriers, but I don't know; I didn't know how far the destruction spread or who else was involved. The outside world was closed to us now, yet here I was trying to reach it again. All of us down here in the Underground had gathered for a common cause. We believed others had survived out there and we wanted to find them, to leave our dystopia and enter theirs. I wanted to break down the walls of our prison. I wanted to find Anna. I found myself staring at Jackson and he shifted a little under my gaze.

"And now? How do you pass the time?" I asked, quickly looking elsewhere.

"I thought we had this all sorted, Josiah?" Jackson said.

"Yeah come on, Alec, I already told you that I'd vouch for him," Josiah reminded me.

Staring at Josiah, I gritted my teeth. I forced myself to let it go and nodded. Change sat uneasy with me. We were close to getting out of this prison and I was anxious about new people joining our team. However, Jackson could be our key to getting out and if Josiah said he was OK, then who was I to argue? I fought the unsettled churning in the pit of my stomach and turned back to Chris.

"OK, so, Chris was just bringing us up to date with everything. Chris?"

"Yeah, sure. As I was saying, it's just the Mechs and the backup system. Since the upgrade, they've added, like, six more firewalls. It's going to take another few days, assuming we're able to stay here that long," Chris explained.

"Sure, sure, Jackson, can you help at all?" I asked, turning to face the newest member of our team. He was peering at one of the old posters on the tunnel wall.

As all eyes flicked towards him, he nodded; shifting the hood of his hoodie and running a hand over the top of his head. He casually reached for the laptop and spun it in his direction, scrolling up and down. I could see the reflection of the screen in his dark eyes as he took it all in. His gaze was unwavering and concentrated.

"So?" I said after a moment. Everyone held their breath, it was palpable. This could be it – the moment we broke through the Barrier. We could begin to make plans and take real action instead of theories and ideas.

He looked up from the screen and met my eye. "They've changed it a bit since I helped put it up, but I should be able to help you. Essentially the programming is still the same."

It was as if the underground was filled with the buzz of the rails and the whoosh of the trains again. The voices of our little group filled the air with a fervour I hadn't heard in years. My skin prickled; in those few words, Jackson had made it tangible – we could almost taste freedom. But I held back. I couldn't quite let myself get swept away in their joy. I cleared my throat; the reality of getting out scared me as much as it thrilled me. No one knew what would be waiting for us out there, if anything at all.

"Can you show me everything you have?" asked Jackson.

Chris jumped forward and started jabbering in 'tech speak' with Jackson nodding along. I watched them for a while before busying myself with a selection of ordinance survey maps. Jennifer and I poured over them, trying to decide on another spot to scout out for the best generation terminal to make our escape from. We needed the quietest one, something out of the way and forgotten about. As Jennifer talked, I glanced down at my watch. Nearly two in the morning. The club would be shutting soon and we needed to get out separately. I clapped my hands and all conversation came to a halt.

"Time!" I called.

Chris tutted. "We were just getting somewhere."

"Next time mate," I said as he saved the file and ejected the memory stick, placing it on the table.

Helping Jennifer pack away, I threw a large sheet over our stuff, and by the time we were done, it looked as if no one had ever been there. We stood by the disused carriage and said our goodbyes. I waited with Lucy and

Chris as Jackson, Jennifer and Josiah disappeared down the tracks and back up into Spectrum. A staggered exit was less suspicious; it helped avoid associations.

Chris, who stood clutching his laptop, opened and closed his mouth a few times, while I listened to Lucy ramble about nothing in particular and I wondered whether I should go back to hers and avoid Cain until after work. That would fuel his banter.

"No!" shouted Chris, and I spun round to face him. He stood frantically searching his pockets with his free hand, then he thrust the laptop at Lucy and began hunting through his bag.

"No," he shouted again.

"Chris?" I stepped toward him.

"It's gone, damn it!"

I seized him by the jacket. "What, Chris?"

"The memory stick," he bellowed, spittle sticking to his lips as his face turned red and his voice cracked.

He pushed me away and turned away from us, but I could see him shaking. He ran his hand through his hair as he muttered under his breath.

"Check again, Chris, I'm sure it's there," said Lucy, ever the quiet voice of reason.

When he turned to face us, I could see perspiration gathering on the nose grip of his glasses. He reached down, and slowly and methodically searched his bag and then his pockets. He came up empty, his brows knotted and his eyes frantic.

"I had it, there on the table," he said, looking over at the empty space where the table had stood, "and then, then…"

His eyes widened and his mouth went slack.

"Chris?" I breathed.

"Jackson, had to be him! He asked if he could take a copy of the file home and I said no, we kept everything on the laptop and the memory stick, no other copies, to keep it safe." Chris started pacing, his hands in his hair.

"Can't you just get another memory stick?" I asked tentatively.

Chris stopped and looked at me, one eyebrow raised. "No, Alec. It's not that simple. There are a couple of files on the memory stick that I don't have on the laptop. I lost some when I had a problem with the hard drive last week. I hadn't transferred the files back over yet."

My throat tightened and I held my breath as I stared down the dark tunnel after Jackson. We were so close just moments ago; now everything was slipping through my fingers like sand. I made to run but the stabbing pain in my chest stopped me dead. Clutching my side, I used the wall for support. What now? What if he was working for the government? Damn Josiah! Damn me for trusting anyone.

"Alec, it's OK," said Lucy quietly, putting a hand on my shoulder.

"No, it's not. Damn it, Lucy! I can't even bloody run after him. We're screwed!"

Shrugging her off, I climbed slowly down onto the tracks. Every step was agony again, and every breath was like a knife in my side. Sitting around, I had been fooled into thinking I felt okay. Pushing through the pain, ignoring Jones, I eventually hobbled out of the toilets and outside into the street, looking aimlessly around, hoping to catch a glimpse of Jackson or Josiah, even Jennifer. But there was hardly anyone about. It was late – or early, depending on which side of the day you lived on.

There was no way I would find him now. He was long gone, and our hopes with him.

"Alec, you don't know that he's not on our side, not yet," said a quiet voice at my side.

I turned to face Lucy. Chris was nowhere to be seen. She was too trusting, too quick to see the good in people. Honesty was a rare commodity when everyone had to fight for their lives. I shook my head, anger gripping my chest.

"Don't be so naïve, Lucy," I scolded.

She looked offended and I turned away. I liked Lucy but she wasn't Anna. I wanted my life back. I knew one day I would watch the tears fall and I'd walk away. This was bigger than one broken heart. This was about freedom.

"Go home, Lucy."

"And what are you going to do?" she said, shoving her bag on her back and beginning to walk into the morning haze.

"The same."

"You can't go home like that, what will you tell Cain?" she asked.

I looked away. She was right; I needed to recover a bit before I faced Cain.

"Come back to mine," Lucy said.

I hesitated. It wasn't a bad idea but I didn't want her to get the wrong impression. I couldn't face her lingering looks and sultry eyes. I started to speak but she interrupted me.

"You can sleep on the sofa."

"Okay, but I'll leave in the morning," I muttered, frowning a little.

"It's already the morning, idiot," she laughed.

I rolled my eyes. Right again.

"Come on. The car is this way," she said, gesturing towards a blue smart car.

I followed her without saying anything else and climbed in. It was a short drive across town to her little one-bed flat. It was in a nicer area than mine and I wondered how she had got it working as a pizza delivery girl. Too tired to object, I let her help me into the flat and onto the sofa, where she quietly took off my shoes and disappeared into the other room before returning with a pillow and a blanket. She placed them next to me on the sofa.

"Want me to wash your clothes?" she asked.

She smiled at me but I shook my head. I knew that smile, it was the one Chris wished she would give him. Shuffling back a little, I avoided her eyes; this was a bad idea.

"No," I said bluntly, then I softened a little – I didn't want to be Cain. "Thanks, but I'm OK Lucy, really."

For a moment I was tempted to tell her who I was, to have someone else know my secret and share the burden with someone who might actually care. As quickly as the urge to be free of my lies had come, it went. I couldn't let down my guard, not even for her. Even her friendship wasn't worth it.

She looked disappointed for a moment, then got up and patted the pile of bedding. I murmured a goodnight as she left for bed, then listened for the door to shut before reaching into my pocket and checking my phone. No texts and no missed calls – good. Taking my jacket off, I shoved the pillow under my head and pulled the blanket over me before closing my eyes and drifting into an uncomfortable sleep.

Chapter 4

The warmth of the morning sun woke me with gentle fingers to my blanket half hanging off the sofa and a silent flat. As I sat up quickly, I regretted it – the ache of last night's fight coursed through my body. Groaning, I carefully moved to the edge of the sofa and reached down for my phone: 11.23 am. I was late for work. I tried to stand up but it was like a knife in my ribs and my legs buckled. *This is not good.* For a moment I sat waiting for the pain to subside to a manageable ache before trying to stand again.

Lucy had left a cereal bowl and spoon on the kitchen table along with a note explaining that she had thought I needed to rest and that there was cereal in the cupboard by the sink and milk in the fridge. She would be back around two. There was a towel in the bathroom for me as well. Already late for work, body stiff and complaining, I decided to make use of the shower but resolved to be gone before Lucy got home.

In the peach-coloured bathroom, I ran the shower hot. On the laundry basket, a neatly folded pink cotton towel waited for me. Lifting it to my face, I inhaled; it smelt like roses, like Lucy, and I tossed it back down again. I envied her for being all the things that I wanted to be. Undressing quickly and feeling as if I were doing something I shouldn't be, I climbed into the shower and washed away the blood and dirt of the previous night. The hot water eased my aching body, dulling the pain until I felt ready to leave. After tidying away the towel and gathering my things, I paused momentarily to search Lucy's medicine cabinet for some painkillers. I came up empty. The pain would have to wait until I got home and faced Cain. The thought of seeing him sent a wave of cold down my back and I clenched my jaw. He wouldn't finish work until six, but that was never a sure thing with Cain. He slipped in and out of the house like a cat, quiet and often unexpected. I prayed I would have time to get out of my bloodstained clothes and to think of some clever excuse for my appearance.

As I made the long walk home, going over last night's events, I breathed the cool air as deeply as I could. All our plans had vanished with Jackson and the memory stick. I had let myself trust someone I hadn't vetted personally and it had blown up in my face. Now everything we had been working on for the last few months was in the hands of a stranger. I kicked a stone hard and it bounced across the street and into the drain. I might as well join it, crawl down and curl up in the filthy effluence where all my hopes were now. As I gazed up from under my hood at the buildings, I pictured myself growing old, someone finding my body moulded into the sofa, sad and alone. Heat threatened in the back of my eyes, and I pulled my hood down further over my face. Women cry but I wasn't a woman anymore. I never had the chance to be; I had Cain to remind me of that.

The time on the scanner outside my block of flats read 1 pm as I placed my wrist under and scanned myself in. Inside, I stood at the bottom of the stairs, pushing the lift button and praying that it would light up but, as always, it was dead. I clenched my teeth and grabbed the hand rail, hauling myself up the steps. The smell of stale cigarette smoke wafted from under one of the flat doors as I paused for a moment to catch my breath. By the time I reached my floor, I was almost crying and a cold sweat had gathered across my skin. Making my way to my front door,

I flashed my wrist under the scanner. There was a click and I pushed the door open. As I stepped over the threshold, I heard movement coming from within and froze. A familiar figure moved around the gloomy room within.

"Alec?"

Closing the door behind me, I turned to face my brother. He got up from the sofa, looking me up and down before he made for me, his hands closing around the neck of my hoodie. He pulled me in close.

"Where the hell have you been?" he said, through clenched teeth.

"Work," I lied.

"Really? Work called. You didn't show up," he said slowly.

His hands twitched at my neck, his nostrils flaring at the metallic tang of blood on my clothes. My heart pounded against my chest, fear freezing me to the spot under his gaze. I wasn't sure why but in that moment, I was scared of Cain, of what he might do, what he might get out of me.

"I wasn't feeling good."

He threw me hard against the door and I collapsed, holding my ribs and gasping for breath.

"Cain, please," I breathed.

"Shut up, Ava!"

He rounded on me again, hauling me up by my hoodie. I closed my eyes and waited for him to hit me; instead, I felt his breath on my cheek, warm and moist. I wished he would hurry up and hit me, get it over and done with.

"Where were you?"

I opened my eyes. His face was so close to mine I could smell his skin. I tried to shift back but my head was wedged against the door.

"I went to Spectrum, got into a fight and was too drunk to come home. I slept it off in a bus shelter. Sorry." I looked away.

"Don't lie to me! You don't drink! I know you were with Lucy. What the hell are you doing with the pizza delivery girl all night and most of today? I know you don't have a dick," he mocked.

He reached down into my t-shirt and ran his hands over my bound breasts. My stomach lurched and I struggled under his grip. Panic rose in my chest, making it even harder to breathe. He'd never touched me like that before. It frightened me more than his fists.

"Nothing, Cain. I was drunk. I slept it off at hers," I uttered, feeling my eyes grow hot with tears.

He let me go and I slid down the door, watching him nervously as he paced the room before sitting down on the sofa and turning on the TV. Eyes screwed shut, I waited for the pain to ease before getting to my feet and making my way over to the sofa. I sat down next to him but he ignored me. His anger radiated out of him like waves of heat. I took a deep breath. I might as well ask him about those men now – what did I have to lose? Everything I had been working on was ruined, might as well carry on.

"I met some of your friends last night," I said quietly.

He carried on watching the TV, but I saw something change in his face.

"They wanted to send you a message," I told him, lifting the bottom of my top for him to see.

After a moment, he glanced down at the large bruise on my ribs, then up at my battered face. He got up and kicked the coffee table. I recoiled, sinking into the sofa. I didn't dare to speak, watching him pace like a caged animal. After a moment, I realised I was holding my breath and I let it go as quietly as I could. His eyes fixed on me and I thought he was going to hit me again, but instead he disappeared into the kitchen.

Tears threatened again in the corners of my eyes and hastily wiped my face with my sleeve. I couldn't let Cain see weakness; he couldn't know he was the only one who still had the power to break me. He appeared in front of me with a bag of frozen peas wrapped in a tea towel and two paracetamol fizzing away in a glass of water.

"Take your tops off then," he said.

I looked at him, hesitant to be vulnerable in front of him. The heat of his hands still lingered on my skin.

"Come on," he urged, tutting.

Slowly, I stripped off to just a t-shirt and, rolling his eyes, he handed me the peas and paracetamol. Downing the water in one, I pressed the peas to my ribs. It was bliss. The cold seeped into my aching bones as I closed my eyes. The worn springs of the sofa gave way to my battered body. I felt Cain sit down next to me. We sat like that in silence, neither of us willing to be the first one to speak; yet I had so many questions for him still.

"Cain," I asked gingerly.

"Yeah."

"What's going on? Tell me."

He didn't say anything for a while and I opened my eyes to make sure he was still there. He was gazing out the window, an exasperated look on his face.

"Cain?"

He turned to face me.

"I owe them some money," he said after a moment's thought.

"Really? How much?"

"A lot, okay," he said, without looking at me.

"Just tell me how much. Maybe I can help?" I moved to touch his shoulder but he shifted and I thought better of it.

"No!"

"Cain."

"Five thousand credits," he murmured.

"What? What could you possibly need that cost that much money?" I yelled.

He fell silent, a dark look on his face, and I felt myself shrink a little.

"It wasn't worth it anyway," he said, storming off and slamming his bedroom door behind himself.

I sat on the sofa, mouth open, mind racing. I couldn't imagine what he needed that much money for. No one who lived in a dirty flat with paper-thin walls and a broken lift had that kind of money. It was almost a year's wages stacking shelves at the Quick Drop Shop.

Getting up slowly to pour myself another glass of water, I passed Cain's door. His voice leached out from under it and I could hear him talking quietly on the phone. Creeping closer, heart in my mouth, I tried to catch some of what he was saying. He was arranging to meet whoever was on the other end of the phone – no names, no addresses. As I leant in closer, I felt something buzzing against my leg and my phone rang loudly in my pocket. Frantically, I fumbled for it while trying to create as much distance between myself and Cain's door as I could. Taking a stand peering out of the window, I answered the phone, my whole body tense as I waited for Cain's breath on the back of my neck, but it never came. A voice on the other end of the phone called my name but I barely heard them.

"I'm going out," Cain said to my back, and I heard the front door open and close as he left.

I took a deep breath.

"Alec? Alec? Hey, what's going on? You there?" I could hear Lucy worrying in my ear.

"Yeah sorry, Luce. What's up?"

"When I got back you were gone, I was just checking you were okay," she said, but I wasn't really listening. My mind was stuck on Cain, on how he had known I was at Lucy's. MTech could track us with the scanners but that information wasn't available to just anyone. And we were nobody.

"Yeah."

"Alec, what is going on?" her voice rose an octave.

"How would Cain know I was at yours?" I asked, not really expecting a proper answer.

"Alec, you're not making sense. What do you mean, how would Cain know? He wouldn't, unless you told him. Or a lucky guess maybe?"

"Maybe…" I trailed off lost in thought. "Look, Luce, I don't feel great. I'm going to bed. I'll speak to you later okay?"

"All right, bye."

Hanging up the phone, I stared out the window as Cain emerged from below and headed off down the street. His head flicked back and forth as he crossed the road and I watched as someone started to emerge from round the corner to meet him but was hastily pushed out of view by my brother. Gripping the window sill, head pressed against the glass, I strained to see more, but they were gone. With more questions than answers, I turned and headed to my room. I emptied my pockets and lay down on the bed, stretching out as much as I could, trying to loosen my tight muscles. Closing my eyes, I attempted to sleep but my head buzzed with things I wanted to ask Cain, and visions of

Jackson slipping the memory stick into his pocket and our plans sliding away with it. With a groan, I sat up and reached for my phone, fingers hovering over the keys. I toyed with the idea of texting Chris, asking about Cain, but changed my mind. It was stupid to involve anyone else – this had to stay between Cain and me. Instead, I went to the bathroom, took a couple of sleeping tablets, and returned to my room. Stripping down to my boxers, I resumed my position on the bed. Waiting to drift off, I tried to push my suspicions about Cain out of my mind, yet I feared they had already made their way deeper into my gut.

Chapter 5

An almighty bang and screaming wrenched my eyes open. It was a woman, high pitched and piercing. Her cries tore through my head like a knife, shaking me roughly from my drug-induced sleep. I sat up and rubbed my eyes, struggling to come round. The screaming drummed on my ears and, bleary-eyed, I forced myself off the bed. Mind heavy with sleep, I fumbled for a t-shirt and headed for the kitchen, skin puckering in the coolness that wafted in through the open window along with the screams. Peering hesitantly out from between the shutters, my stomach did a somersault. Our flat looked over the front of the building and beyond it a bleak tower block skyline stretched for miles and miles, but down below I could see a familiar bus parked half on the pavement, the front end wrapped around a lamp post. People had already started gathering around it, filling the air with a tense buzz of chatter.

One hand across my mouth, I staggered back from the window, nausea rising in my throat and a heaviness lodged itself in my gut. *Bernie.* In a blur of sweaty panic, I grabbed my trainers and fresh clothes, pulling them on as I made my way towards the front door. Thrusting my keys into my pocket and closing the front door behind myself, I headed down the lengthy staircase, ignoring the pain that splintered through my chest, one hand on the railing to steady myself, until I reached the bottom. It must have been early evening, as the sun was sitting low in the sky and dusk was starting to fall, bleaching everything to sepia. Digging my fingernails into my palms, I stepped out of the doorway into the chaos.

The bus appeared to be empty, apart from one lone passenger slumped on the back row of seats. My skin prickled as I pushed my way carefully through the gathering crowd, and glancing up at the bus number as I passed the front, my heart stopped. It *was* Bernie's bus. Panic spread like fire across my skin as I forced myself between people, not caring if my aching ribs were crushed in the process; I had to get closer and see who was on that bus. When I finally made it to the front of the crowd, the screaming had stopped. People were taking photos, noses pushed up against the windows, but no one had dared get on board. As I approached the crumpled doors and reached inside to force them open, the crowd fell silent, holding their breath. The tang of blood stung the air. I swallowed hard and squeezed myself painfully between the doors. Before I had even made it half way along the bus, I knew it was him. His dead eyes stared straight at me, making my skin crawl. My blood had turned cold and the world around me started to shift as a thin film of darkness began to cloud my vision. Yet I edged closer, my trainers spreading the crimson river of blood that flowed down the bus. Bernie's throat was sliced open with one clean cut and he was soaked in his own blood, a permanent look of terror on his dead face.

"Oh Bernie, I had warned you. I told you to be careful," I breathed.

I finally reached him and carefully closed his eyes; it made him look more peaceful in the carnage that surrounded him. Then I turned and left. Sirens rang out in the distance already and I couldn't be here when they arrived. Squeezing out of the doors once more, I ignored the horrified looks of those around me as I pulled my bloody trainers off, fighting the urge to run for the front door of my building. Every eye clung to my back, boring into my skin as I walked away bare foot and opened the door as casually as I could manage. A small moan, strange and tight, escaped my lips as I forced myself to take the stairs as quickly as my aching body would let me – the vision of Bernie burning its way into my skull, chewing up my insides. Flinging open the flat door, I dived inside, leaning hard against it, trainers clattering to the floor beside me. My heart drummed hard against the door, vibrating through it and into the walls – surely everyone could hear it? I concentrated on my breathing, slowing it down, feeling the rise and fall of my chest fall into a calmer rhythm; clarity would follow.

"Damn it, Bernie!" I muttered, banging the door with my fist.

I caught sight of my bloody trainers, the smear of blood on my sleeve and the streak of deepening red seeping into the carpet around the shoes. There had been so much blood. My legs quaked and my stomach churned. Throwing myself towards the sink, I retched until my throat burnt with stomach acid, yet the heaviness refused to leave. Standing back, I wiped my mouth with my sleeve and glanced back at the trainers still abandoned at the door. I couldn't leave them like that, blood-spattered from the carnage – and now my footprints were all over the bus. I should have walked away the minute I recognised the bus – headed for the car park and driven into the night. But I had to know if it was him; I'd needed to know if I had caused a good man to be murdered.

Retrieving the shoes, I returned to the sink once more and ran the hot tap, shoving my trainers under it. I stood, unmoving, watching them fill with water, the blood paling to pink and washing away down the plug hole; if only it were that easy to wash away bad memories. Unable to pull my gaze away from the diluting blood, my mind span. I had to speak to Lucy. Cain hadn't come back from his strange meeting. My heart sunk at the thought that he might have been involved in this. A whirlwind of doubts flooded my mind. Cain, my cold, hostile brother – we didn't share blood, just parents. Parents that had been lost because of this Barrier, because of MTech, because of me. There was a part of him that hated me simply because I was me, and it filled me with a sickening dread.

But then Cain was all I had. My security. He didn't know anything about my secret meetings; he had never met Bernie. Yet he knew exactly where I was last night. My head fought my heart, a draining tug-of-war. If not him, then perhaps those guys Bernie had rescued me from; he had stood up to them and they had done him over. My skin turned clammy, guilt tightening knots in my chest. The nausea returned. I should have taken the beat-down, gritted my teeth, and got on with it – been a man. One way or another, I had caused this. It was my fault.

A warm sensation seeped into the soles of my feet, shaking me from my mental battle. Hot water spilt over the edge of the sink, splattering on the floor. It was just how I imagined Bernie's blood had poured from his neck – a torrent of warm crimson. Guilt twisted inside me again as I reached for the tap, stemming the flow. I shifted the trainers in the sink, unclogging a clod of gritty earth and blood from the plug hole. I stood, numb, for a moment, staring at the puddle of water on the floor, eyes drifting to the sodden, stained trainers in the sink and my mind turned to Lucy. My fingers trembled as I reached into my pocket and pulled out my phone, then brought up her name in the message box. I hesitated, picturing the tears she would cry for Bernie. Not now, I couldn't tell her.

Coming for pizza this evening. Last orders. Make sure there are plenty of jalapenos. Alec. Send. A few moments later my phone buzzed and Lucy's reply came through. *Will make sure we are stocked with jalapenos. Lucy.*

With a sense of urgency, I bundled the sodden trainers into a carrier bag and slung them back in the sink. Shoving clean trainers on my feet I fetched the blood-stained t-shirt I'd been wearing last night, bunched it around the trainers to soak up the worst of the water, and grabbed the Land Rover keys. My vehicle was waiting in the underground car park, nestled between a clapped-out old Vauxhall and a blue people carrier. Cars were a forgotten commodity – left to rot after petrol stations ran dry, too expensive to convert to electric, and with nowhere to go, they had become a status symbol. I had saved for years and gone without so I could convert the Land Rover. It had been Dad's; he had taught me to drive it when my feet had barely touched the peddles. Unlocking it, I climbed inside and pushed the key into the ignition. It roared into life, echoing around the concrete car park. I flicked the lights on and plugged in my MP3 player. As I pulled away, I could see the decimated bus that contained poor Bernie's body in the wing mirror while Mech vehicles flooded the area with their blue flashing lights and wailing sirens. Eyes fixed on the road ahead, I drove into the fading light.

As the blue lights disappeared, I turned the music up loud and let it fill the car, drowning out the guilt and fear that was tearing away at me. Every now and then I caught the sight of the carrier bag out of the corner of my eye, inconspicuous but hiding such horrors inside – and a new wave of nausea rose within me. Fixing my eyes on the road, I drove until I could no longer see the street lamps and high-rise buildings, and the roads opened out into countryside. I knew where I was going. There was a little piece of woodland on the edge of a small village that Dad used to take me to when I was still Ava, where Cain and I used to play before he was a jerk. That was before Dad started drinking; before we realised this new state of play was permanent. It was quiet and peaceful there, a place where I could forget that we were imprisoned by the Barrier, controlled and monitored.

I drove until I saw the familiar higgledy-piggledy rows of trees, and pulled over into a layby, letting the car fall silent. The inkiness of night was falling fast as I climbed out of the truck and grabbed the bag from the passenger seat. I rummaged in the boot until I found a hammer in an old toolbox that had belonged to Dad, a box of matches and a couple of half-empty lighters left over from when Cain used to smoke, then headed into the woods.

I had no idea what I was doing but it was the only thing I could think of – to burn the clothes and bury them; maybe bury my guilt with them. I walked and walked, trudging through the damp, earthy-smelling undergrowth, until I found a clearing. Kneeling down, the wet grass soaking into the knees of my jeans, I thrust the hammer as hard as I could into the tightly packed earth. I dug until my muscles burned, forcing me to stop, then I peered down at the roughly hewn hole.

Sitting back heavily, I ran my hand through my hair, a smudge of earth sticking to my damp forehead as I let all the breath escape my lungs. I stared down at the hole, imagining what it might be like to curl up in the cold, damp earth and waste away; to disappear back into the ground, lost once more, just like my hopes of escape. I didn't know whether to cry or scream. We had been so close. Punching my fist into the ground, a breathless cry escaped my dry lips – the thinnest wisp of anger left in my aching chest. The trainers were heavy as I pulled them from the bag and threw them in the hole before emptying lighter fluid all over them. I wished it had been Quinn's body I had seen on the bus: a stranger who had deceived me. Striking a match, I dropped it into the hole. It quickly fizzled out. The second and third matches did the same before I realised that the trainers were still soaking wet, sodden with water and Bernie's blood.

"Damn!" I shouted, kicking the loose earth. I crumpled, clutching at my ribs, all the air stolen from my lungs. Catching my breath, I roared with anger, pain, and exhaustion. Everything was falling down around me. I crouched down and pushed my hands into my hair, the weight of what had happened in the last couple of hours pressing me into the ground, forcing me down. I stayed there until my legs went numb and until the world seemed to drift away in the blackness of it all.

Cold and exhausted, I finally stood up. The blood rushed back to my legs and feet, sending agonising pins and needles through them as I grabbed handfuls of dirt and began covering the trainers. It felt like an anti-climax: I couldn't even burn a pair of trainers. The child inside me wanted to talk to my brother, for him to tell me I was an idiot and it was nothing to do with me, to man up and that everything would be okay. I wanted to feel Dad's arms around me, his aftershave filling my nose and his beard tickling my neck. Yet the thought of the gash in Bernie's neck and river of blood running down his bus forced thoughts of telling Cain what had happened out of my head and dissolved the memory of Dad.

Trainers buried and covered with leaves, I trudged through the trees, head down and shoulders hunched, unable to shake Bernie's blood-soaked body from my head. I barely noticed where I went; my chest ached and a chaos of emotion had swept me up in a strange daze. Then I saw it: dim lights through the trees, no more than pin pricks of white illuminating the foliage around them. Reaching back into my memories, I couldn't remember it being here when I was a child – in the depths of my mind I found nothing but birdsong and running games, Dad's warm smile that guarded a broken heart, and checkered picnic blankets. I was sure the terminal wasn't there then: this angular, grey, block hidden by trees.

Adrenaline and excitement pricked at my skin as I edged closer carefully until I could make out the large bulk of a building in the pale light. A Mech stood outside keeping guard, gun poised, emotionless eyes scanning the woodland where I lurked like a shadow. The hum of the Barrier was much louder here; it was in the air, buzzing like electricity and making the hairs on my arms stand on end. Biting my lip to stop the shout that tried to erupt from my throat, I stood wide-eyed, staring up at the shape that had grown up between the twitching leaves. I had found it – finally – the generation terminal we had been looking for, for the last few months. Heart pounding, I crept silently around the building, giving it and its Mech guard a wide berth until I reached the pulsing Barrier itself. Except for the one guard, no one else was around; it was quiet, remote. No one came out this far, no one left the city – it was empty and still here, not even the birds sang. The village I had driven through was quiet and run down, most of the houses in a state of disrepair, although the twitch of curtains as I drove through assured me that people were still living here, barely surviving in their own squalor.

The Barrier was almost invisible to the naked eye, save for a gentle pulse that buzzed across the perfect image that it reflected back at me. Here at the edge of the woodland, the trees with their dark leaves and fluttering shadows bounced off the Barrier in a near-seamless reflection. In the city it reflected the pale, sky-high, towers of flats or offices, or the flashing traffic lights and glaring MTech signs. It was like looking into a mirror holding a mirror – an image that went on and on; yet you could see the flaws if you took a moment to be still and open your eyes.

Gingerly I reached my hand out so I was almost touching it. Static shot across my skin, carrying with it a warmth that exuded from the Barrier. With a sharp intake of breath, I pushed my fingers into it and for a moment, I thought they might go through. But a burning pain coursed down my arm as if my nerves were on fire. Yanking my hand away, I cradled it like a child, while in the distance an alarm wailed, splitting the silence. I ran. Tree branches tugged at my clothes and tore at my skin as my feet pounded against the damp ground until I emerged at the roadside once more where the Land Rover stood waiting, draped in moonlight. In the inky blackness I fumbled with aching hands for the keys. My stomach rumbled as I threw the hammer and lighters in the boot and climbed into the driver's seat. I hadn't eaten since breakfast and now my stomach was eating me from the inside out. The overwhelming nausea after finding Bernie had subsided, replaced by excitement and a craving for something sweet. As I fired up the truck, the old CB radio began to crackle and click. I picked it up. Silence. I think I had seen Dad use it once, back on the outside – as we raced down green lanes, mud splattering up the windows, crackling voices laughed through the radio. I stared at it, willing it to make a noise, anything. I made to shove it back into its cradle but as I did, it sprung into life again. This time I could hear a voice so quiet and small it was almost lost in the static. I sat there, lips parted, one hand on the radio, the other on the steering wheel, words stuck in my throat with disbelief.

"Hello?"

Static.

"Hello, over?" I tried again.

Nothing but static once more. With a small shake of my head, I put the radio back and fired up the car; I was hearing things. Exhaustion was catching up with me and playing tricks on me; the day had been traumatic, and my mind couldn't focus. I needed to eat, to sleep, to plan. I needed to speak to Lucy and the others, tell them what I had found. Despite my stiff body crying out for sleep, it was time to take action. I couldn't go home, not yet. The thought of Bernie's bus hovered in my mind once more. As I peered down at my phone, I decided to go to Clements, a little café in the back end of nowhere, but the coffee was always fresh and hot, if a little weak. It was open late and I knew it would be quiet. I could nurse a coffee there for a while, maybe eat something and wait until it was time to meet Lucy.

I drove back into London in silence, the weight of my decisions resting heavily in my gut. We couldn't wait any longer to make our move; it was now or never. If Jackson was working for the government, if he had the memory card, there was a chance it was already too late. In my mind, I saw the Mechs waiting behind my front door, Cain strapped to the kitchen chair, his face bloody, nose broken, head lolling as he rolled in and out of consciousness. I clenched the steering wheel, my knuckles turning white; Lucy's name might have been extracted from between his swollen lips.

The street lights soon grew more frequent as the countryside receded, their dim lights illuminating the darkness of the truck. Other cars joined me on the quiet roads until I was sitting in a flow of traffic. As I pulled off the main road and down a side street, my phone lit up the passenger seat and I glanced over. It was Cain. He must have come home, seen the mess outside our flats and wondered where I was. Pulling into the curb, I cut the engine and answered the call.

"Hi."

"Alec, where are you?" he sounded concerned.

"Out."

"Stay out, alright? It's carnage here. Mechs everywhere. Some dead guy on a bus."

I cringed at his tactless words.

"Yeah, I saw something as I left. I got out quick."

"Good, go see Lucy or something, yeah?" he told me.

"Yeah I was thinking I might crash there, or with Jones," I said.

"Jones?" he repeated.

"Yeah, you know my mate that works at Spectrum, the one with a job worse than mine!" I laughed, trying to lighten the mood.

He didn't say anything for a moment, then: "Stick with Lucy!"

"I think she's at work."

Shuffling in my seat, I attempted to reach my wallet as I spoke to Cain. He mumbled down the phone at me about sitting outside her door or finding a work friend to hang out with. Finally freeing my wallet, I chucked it on the passenger seat, glancing out of the passenger window as I did. I froze.

It was the slightest glint, the smallest flash of street light on metal, the hint of a gun; a movement that said, '*follow me, don't argue!*' Two figures bathed in the lurid light of the nearby kebab shop on the opposite side of the street stood facing each other, one in black, one in a suit, and though I couldn't hear the hushed whisper of their conversation, their bodies were stiff with the tension of it.

There was a shuffle of clothes and a brown, well-packed A4 envelope, emerged from beneath the suited man's jacket. The man in black shifted on the spot and there it was again, words unspoken. '*Follow me, don't argue!*' The two disappeared between the grimy bins into the darkness and I followed them with my eyes, caught up in the affairs of these two opposites and an envelope full of money; curiosity had stolen my caution.

There was a muffled gunshot and my blood ran cold. The street I had stopped on was empty; there was no one else around to hear it but me. No one came out of the fast-food restaurants, no one peered out of their windows. No one asked questions anymore. The street was even more silent than it had been before. Throwing myself back in the driver's seat, I reached for the keys in the ignition, eyes itching to look but self-preservation forcing me to sit back, act natural – I had stopped for a phone call.

My stomach flipped as out of the corner of my eye I saw the man in black exit the alley. Despite the hat pulled down and his hood up, I recognised his face beyond any doubt.

"Quinn!" I breathed, wrenching my eyes forward again.

"What? Alec, what did you say?"

Cain, momentarily forgotten at the other end of the phone, sounded panicky.

"I have to go, Cain."

"No, Alec wait. Did you say, Quinn? Jackson Quinn?"

I hung up the phone and sat back up. Watching Jackson casually cross the road in front of me and walk away, I made a snap decision: grabbing my beanie from the glove box and shoving my phone, wallet, and keys in my pocket, I jumped out of the truck and followed him. My heart raced.

My head whirled with wild theories about Jackson as, teeth clenched, I quickened my pace to stay a few metres behind him. He was not a Mech and he didn't look like the typical kind of government official, all slicked back and suited up. He carried a gun. The thought made my feet stutter, his dark form ahead of me grew smaller. Did he take the money? The streets were getting busier as we walked and I could feel my heart pounding in my ears as my resolve returned and I hurried to keep up with him. After about five minutes, he stopped and walked up a narrow flight of stairs, disappearing under a glowing neon sign: Needles Tattoo Parlour. I hesitated at the bottom of the stairs, wondering whether I should follow. I was safe out here on the street in clear view of other people. The earlier gunshot still rang in my ears; I knew he was prepared to kill. Knuckles white and nails digging into my palms, I dashed up the steps and entered the dark parlour.

In the waiting room I was met by a girl with multi-coloured dreads, her face full of metal and every inch of skin inked. She had a face that said, *'I don't give a crap'*. She looked up from behind the counter and raised her eyebrows.

"Hey newbie, can I help you?" she smirked.

I tried to look casual, despite the sweat that was gathering under my arms, whilst attempting to spot Jackson. The waiting room was small and dimly lit; it smelt a bit like weed and latex gloves, and was kitted out with faux-leather sofas and rows of black ring binders. The walls were painted black and covered in tattoo designs and photos of previous customers' new artwork. There was a large window into the parlour itself and, as I sat on one of the sofas, I could just about see the empty chair.

"Hey, you want something?" said the girl.

"Oh yeah, sorry, I just wanted to check out some designs, bit undecided," I lied.

"OK whatever, Dan will be a while anyway – he's got someone else at the moment."

Nodding, I picked up a binder, opening it and flicking through the designs without looking at them. After a moment, Jackson entered. I watched him as he sat bare-chested in the tattooist's chair. His dark skin gleamed in the bright artificial light, the tattooist's pale, latex-gloved hands stark in comparison, moving over his skin, pulling and pushing the ink into his flesh. He gritted his teeth against the pain, eyes closed, head back, feeling every stab of the needles and dot of blood that oozed from the design birthing on his skin. There was something familiar about him that took me off guard as I watched the tattoo on his shoulder joining the map on his skin, something that flung me back to my childhood and Dad.

"See something you like?" said Dreadlock Girl.

"Pardon?"

"A tattoo? Or are you more interested in him?"

I caught myself and looked down at the binder, pulling my hood up over my beanie. I needed to leave. Glancing up once more at Quinn, I saw the tattooist wipe the blood from his skin and sit back, admiring his handy work. Quinn opened his eyes and glanced down. He must have sensed me there as he looked up at the window and our eyes met for an instant.

The binder clattered against the table and landed on the floor as I leapt up and legged it. The girl called after me, something expletive and coarse, but I didn't stop. Darting between disgruntled-looking people, my shoulders colliding with anyone who didn't move in time, I ran until I was back at the truck. I didn't dare to look behind me, unable to bring myself to stop to see if Quinn was following. Pulling open the Land Rover door, I jumped in, thrust the key in the ignition, and pulled away, not bothering with my seatbelt. As I did, I saw Jackson Quinn calmly walking up the street. Fixing my eyes on the road ahead, I prayed that he hadn't seen me and that the lights at the end of the road would stay green.

"Come on, come on!" I muttered to myself as the car in front of me dawdled along up ahead.

My heart continued to thud against my ribs until I reached Clements, where I ordered a large black Americano with an extra shot. Chucking a large spoon of sugar in and stirring, I watched the dark liquid swirl around in the chipped mug. The contents of my pockets sat on the table as I stared at the dark, steaming liquid, feeling its heat burning my hands through the porcelain mug. I tried to comprehend what I had just witnessed: Jackson Quinn had shot that man and left him to rot in that alley between two late-night takeaways. And I had just left – what if he had still been alive? I doubted it, but I hadn't bothered to check. What kind of person did that make me? Distractedly, I picked up the spoon and stirred the coffee again. I was turning into a jerk just like Cain. The phone in front of me buzzed and I looked down to see my brother's name flash up on the screen. It danced across the table until he hung up. Six missed calls from him. I tried to recall our last conversation. Did he mention Jackson Quinn as I hung up? I wasn't sure; I wasn't sure of anything anymore. No one was who I thought they were – myself included.

Picking up the phone, I texted Lucy. *Scrub tonight. Need a new pizza place, the old one is dirty. Start the text chain. I will message in the morning with a new location for pizza. I found something.* Send. After a couple of moments, the phone buzzed. It was Lucy: *OK. You heard from Bernie?* I tapped back a message and then deleted it, trying to decide how best to tell her about him. In the end I went straight to the point. *Bernie's dead. Foul play suspected. Will talk tomorrow. Sorry.* She didn't text me back. I could picture her, sat in her flat, her eyes red from crying; the one person she thought she could rely on gone – murdered. I was her friend, I should have been there to comfort her, but I couldn't bring myself to go. Despite what Cain said, I couldn't go and see her. With everything I knew about Jackson Quinn, I began to wonder if I had a new suspect for Bernie's murder. He could be out looking for me, too. One death on my conscience was already one too many. I brought the mug to my lips and swallowed a mouthful of hot, sweet coffee. It burnt in my chest. No, I had to lay low now – on my own. If Quinn was working for the government then they would be after me, too. No one got out; no one tried. If the people in charge knew about me, then I was already dead.

Chapter 6

The red and black hands of the plastic wall clock ticked by slowly, the last dregs of over-sweetened coffee growing cold in the bottom of the mug as I mulled over the unexpected direction my life was taking. The more I thought about it, the more I realised it was the right thing; this was the push we needed to break free. Yet freedom had an unexpected bitter-sweet taste to it. I had always said I would get out and find Anna and Mum at all costs but now that Bernie was lying dead in that bus, his blood running down the drains outside my flat, I found my resolve wavering. Was it so bad here, as a man, living like this? Living a lie?

The bell on the cafe door tinged and I flicked my eyes towards it, tension rising in my chest but it was an older woman with fair hair and tired eyes, not Quinn. Releasing my knuckle-white grip on the mug, I knew it was time for the lie to end: every fibre of my being knew it was. I had to make sure that Bernie hadn't died for nothing and that I didn't end up just rotting in this hole. Compliance and indifference were the beginning of the end. Pushing the metal chair back across the floor with a screech I stood up, rammed my belongings back into my pocket and headed back to the car. There had to be a new place for us to meet, a place that we hadn't been to before. If this was going to be our last meeting, then I had better make it count.

The night air was cool and refreshing, making my skin tingle and clearing my head as I fired up the 90. The recharge light clicked on as I turned the corner back onto the main road, and I remembered passing a small charging station in the village I had just left. It would be open, and quiet. Taking a left, I headed away from the lights of the city once more, back the way I had just come and, after a few turns, I finally found the charging station. Pulling up to the charge point furthest from the shop window, I climbed out. As I pulled my hood up, I saw the cashier lift his hand in greeting but ignored him, shifting so he couldn't see my face any more than he already had. I plugged in, grateful for the invention of lightning charging, and watched the numbers turning on the gauge. Once it hit eighty credits, I stopped and unplugged it, before waving my wrist under the scanner. I hated that paying for things meant that the government knew where I was, but there was no other way of doing it. Physical money had become obsolete years ago when resources started to dwindle; they couldn't print anymore, couldn't find the paper or ink to print it with. It was just one of the many things they didn't foresee. The implants were used for so many things, people had become so used to them that they didn't think about it anymore and didn't remember a life before them – that generation was gone.

The truck rumbled as I swung round on the forecourt, headlights bouncing off the grimy windows of a cluster of abandoned shops opposite. I paused, my foot hovering over the clutch, and peered out into the darkness. A small sign that read 'customer parking' pointed down an unlit side street, and I smiled at the abandonment before me. Shifting into gear, I drove away from the fuel station and parked the car a little further down the street before killing the lights. I sat, waiting in the heavy darkness, the bright, twitching, lights of the petrol station behind me only light around, and listened. The lonely street was quiet, no people, no cars, no life – swept clean and neat. Sterile. As I climbed out of the Land Rover, something inside me hung back, clinging to the safety of the truck. I craned my neck, peering down the still street. Though it was as empty as it had been a moment ago, something had changed. Resisting the urge to get back into the truck, I pulled my hood up again and zipped it up against the cool air, my feet leading me back to the shops. I paused at the side street, glancing down at my phone. It was gone eleven. There was still no reply from Lucy. Pushing my phone back into my pocket, I headed down the street.

The small car park, with its faded parking spaces, was empty save for an old skip half full of broken shop fittings and rubbish. There was a smell of must and mildew, of things unused and unkempt, which was unfamiliar in the inner city. It was dismal but perfect. The buildings that overlooked the car park seemed quiet and dark, no curtain-twitchers or nosy neighbours – no one that cared. The shops that backed onto the car park were in a state of disrepair, doors hung from their frames like broken limbs, and glass was scattered over the ground, glinting in the moonlight. I stood at the broken threshold of one shop, waiting for my eyes to adjust to the darkness, before cautiously climbing over the broken door and into what looked like an old butcher's shop. Anything of any value was gone, but the metallic smell of blood still lingered, accosting me as I entered. It clawed at my throat and I gagged a little, backing out. The next two shops had once been a florist and a newsagent – both stripped bare except for a sea of animal faeces that covered the floors. The smell was inside acrid, ammonia and decay thick in the air, but we didn't need the place for long, we didn't even need to plug anything in; we just needed to decide on a time and place to break out of this hell hole. My heart beat a little faster and I clenched my teeth excitedly; I could almost taste freedom. I was days, maybe even hours away from discovering what was out there, what the government had kept hidden from us for so long. A terrifying sort of elation swelled inside of me. The idea of being Ava again was so close, so tangible.

Leaving the abandoned shops, a skip in my step, my thoughts turned to Cain. Maybe it was time to bring him in on all of this. The idea of leaving him behind weighed heavy on me, but there was something about him recently that made my skin crawl. The strange game of cat and mouse that we seemed to be playing, one minute my caring brother, the next his cold, hard hands finding their way under my clothes. I could still feel his breath on my face, his hands forcing their way between my t-shirt and my flesh. My shoulders tensed. He was a man I no longer knew, a stranger I still called brother. As I turned out of the side street, heading back to the truck, the blink of torchlight on the empty road made my feet falter; my breath caught between my teeth as I dived back into the side street, pressing myself against the rough brick wall, praying I was mistaken. Hardly breathing, I peered around the corner. The dark figure of a man torch in his hand peered into the driver's side window of my truck. A motorbike was parked a little way down the road. I recognised the broad shoulders and dark clothes. *Jackson.*

Sinking back into the shadows, I waited, cursing every breath that seemed to echo down the narrow street. The shelter of the skip surfaced in my mind but it was too obvious – too full of tetanus-inducing needles. My eyes lingered on the shadowy shop entrance. I took a deep breath and forced myself to pad silently back towards the shops. Skirting around razor-sharp shards of broken glass, I dived behind the counter and crouched down in the stinking filth, acutely aware that something must have died under the floor back here. The stench of it wafted up from between the stained floorboards and I fought my wretch reflex.

As the minutes passed, I pushed my fingers into the screaming muscles of my legs, shifting as noiselessly as I could. From where I waited; the world outside seemed unnervingly quiet, the drum of footsteps never sounded, the flash of torchlight evaporated, soaked up by the night. I let the breath that had been fighting to get out slide from between my dry lips. Trying not to make a sound, I emerged from behind the counter, legs stiff as I tried to walk. The shop sat in the same darkness as when I had entered it, nothing had changed. The street outside was also quiet; nothing moved in the pale glow of the street lights. As I peered around the corner, the coast seemed clear; I couldn't see Quinn or the motorbike. Relief swept over me, warm and new, as I headed for the truck, eyes fixed on the door handle, fingers already wrapped around my keys. As I unlocked the door, I heard the click of a torch and looked up, eyes searching for him. He appeared in front of the Land Rover, his motorbike parked on the pavement, hidden by the hulk of the truck. His dark eyes were desperate as he rounded the truck towards me, shouting something I couldn't hear over the panic in my head. Flinging open the door, I jumped in, fired up the truck and floored it. I swerved around him as he blinded me with the torchlight, and felt something crunch horribly under my tyres, but I didn't stop. As the sounds of the world filtered back to me, I dared to glance in the rear-view mirror. Quinn stood in the middle of the road, staring down at the remains of his torch spread across the tarmac. I watched him fade into the darkness, a dark, ominous shadow. The blare of a horn pulled me out of my fear and back to the road with a lurch. I swerved again, narrowly missing the only other car on the road. The driver flashed angrily at me and whacked the horn repeatedly. Quickly, I flicked on the lights and tried to focus. I glanced down at my hands, fingers white against the steering wheel. My teeth were so tightly clenched that my jaw ached with it, and my toes were screwed up inside my trainers. Taking a deep breath, I tried to unfurl my body from my panicked state of rigidity. I glanced in the mirror but even the tail lights of the car I'd narrowly missed were gone. There was no Quinn, no motorbike stalking me in the darkness.

I'd head home, park up and try and sneak back into the flat. I turned the music on again and tried not to think about Jackson Quinn or the gun I knew he carried. But his face was lodged in my head, his lips mouthing words I couldn't make out, drowned out by my panic. The more I thought about him standing there watching me go, his crushed torch at his feet, I began to doubt I'd made the right choices.

It was just gone one in the morning when I pulled into the car park under the flat and made my way up to number 625. Removing my shoes, I winkled open the front door as quietly as I could, the memory of Cain's anger still imprinted on my skin. Light seeped out from under Cain's door and I could hear the muffled drone of his voice as I entered unhindered. I went straight to my room and closed the door behind me, overcome with a tired relief. After stripping off, I collapsed on the bed, my side aching from the previous night's beating, my mind reeling. Fighting the encroaching blackness that pressed in at the edges of my eyes, I sent a quick text to Lucy with the name of the newsagents and a time to meet: *1 am. Be ready*. Send. She didn't text back but I knew, as sleep caught up with me at last, that she'd get it and spread the word.

Chapter 7

The smell of burning greeted me early the next morning. The clatter of pans and plates breached the thin walls as Cain fumbled about in the kitchen. I reached for my phone. 7.14 am. Groaning inwardly, I hauled myself out of bed and threw on some clothes. I emerged from my room rubbing my eyes, only to be enveloped in a cloud of smoke.

"What the hell are you doing, Cain?" I called through the smog.

Cain appeared from the smoke like a spectre, wafting a tea towel and coughing.

"Get the window," he managed to sputter.

I dashed over and swung it open. The morning breeze swept around the room and the kitchen slowly reappeared. Cain stood at the hob, pushing a charred-looking something sadly around a pan.

"I think it's done," I said, peering over his shoulder.

"Yeah, I know," he said, picking up the pan and tipping the contents into the bin.

"Since when do you cook me breakfast?" I asked. "What did you do?"

"Shut up!"

Cain sat down heavily at the table and poured himself a coffee from the cafetiére. He stared at the mug for a moment before clearing his throat.

"Look, I'm sorry about yesterday, all right. I should have told you about the credits."

He paused, not looking up from his coffee. When he spoke again, his voice was subdued.

"Sorry about the other stuff, too."

He got up, taking his coffee with him, and leaned out of the window. I waited for a moment, trying to work out how to tell him. He seemed receptive, like the Cain I used to know; he was once more the brother who had sat with me while I cried myself to sleep in the days after Dad died, who had come home with men's clothes brought with his own credits to cheer me up – now was a good a time as any. After today, there would be no more time; for all I knew, I would bring down the Barrier and kill us all. But at the same time, I might find Anna; I might find the truth – and for that I'd give everything.

"Cain…"

He glanced at me over his shoulder, then back to the view. I edged closer, taking a seat behind him, out of arm's length. "We need to talk."

Finally, he turned to face me, draining his coffee cup and letting it dangle from his fingers by the handle. I clocked it as a possible projectile. He shrugged his shoulders, nodding at me to begin.

"Are you happy here?" I asked nervously.

"What, here at Foxgloves?"

"No, here! You know…inside the Barrier."

My throat felt tight as I forced myself to speak, sharing my deep darkness.

"It's OK. I mean, what can I say, Alec? This is life. This is just how it is now," he said with a shrug.

He crossed his arms over his chest and stared at me. His eyes like needles penetrating their way into my skull.

"Cain, I hate it. I need to get out and I want you to come with me."

"What kind of bull is this, Alec?" he shuffled his feet a little. "You know that's impossible. You have no idea what kind of world is out there, if any at all."

His voice was steady and calm.

"There must be something out there. Otherwise we wouldn't be in here, would we? What if Anna is still alive out there? What about Mum?" I asked.

"Alec, come on, don't be silly. You heard the explosions – you *saw* the missiles. Come on, there's nothing out there for you. It's all gone," Cain placed the coffee cup on the table.

"But how do you know? You don't know why the bombs were sent. You don't know if anyone survived."

A heat welled behind my eyes and I gripped the edge of the table; this was not how I wanted the conversation to go.

"Alec, really? Let this go, please!"
This – his pity – was worse than his anger.

"No, Cain, I'm going. I'm getting out!"
Something changed in his eyes and it frightened me.

"What?"
His eyes narrowed and I saw his hand twitch. That single word made my whole body tense. A fresh wave of adrenaline started to pump through my blood, sweat gathering on my upper lip. I was wrong, the anger was worse.

"I'm going, with or without you. I finally have a real chance," I said, fixing my eyes on his.

As quickly as his anger had come, it disappeared and I saw something else take its place. I wasn't sure what it was but it made me feel even more on edge.

"What do you mean?" he asked softly, "a real chance?"

"We've worked out a way to get the Barrier down. Only for a moment, but long enough for those that want to get out," I explained quickly.

"We?"

"Yeah, it's not just me."

"Hmmm," he murmured, his eyes fixed me to the spot, "who else?"

"It doesn't matter, Cain. We've finally got a chance."

He turned away and looked out of the window again, as if the dreary cityscape would inspire an answer. He beckoned me over and I approached him cautiously. I stood just behind him, waiting for him to face me so I could see his expression. He patted the window frame and, unclenching my fists, I leant next to him. Pushed against him, I was surprised at how solid he felt through his clothes. He was slight and angular and though he pushed me around, he would be at a disadvantage against a bigger man. Then again, he had a violent temper.

"Tell me," he said.

Taking a deep breath, I explained to him about the others, about our secret meetings in the deserted underground station, and how we had found a way to interrupt the Barrier. I explained how we had been discovered, that I was being followed, and that I had someone after me. Lastly, I told him about the little parade of abandoned shops where we planned to meet in the early hours of the morning to formulate the last part of the plan and to finally put it into action. I could feel myself speaking faster and faster, excitement rising in my chest.

"So, they've finally done it, finally found a way out," he said when I had finished.

I creased my eyebrows in confusion.

"Yeah, we did it. Tonight…I'm leaving tonight," I swallowed hard. "Are you in?"

He gazed out at the buildings once more, the answer still eluding him. After everything I had told him, he still had to think about it? What was there to contemplate? I couldn't understand him. I opened my mouth, about to spew my irritation on him like a swarm of bees when there was a hard bang on the door. Loud and persistent, the banging filled the flat and shook the badly fitted windows. Panic filled my body, freezing me to the spot. I could barely breathe. I looked desperately at Cain, who shrugged. Was the caller for me or him?

"Alec Scott?" came a male voice through the door.

Recognising Jackson's voice immediately, I grabbed hold of Cain.

"It's him – it's Jackson Quinn," I hissed.

There was a glimmer of recognition in Cain's eyes but it was gone in an instant as he dragged me into the bathroom and pushed me into the bath, pulling the shower curtain across.

"Stay here and be quiet," he murmured into the darkness.

I sat down in the bath, hugging my knees, all the self-determination and confidence I had only moments ago, gone. The shower curtain felt like a flimsy defence against the barrel of a gun. I pictured myself: brains splattered across the bathroom wall, the stripy shower curtain ripped from its rail and slung on the floor, blood seeping thickly down the plug hole. I had gone from Alec Scott who could take on the world, bare-fisted and bold, to the Alec Scott I used to be, scared of the world and everyone in it. I thought this version of me was long gone yet here it was, rearing its pathetic head. I was so close to being free that the idea of being gunned down in my own bathtub turned me into a pitiful mess.

Barely breathing, I listened as Cain opened the door; I could just about hear Jackson's voice, soft and deep, through the walls, and then Cain's. I waited for the shouting, for the sound of Jackson Quinn barrelling into the flat, for the sound of his gun. But their voices didn't even change octaves and after a tense moment, the front door clicked shut. The bathroom door squeaked over the Lino floor and I prayed it was Cain as the footsteps approached. The light clicked on and the shower curtain was drawn back.

"Get up, you pussy!" Cain said in his usual manner. But I couldn't move; I just stared up at him, motionless, mouth open like an idiot.

"Look, he's gone. Just get up!"
Taking the hand Cain offered to me, I stood up slowly. Disappointed in myself, I couldn't look at my brother. Once again, I had had to rely on him to keep me safe. Alec Scott, the permanent burden. Not for much longer.

"What did you tell him?" I asked.

"That you weren't here and I hadn't seen you for a couple of days," he said with a shrug.

I nodded and followed him out of the bathroom and back into the kitchen, where he turned to me.

"I'll come, okay. I just need a little time. Sort a few things out."

I looked at him in disbelief, unable to hide the grin that was erupting across my face. "Really, Cain, you mean it?"

"Yeah, okay – look stay here until the meeting, get your stuff together ready and I will meet you there okay? One a.m., right?" he confirmed.

I nodded and he smiled at me. He reached over and patted me on the shoulder; for a moment, he looked as if he had something more to say but it never came. Instead, he turned away and disappeared into his bedroom without a second glance, leaving me excited but still confused.

Following Cain's lead, I headed to my room, collecting the holdall from the cupboard and emptying it onto the bed once more. This time I didn't make an effort to flatten the creases or lay out the clothes; it was as if I were casting aside all of the things I'd been holding onto and the person I used to be. I was going to be Ava again – but not the Ava I had once been, that little girl was never coming back; I knew that much. No, I was going to discover who Ava was now she was a woman. I was going to be reborn.

I shoved a handful of underwear into the bag, followed by some t-shirts and two pairs of denim jeans, one blue and one black. Leaving the bag on the bed, I went to the bathroom and packed some toiletries into a wash bag before returning to my bedroom. Lastly, I grabbed my warmest jacket, a khaki-green trench coat, and slung it over the holdall. I was ready. I was bricking it. I glanced down at the discarded girls' clothes on the floor and felt drained all of a sudden; I wanted to lie down on the bed and just sleep – deep, restorative sleep. I checked my phone: it was only 8.36 am. Still, time to get to work. I should go to work. Act normal, pretend nothing's going on. And the best way to do that was to go to work.

I was pulling on my Quick Drop Shop uniform and tying the garish red apron around my waist when there was a knock at the door.

"Yeah?" I called out.

Cain peered around the door frame.

"Off to work?" he asked.

"Yeah, I didn't go in yesterday and I didn't call. I'll get flagged up if I don't go in today. Don't want people asking too many questions. They might send a drone," I told him.

"They wouldn't send a drone for you," he smiled - but it was unsettling. "Got to stay invisible, right?"

"Indeed, indeed."

"Well, I've got to go sort out a few things before we make a break for it, so I will see you later. Don't wait for me, I'll just meet you there."

"Yeah, you said," I replied, wondering why he felt the need to repeat himself.

"Okay bro, catch you later!"

"See ya."

"Cain. Wait! The password…it's 'jalapenos'."

A realisation crossed his face, then he shook his head and shut the door. I listened to him leave as I stood in the middle of my room, alone once more. Without thinking, I stepped quickly after him, then I faltered. My hand rested on the door handle as I puffed out my cheeks and tried to ignore the urge to follow him. I bit my lip. It was his day off, so I assumed he wasn't going into work, or maybe he was going hand in his notice – but surely that would raise suspicion? Reaching for my equally blinding red work cap, I shoved my phone and wallet into my pocket. Something was up with Cain and I couldn't work it out; I hadn't felt this anxious about him since that day a couple of months ago when he had stormed out and come home a week later a different person. As I headed out of the door, I felt my phone buzz in my pocket. Whipping it out, I saw a text from Lucy on the screen. The message preview showed that it contained only one word: *Done*. All I had to do now was wait.

Chapter 8

The little red hands on the Quick Drop Shop clock crept slowly around its face, taunting me with its second hand, which seemed to linger a little longer than it should over each passing second. Every hour dragged its heels, kicking and screaming, until finally the clock hit seven and I tore my name badge from my shirt, chucking it in the tray by the scanner and swiping my wrist under the little red, pulsing light. Escaping into the dusky evening light, I scanned the streets, pretending to check my phone and adjust my earphones as I loitered outside work hoping I didn't catch a glimpse of Jackson Quinn in his killing garb or the Mechs with my face flashing across the screens built into their chests, the way they did when they were looking for someone.

The street appeared to be clear; people wandered up and down, minding their own business. It was a far cry from Spectrum, where these same people pushed up against each other, sweating and grinding, forgetting the prison we lived in for one brief moment. Out here, virtually no one so much as met my gaze – relief calmed the churning that filled my gut. Head down, music blaring in my ears, I made the short walk from work to the flat in under ten minutes, my body feeling better with each step.

Swinging open the door, I called out a greeting but was met with silence. I had either missed Cain or he hadn't returned yet. I scanned the open-plan living room and kitchen, but nothing seemed to have changed. It was exactly as I had left it this morning. The picture of my family, in its usual place on the end table, caught my eye and for a moment my hand hovered over it. Letting one finger trace over the faces of my family, I stored them to memory once more, fixing them firmly in my mind.

"Soon,' I murmured, the sting of threatened tears forcing me to look away.

I deliberately spent the evening as I normally would, showering, eating, watching television – being ordinary was the best way to stay hidden in plain sight. As the hours wore on, I struggled to concentrate on the meaningless words that poured from the mouths of people on the TV, twitching every time voices passed by my door or keys turned in the doors of other flats. Despite Cain reiterating that we would meet there, a part of me longed for him to come through our door so we could go together, sister and brother once more. Another part of me hoped he wouldn't turn up. There was something about him that still made me nervous, in the way he had looked at me as I had explained about our escape plans, that made me feel like I was betraying the others. He was safety and fear all bound into one person.

Around eleven I headed for the bedroom, kidding myself into thinking I could sleep for an hour. Lying on the bed, I gazed up at the ceiling in the darkness whilst my mind buzzed with a combination of nerves and excitement. Waves of delight at the thought of seeing Anna and Mum again peaked like mountains inside me before plummeting down into pits of hideous cold, dread and doubt. What was I doing? What would I find out there, if anything? I tried to picture the faces of those I longed to see, waiting for me, arms open wide, eyes filled with tears of joy but every time I closed my eyes their faces melted, blistering with an infernal heat. Their bodies blackened and charred, slowly turning to ash as I tried to reach out to them. And then again, there might simply be nothing out there – just a void into which I had poured everything I had. Those thoughts gripped me as I tried to push everything to the back of my mind, tucked away with my fears about what I risked letting into this prison. Radiation? Chemicals? Deadly diseases? It could be the end of the rest of humanity. But I had to do this. I had to get out. It was all a lie. It had to be – and in the lonely darkness I told myself so, over and over.

The shrill ringing of my alarm shattered the light sleep I had managed to drift into. I rubbed my eyes and sat up, head thick with a groggy haze. The sight of the holdall on the floor beside my bed filled my stomach with butterflies, pulling me out of sleep like an electric shock. Scrabbling out of bed, I dressed and gathered the last bits I deemed essential. Taking one last look at the flat, quiet and still whilst inside I burned with a nervous energy, I picked up the Land Rover keys and left, closing the door once and for all on everything I hated about my prison, about my life. Taking the stairs down to the car park, I unlocked the truck, throwing my kit in the back and jumping into the driver's seat. Then I drove. I drove and drove until I finally came to the parade of abandoned shops and parked a little way away. The thickness of the night pressed in on me as I sat in the truck, staring at the side street where so many things were about to happen. I knew they were there, that this was it, but I couldn't move. Winding my fingers around the keys, I gripped them so tightly in my trembling hands that I felt the sting of pierced skin. The stab of pain was enough to shake me free from the weight of the promise I had made to all those waiting inside for me. Jumping out of the vehicle, I headed for the boot, hunting by the torchlight of the phone for a battered-looking map that Jennifer and I had used down in the underground. It was crushed between the 90's body panel and a heavy ammo box full of useful tools and knick-knacks that Dad had assembled himself, imprinting its value on me. With the map in my hand, I locked the Land Rover and headed for the meeting place. As I rounded the corner into the car park, I could hear the shuffling of feet and the low murmur of voices. It seemed dark from the outside but as I pushed the door to the newsagents, I could see the glimmer of torchlight sliding out from under the back-office door. Heart in my mouth, I approached quietly, knocking softly on the battered door.

"Jalapenos," I whispered to the closed door.
There was the briefest of movements behind it, then it was cautiously pulled back to reveal the face of Jones. He gave me a toothy grin and beckoned me in. The office was bigger than I had anticipated, with a small, dirty, kitchenette and an en-suite toilet. There was a narrow set of stairs that I guessed led up to another storage room. Inside, Jennifer and Chris were already seated at a wobbly table, murmuring quietly to each other.

"Hey," I said quietly. "All okay, guys?"

"Hey, Alec, how you feeling?" asked Jennifer.

"Yeah, okay thanks, bit sore but I don't think it was as bad as I thought it was," I told her.

Chris gave me the smallest of glances, his laptop case on his lap, hands clasped tightly over it, protecting it. As I sat down, there was another knock at the door and I looked around to see Cain standing in the doorway. His eyes went from Jones to me and back again. I couldn't see Jones' face but I could tell from Cain's that he wasn't expecting to see him there.

"Cain, come in," I said, watching him as he plastered a thin smile on his face and headed over to where I was stood. "Everyone this is my brother, Cain. He's coming with us."

The others looked up at him and I was about to introduce them when there was yet another knock on the door. Jones pressed his ear to the door, and after a moment he opened it and Josiah and Lucy walked in. Everyone sat down as I introduced Cain to them all – Josiah opening and closing his mouth like a fish a few times and then thinking better of it, remained silent.

"So – I'm sorry to have to start on a downer, but Jackson Quinn turned out not to be what we thought he was," I began.

"He kinda was," murmured Chris, a sly smile creeping into the corners of his mouth.

"Pardon?" I turned my attention to him and he shuffled a little under my gaze. I was glad I made him feel uncomfortable.

"He did help me. With the info I got from him, I was able to find a frequency to temporarily shut down the Barrier for longer than we had previously and I was able to create a virus to reboot the Mechs. It will shut them down for about seven-and-a-half minutes," Chris explained.

"And you kept this news secret?" I asked him, heat rising behind my eyes. I balled my hands into fists.

There was a horrid smirk on his face as he answered, as if he had got one up on me. I noticed he didn't mention the memory stick.

"I only finished it this morning. I texted Lucy."
I turned to her; she hadn't mentioned it either. But she just shrugged her shoulders and continued to stare into the middle distance.

"Well, that's great news, I was under the impression we were just going to have to wing it with what we had," I said.

"Not anymore."

"No, I guess not," I gritted my teeth. "Well done, Chris!"

The words tasted foul.

"OK, well, that brings me nicely onto the reason we had to change venue, which is also the reason why we have to act now. Tonight, in fact," I took a breath. "We can only assume Jackson Quinn stole the memory stick - I wasn't able to get it back."

Chris instinctively looked away, his hands fiddling with the laptop, all the smugness gone from his face.

"I don't know who he is working for or whether he has gone to the government with the info yet, but he found me last night…after I saw him kill a man."

"What?" exclaimed Lucy, forgetting to keep her voice down.

All eyes darted from me to her and then back to me again, the realisation of what we were getting into starting to really sink in. The reality of it filled the air, thick and choking.

"Look, he approached me in my car and I just managed to get away. This is why we need to act now. We are no longer safe, we either go ahead with the plan or we destroy everything and go our separate ways, never see each other again – change our names if we have to. This group never existed."

I paused, holding my breath, praying that everyone wanted to go ahead with the plan. Their hesitation was tangible but after a gruelling minute, Cain stood up.

"I'm in," he said, patting me on the shoulder.

Then Lucy followed his lead, and soon we were all standing around the small, grubby table, grinning at each other nervously, my stomach churning with anticipation.

"Okay then, are you all ready?" I asked.

There were nods from around the room. I slapped the map down on the table and unfolded it, flattening out the heavy creases as best as I could. The others leaned over to get a better look, and Cain held a torch over it to illuminate the colourful lines and road names.

"Here," I said pointing to a large area of woodland, "this is the section of the Barrier that we are closest to. I found it yesterday. There is a guarded generation terminal lurking in the woods. If we can plug into here, we can get the frequency up and running and shut down the Barrier for what – five minutes? You got another memory stick, Chris?"

He nodded and placed a small, black drive on the table. "And it's four minutes!"

"And the Mechs?" said Josiah.

"Weren't you listening?" asked Chris, his bad mood spreading to Josiah.

"Yeah but…" Josiah began.

"I've got it sorted, we just have to upload a virus into someone's ID chip and let one of the Mechs scan it. They are synced so it should take out all of the ones in the vicinity. It won't get as far as the ones in the city centre, it'll burn out before then but it's enough for what we need," explained Chris.

Everyone shuffled, eyes suddenly fixated on the gnarled table top.

"I'll take the virus," volunteered Cain and Jones at the same time.

The pair of them flicked glances at each other, something unspoken passing between them, missed by the downturned faces of the others, before Jones stepped back. I searched for Cain's eyes with mine, but he didn't meet them. A murmur ran through the others and I made to take Cain by the arm but he edged away from me.

"But you barely know us? You'd take the risk?" asked Lucy, her eyes narrow.

I felt the situation slipping out of my control, the others looked from me to Cain and back again.

"He's sound," I assured them. "He'll be with me. In fact, upload it to both of us, just in case."

Cain opened his mouth and closed it again. He smiled at me, his eyes tracing the features of my face in the darkness. Everyone around us was nodding in agreement. I could see the excitement in their eyes despite the shadowy torchlight as I stepped forward and offered my arm to Chris. He plugged his makeshift scanner into the computer and placed it over my wrist. There was a low beep and Chris gave me the thumbs up. With the virus installed, I cast a glance around the group but couldn't see Jones. I stood back from the map and looked around the abandoned room. I hadn't heard him go; he hadn't said anything. A nasty feeling struck me in the pit of my stomach, causing my throat to close and my mouth to go dry. I turned to Cain, who was stood with his wrist under the scanner, and grabbed him by the arm, pulling him closer to me. There was a beep from the scanner and Chris looked up at me, eyes piercing.

"What are you doing, Alec? It wasn't done," snarled Cain.

"Wants all the glory!" muttered Chris, his face sneering.

106

I shook my head. "Where's Jones?"

Everyone else looked up, eyes searching around the room. No one dared to call out for fear of being heard. I shuddered, the hairs on my arms standing on end. Something moved outside the door.

"Turn off the lights," I hissed.

The room went dead. In the inky darkness I could barely see anything, the faint light of the distant fuel station throwing a slice of illumination across one end of the room. I listened hard, heart in my mouth. Lucy's fingers intertwined with mine, the heat of her body leeching into my shoulder; I couldn't bear to push her away, to rip that last bit of comfort from her in the darkness. It reminded me of that day when this all started, when my Dad held me in the darkness, in the unknown – and that had been enough for me; with him holding me, I knew it was going to be okay.

Soft, calculated footsteps approached outside the door and I recognised the gentle hum of the Mechs, the sound of technology that always gave them away. Once they were close enough for you to hear the cogs turning inside them, it was too late. You were already dead.

"Run!" I shouted.

There was a hiss and the room filled with smoke and the door slammed down onto the ground as it was kicked from its hinges. Mechs came pouring in, firing round after round into the smoky darkness. There was the thud of bullets hitting the walls, ricocheting off the kitchenette, sinking into flesh. Lucy tensed next to me, numb in the chaos. I didn't speak, dragging her across the smoke-filled room towards the narrow stairs. She followed limply behind me, crying softly. I could hear the others screaming. I could hear them dying. Where the hell was Cain? I

107

couldn't stop. I had to get out, had to keep going. I couldn't die, not now.

Dragging Lucy up the stairs, we barrelled through a door into a large storage room, dusty and stacked with boxes. Clocking the window on the far side, I made for it and peered out. On the street below, a row of Mechs' motorbikes were clustered in the road, and a mound of stinking rubbish bags lay a little to the left of the window. The rubbish would be our best bet; we might actually survive. Downstairs the gunfire had stopped, but the blood-laden screams of my friends still hung through the air. Through the terror, I could hear boots on the stairs and spun round, scouring the room for a weapon and pushing Lucy towards the window. I found a crowbar lying in the dust; it was a poor weapon against the guns of the Mechs but it was the best I could do.

I turned to Lucy. Tears streamed down her face, her eyes red from the smoke bomb. A pang of guilt made my chest tighten.

"Out the window," I told her.

But she just stood there, frozen.

"Lucy, get out! Now!"

She shook her head, staring at the stairs. There was a flurry of footsteps and Cain appeared, a deep cut across the right-hand side of his face and he clutched his left shoulder, but there was no blood. I was flooded with relief at the sight of him, but it was short-lived.

"I've slowed them down. Go, get out!" he shouted at me, shutting the door behind him.

Turning, I took Lucy by the arm. Cain pushed past us and kicked the window hard, sending glass cascading down to the street below, then he leapt out. I dropped the crowbar and pushed Lucy forwards but she pushed back against me.

"Go, Lucy, Cain is down there. He'll help you," I told her.

There was a crash from downstairs as whatever hasty defence Cain had managed to erect was torn down. There was no time – we had to go now. I took her hand.

"Together," I said, and she finally tore her eyes from the stairs and nodded. "Aim for the rubbish bags, okay? Bend your knees and try to roll out of it."

We turned to face the window with the sound of the Mechs ploughing up the stairs, so loud in my ears. I wanted to cry, too.

"1."

Thud.

"2."

Thud.

"3."

The door at the top of the stairs swung open. There was gunfire. I held Lucy's hand hard and jumped. I felt her body slump as I stepped over the window sill, her grip loosened as we fell. She made no attempt to steady herself as we landed in the pile of rubbish bags. Instead, she hit them with a sickening thud. Something wet splattered over my face and I tasted blood, still warm, still pulsing. With trepidation, I looked over from where I had ended up, my legs trembling with the impact of the jump, pain coursing through my already broken body. I crawled towards her and threw up onto the street.

She lay there, surrounded by old takeaway containers and rotting food. Her eyes were staring up at the night sky, a look of terror on her pretty face, except now she frightened me. The trickle of blood that oozed from the bullet hole in her forehead turned my stomach. I didn't want to look at her yet I couldn't tear myself away from her hideous death. There was a hand on my shoulder and I looked up. Cain. He pulled me to my feet and started to run. I staggered after him, not caring who saw us or who heard us. The sound of gunfire rang in my ears and the sight of Lucy sprawled across the pavement burnt into my eyes.

No one stopped us, no one chased after us as we ran; my heart pounded and my head span until finally, we came to a stop, sliding into a dank, rundown side street. It was lifeless and silent. Leaning against the wall, my breath came hard and fast, vomit rose in my throat again, burning as I forced it back down. I looked up at Cain, who was also breathing hard. His eyes met mine and something in them changed; something that I sensed had been bubbling below the surface for some time now. His eyes were all over me, nipping and biting like insects. He took a step towards me and I instinctively stepped back.

"Cain, what's the matter?" I stammered.
He didn't say anything, continuing to edge towards me. Something dark exuded from him, and my body trembled, fear gripping my chest tight and cold.

"Back off, Cain!" I cried.
As the words escaped my lips, he was on top of me, pinning me to the floor with his knees, tearing at my skin. The damp ground beneath me soaked through my clothes and made my skin prickle. I struggled, kicking and thrashing, but despite his narrow frame, he was strong, solid. I swung desperately at his face, catching him square in the mouth. The force of the blow split his lip but it only seemed to spur him on further, his eyes full of hate and a strange, tainted blood-lust. He grabbed me by the throat,

110

paying no heed to his injury, his finger feeling for the implant at the back of my neck and switching it off. Screaming, my skin shifted over my changing flesh. The guise of manhood slipped away in an instant to reveal my real face. I cried out, desperately fighting with all I had, until he pulled back and head-butted me, hard. Pain radiated through my skull and burnt at the back of my eyes. I saw him reach into his jacket and pull out a knife. I stared at the blade, seeing but not comprehending it. Eyes shut, I tried to leave my body, to drift away; I had nothing left to live for, everyone I cared for was dead. The man who had protected me for almost a decade was about to kill me. I had nothing. I was finished. I wanted to feel numb, to shut it all out, but I couldn't. I lay there, feeling his hot breath on my face, his rough lips on my skin like cigarette burns.

"Good girl, keep still," he whispered, his lips close to my ear.

His breathing changed and I felt the cold of the knife's blade across my stomach. Forcing myself not to feel, I let my mind wander to people and places that made me feel safe. I pictured Lucy, and then her face became Anna. I prayed to a God I had disregarded long ago that whatever demon possessed him would go, that he would change his mind and leave me alone. With a last ounce of strength, I twisted under his grasp but he pressed in harder with his knees, crushing my joints and forcing the air out of my lungs.

"You couldn't just let me take the virus, always the bloody martyr!" he growled.

Suddenly his hands shifted, no longer slow and teasing, instead, pulling my wrist towards him. A sharp slice of searing pain cut across my wrist and my eyes flicked open as a wail of agony escaped from my lips.

Cain stopped as my cry evaporated into the gloom, and the click of a gun being cocked echoed in the silence. I dared to breathe.

The weight of him was on top of me, still pressed down on my legs as he straddled me like an animal, but now he sat stock still, his hands in the air. Over his shoulder, I could see Jackson Quinn with a gun pressed to the back of Cain's head, his features twisted into a look of pure disgust.

"Get up," he said, his voice quietly terrifying.

A sickening grin spread across his face as, slowly, Cain did as he was told, turning to face Jackson and placing his hands back on his head, concealing his knife.

"All yours mate, I was bored of her anyway," said Cain, scathingly.

With hate in his eyes, Jackson smashed the butt of the gun into Cain's arrogant face, sending him sprawling onto the ground, the knife flying out of his hand.

"Run," Jackson told me, eyes fixed on Cain and his gun still raised. "I said run!"

Cain got slowly to his feet, spat a dislodged tooth out and stuck his middle finger up at Jackson. "This wasn't what I paid you for, now, was it?"

There was a crack as Jackson fired the gun. I froze in horror as the sound of metal on metal echoed around the street and Cain was sent reeling once more. He lay motionless, sprawled on the ground. My stomach lurched as I clambered to my feet, unthinking, and took a step forward. But Jackson put his large arm across me and held me back. I didn't fight him, instead, I stood trembling, barely able to breathe, and struggling to get my head together. The chill of the night air seeped into the skin on my bare chest, a feeling I hadn't had in a long time, but it was barely a whisper, a feeling felt in my subconsciousness. The edges of my vision were dark and hazy; all I could do was stare at Cain's lifeless body. I pushed against Jackson's arm again, but he held me back, turning to face me, a dark look in his eyes.

"Wait," he said quietly, anger still in his voice.

As he spoke, out of the corner of my eye, I saw Cain move and a wave of relief spread through my body, yet as the wave peaked it threw me down into the fires of rage, my fists clenched and my jaw stiffened. He had forced me to the ground, cut me, scared me. He was my brother, the only one that knew my secret. He was all I had, and now I had nothing, no one. He hated me.

The words I wanted to shout at him stuck in my throat and the foul names I wanted to fling at him like bullets burnt inside my head. I wanted to feel the splintering of his skull beneath my hands, see the red of his blood run down the grimy street, but I didn't have the strength; it was like his final betrayal had sapped everything from me. Jackson's arm remained hard against my chest and it was a moment before I realised that I was no longer fighting him but leaning on him. Cain got to his feet, a manic look on his face, anger boiling behind his eyes. He walked toward us as if he were invincible.

I wished he would just turn and run, just leave. But he advanced like a machine, his eyes fixed on me. Jackson fired another shot but it seemed to ricochet off him again, only slowing him down for an instant. Fear rose its ugly head again and I stumbled back, landing on my backside once more. Jackson adjusted his aim and took another shot. Nothing. Cain didn't even flinch or miss a step.

Jackson pumped shot after shot into him, until the gun was empty. The world around me seemed to slow for a moment, then suddenly Cain was on him, beating him to the ground, burying angry fists into his face. Jackson used his size to throw Cain off, but he came back again with just as much ferocity. The two fought hard, blood spraying over the ground and the walls, neither relenting. Then the fight seemed to turn and Cain appeared to have the upper hand. I stood watching, forgotten by both of them.

"No," I managed to murmur as Cain forced Jackson to the floor, battering him senseless; his head lolled sickeningly as Cain's fist mangled his swollen face.

As if in a dream, I scoured the street for something – anything – I could use to stop Cain. My eyes fell on a length of blue nylon rope. I snatched it and dashed towards my brother, wrapping it quickly around his neck and hauling him off Jackson, twisting it tighter and tighter in my hands and leaning back. He choked and gagged, clawing at the rope but I held firm. I held onto that rope until my fingers went numb, until my arms were dead with the effort. I held on long after Cain dropped to the ground, the smell of piss filling the air. I held on long after he stopped struggling. It was as if I, too, had entered a state of rigour mortis; if I let go then it would be real, he would really be dead. I would really have killed him. Collapsing down on top of him, I finally let go, pressing my face into his back. I inhaled the smell of his aftershave mixed with the washing powder we both used. Hot tears ran down my face into his jacket, silent and desolate. I lay there for an eternity, feeling the heat leach from his body into the night air and into the ground; I felt him turn cold beneath me. I knew the anger would come, I could feel it lurking inside me, biding its time. As much as I tried to deny it, I had a temper, too. But for now it could wait: grief had me. I cried for Cain, for Lucy, for Jennifer and for Josiah. I even wept for Chris and rat-faced Jones. I cried for Jackson and for myself: all the tears I had sucked up and fought back over the years.

When the tears finally stopped, I peeled myself away from my brother's body. As I got to my feet, I immediately threw up whatever was left in my stomach. It wasn't much. I looked down at Cain. I had seen people die, this world was full of it now; there wasn't a man or woman alive that hadn't. But I hadn't seen it so close up. I hadn't killed anyone before. I killed someone. I killed my brother. I let out a small moan. I killed my brother. I murdered Cain.

Chapter 9

All at once I felt the chill of the night air, harsh on my trembling flesh, acknowledged the heavy cold drops of rain that had begun to fall unnoticed, smelt the blood on the ground and tasted it in my own mouth. I pulled my jacket around me and zipped it up, quickly flicking my implant back on; gritting my teeth as flesh moved over bone. Movement on the edge of my vision caught my attention. Jackson Quinn was pushing himself up into a seated position against a wall, tentative fingers feeling the damage done to his face. He said nothing, watching me through swollen, blood-shot eyes.

He scared me; maybe more than Cain did. Yet I had chosen to save him over my own brother. Then I remembered why: the feeling of Cain's hands all over my body, his lips pressing against my ear, his blade slicing into my flesh. I wanted to be sick again but there was nothing left. I was hollow. I strode over to Jackson and placed the heel of my boot on his fingers. Bones crunched under my foot. He winced in pain but didn't look away.

"What did you mean?" I enquired. "What did Cain pay you for?"

Jackson looked up at me and shrugged. His head tilted back against the wall and he closed his eyes.

"Tell me!" I growled, crushing his fingers a little with my heel.

Pain radiated across his face: "To kill you!"

"What?"

The revelation took my breath away and I stepped back off of Jackson's fingers, catching myself with one hand against the wall.

"What did you say?" I stammered.

"He paid me to kill you," he repeated.

"No," I murmured, half to myself, half to Jackson.

I turned to look at Cain's body; he looked small and pathetic in death. Now the rage was coming, yet it was soured by confusion; the back of my throat burnt. Finger nails cutting into my palms, I took a deep breath.

"Why?" I managed to say.

"He wanted information about an escape plan, about the Barrier. He wanted to know what you knew and how legitimate your plans were. Then he wanted you dead," Jackson Quinn informed me.

"If he had just asked…" I murmured, the feeling in my legs wavering, and the damp of the wall pressed against my skin as I slid down next to Jackson, "I would have told him."

"It wasn't for him, the info…Government snitch, you can smell them a mile off," he laughed to himself, but quickly drew his breath in through his teeth in pain. "I wasn't expecting *that,* however."

He nodded at Cain's body and I turned to look in the direction of his gaze. Cain lay where he had fallen, one arm underneath his chest, face pressed into the dirty, wet, tarmac.

"Go and look," he said.

All I could do was stare for a moment at the body of my brother as rain soaked into my hoodie, plastering my hair against my face. Jackson took a deep breath, a deep groan rising up out of his throat, shaking me out of my stupor. I made my way over to Cain and knelt down, before rolling him onto his back with some effort. Again, despite his small frame, I was surprised at how heavy he was. I closed his eyes, trying to avoid the judgement they pierced me with. Hands quivering, I ran them over his chest, fingers finding the ragged bullet holes in his shirt. It was ripped to shreds but there was no blood. Several of the holes were directly over his heart and lungs – Jackson was a good shot – yet Cain seemed unharmed. I ripped open his shirt to reveal his chest and stumbled back, hand clasped to my mouth, shaking my head.

Beneath a torn cover of skin, I could see metal gleaming in the glow of the street light. My throat tightened as I forced myself to get close again, making myself touch him. My fingers touched the cold metal, hard and synthetic next to his skin – if that was even his skin? I pushed back the folds of flesh as far as they would go, my breath stuck in my lungs, until his entire chest was on display. He was metal from the waist up to his collar bone, and it appeared to continue across his right shoulder.

"What the…?" I started, the words catching in my throat.

"I've seen it a couple of times before," Jackson called out, shifting himself awkwardly against the wall, "but he's better than the others."

I sat back on my heels and stared at him, at the machine that resembled my brother. The memory of that week all those months ago when he had disappeared surfaced in my mind. Now it all made sense. Something had happened to him far worse than a beating. Something far, far worse.

"He's not your brother anymore, you didn't kill him, if that makes you feel better," said Jackson.

"I don't understand…I…" I mumbled, unable to take my eyes off of Cain.

"It's all part of the big brother thing MTech have had going on since the Barrier appeared. They find people that have been in accidents, messed up and half-dead, and they give them a second chance. Rebuild them and use them as informants. Pair them up with people of interest," Jackson explained between breaths.

"People of interest?"

MTech had known. Nothing had been a secret.

"Guess they thought you were a threat to the Barrier and to MTech," he said.

I glanced in his direction to see him pushing himself unsteadily to his feet. He was such a big guy but he looked like a baby deer in the hazy morning light.

"We need to leave," he told me.

I shuddered. Leave? Go where? My thoughts were singular, monosyllabic; nothing else would process. I was watching my life play out through frosted glass.

"Before they catch up with you. Come on."

As he approached, I stared up at him. He loomed over me, his breathing still a little ragged. Letting my eyes drop to the ground, I felt the words barely leave my lips.

"No!"

"Alec, we don't have time for this. Let's make the most of the time that machine has brought us, it won't be long before they realise his signal is down. They will come for the body, and fast. Tech like that won't be left lying around for long," he pushed.

"Why would I go with you? You stole the memory stick, you were sent to kill me! Who the hell are you?" I shouted.

"Quiet," he hissed at me, resting a large, heavy hand on my shoulder. "Look, I can explain but not here, not where we are vulnerable. You have to believe me, Alec: I'm not the enemy. In fact we need each other, I've been waiting for someone like you. I had to see it to believe it."

His eyes fixed on mine pleadingly. What had I got to lose? Go with the man sent to kill me or wait for the Mechs to come and haul me away?

"Give me your gun," I demanded, brushing his hand off of me.

"It's back there," he said letting me go and gesturing over his shoulder. My eyes followed to where it lay in a puddle on the floor.

"And anything else you might have," I said.

He shook his head. "Just the gun, everything else is with the bike, but it will have to stay there. It's too dangerous to go back for it. You will have to leave yours, too."

I went over and collected the gun. It was empty and useless, but I took it anyway. I, was not, however, prepared to leave the 90; it was the one thing I had left.

"I'm not leaving the 90," I told Jackson. "But first…"

Gun safely tucked away, I headed back to Cain. Even if only a small part of the virus had uploaded onto his ID chip, I couldn't leave it for MTech. I couldn't leave them a key. If they were still interested in me, then there was a part of the puzzle they were still missing. Now I knew why Cain was so keen to volunteer to take the virus.

Remembering his knife, I scanned the ground for it and spotted it lying a few feet away, the blade catching the street light. A moment later, teeth clenched, I was pushing the blade into the skin of his left wrist. The knife was dull and snagged on his artificial flesh as I gouged out a hole big enough to get my fingers inside. Finger forced between metal and skin, I dug around until I finally freed the ID chip. As I pulled at it, it emerged, attached to a long stream of wires that followed it out like veins. I cut them to free it

120

and pushed the chip into my pocket, white-knuckled as I gripped the knife in my other hand. Jackson stood watching me, his face full of questions. But he remained silent.

With one last look at Cain, I let him go – he was dead to me now, whoever he was. I forgot about him, blotted out his memory and shut away that part of my life. No looking back. I turned to Jackson.

"I thought you were in a hurry to leave?" I said, pushing past him in the direction of the 90.

Jackson was calling to me as quietly as he could but I ignored him, letting my feet carry me away. I couldn't stop. If I stopped then I would have to think; I'd have to let the situation become tangible. A few moments later, I heard ragged breathing at my side and turned to see Jackson there, his face was a mess and he was covered in blood but he managed to keep up with me despite the pain.

"You'll get us killed," he said.

"That will save you the job," I retorted as we turn the corner.

To my surprise, the street was still dangerously empty. The Mech's motorbikes were gone but I could still see Jackson's bike. The small pile of rubbish bags in the distance made my step falter. Lucy's face flashed into my mind, the fear in her eyes and the wet streaks carved down her filthy face, the limpness of her hand in mine as we had jumped. I swallowed, trying to ignore the shattered windows of the shop and the lingering scent of smoke bombs.

The Land Rover waited a short distance away and I made a beeline for it. We reached it without event and I unlocked the driver's side door. Climbing in, I threw the knife in the back before pushing the keys into the ignition.

I reached across to open Jackson's door and hesitated; I could just drive off, leave him here to fend for himself. Hesitantly my fingers brushed the lock and out of the corner of my eye, I saw something move. A rain of shattered glass filled the cab, slicing into skin, as a bullet came whizzing through my driver's side window. I wrenched up the lock and Jackson jumped in.

"Go!" he shouted as Mechs started pouring out of the neighbouring houses, guns blazing. I turned the key, pushed it into gear and floored it as the bullets bit through the metal cab of the 90, splintering glass all around us. A cloud of smoke billowed out of the exhaust, temporarily slowing down the Mechs – but only for a moment. The drone of their motorbikes rang in the air, gaining on us as we went. I loved the Land Rover but it wasn't built for speed. I knew they would catch us up and kill us both. We had minutes at most.

"You still have the memory stick?" I shouted at Jackson over the roar of the engine.

"Yeah," he fumbled in his pockets and produced the small, white stick.

"And you know the new frequency I'm guessing?" I asked.

He nodded. "Not just a pretty face."

"The weak point in the Barrier is about five minutes from here, but we will have to get to the generation terminal on foot. Can you run?" I asked him.

"I don't know," he groaned, "your brother did some serious damage."

"Okay, you need to just trust me. Got your seatbelt on?"

Egging the truck on, I drove as hard as I could away from the little village and towards the clump of woodland that was home to the generation terminal. The Mechs, rapidly catching up on their motorbikes, grew larger and larger in the wing mirror. As the thrum of an engine on my right told me they were upon us, I slammed on the brakes sending a couple of them blazing into the back of the Land Rover; the whole vehicle shook, sliding across the road, and collided with the bike to the side of us. My head ricocheted off the steering wheel and the seat belt ratcheted tight against my chest. I felt the warmth of blood on the side of my face as I glanced over at Jackson, who hung in his seat, unconscious. Praying I hadn't killed him, I clambered out of the smashed driver's side window and out into the open. Standing face to face with a Mech, I turned off my implant. I grimaced as I became Ava; the pain of changing never seemed to get better. An army of Mechs surrounded me, sent for me and my little army of rebels. I heard them arm their guns in unison.

The Mech before me pushed its in-built pulse gun into my face as I thrust my left wrist out towards it, ignoring the hot barrel kissing my forehead. No need for traditional bullets here, a shot from the pulse gun would fry my brain, no problem.

"Go on, scan me," I shouted at it, spitting my words into its blank mechanical face.

The machine obeyed, its programming making it follow protocol; my face was not the one it was sent to kill. I could almost hear the mechanical cogs turning. I was Ava, not Alec. There was a beep as the Mech scanned my wrist, followed by two more beeps in quick succession, incorrect scan data. Then it took a step back to do a full-body scan. The world seemed to slow down as its eyes swept over my body. I threw my arms wide and laughed; a laugh that didn't sound like mine, that seemed to come from somewhere outside of my body and take on a life of its own. I watched, my smile reaching my eyes, as the light behind the Mech's eyes flickered and went out, it dropped to the floor at my feet like a pile of scrap metal. I could hear them falling all around, powering down and clattering to the ground.

Setting the timer on my watch for seven-and-a-half minutes, I spun round and clambered back into the car. I tried the engine a few times but it wouldn't start. Cursing, I reached over to Jackson and gave him a shake. He gurgled groggily and opened his eyes, his hand going straight to his head.

"Wake up, we need to move now!" I told him, undoing his belt and then reaching over the front seat into what was left of the back of the Land Rover. Grabbing the holdall from where it was wedged between the front end of the motorbike and a dented body panel, I jumped out, heading to the passenger side. Placing a foot against the body of the truck, I wrenched Jackson's door open and he slumped towards me, catching himself on the slack seat belt. Barely able to stand, he pulled himself up right, planting his feet on the tarmac and leant against the bonnet. It was a moment before heavy silence and the sea of Mech bodies scattered across the road sunk in.

"It worked…" he murmured, eyes wide as he took it all in.

"We don't have long, less than six minutes now before they all wake up and shoot the crap out of us," I said glancing down at my watch. "Grab a bike and let's go!"

Jackson did a double-take as his eyes met Ava's eyes not Alec's, but he did as I said and heaved himself onto a bike with a groan. His engine roared as I fired up mine; the bike trembled beneath me as I let it loose, my eyes fixed on the woods ahead of us. I couldn't think, couldn't breathe, yet the wind that whipped around my face and over my skin made me feel alive. In the midst of all the death and destruction, I felt free. This was it: if I died now, at least I was going out fighting. Our bikes ploughed into the thin scattering of trees, shaking us hard as we ran over tree roots and mud. I squinted a little to protect my eyes, and pushed on.

The generation terminal was less than five hundred metres into the woods, a large gun-metal grey building that buzzed and hummed like the Barrier itself: a great grey beast lurking in the woods, waiting for us – waiting for me. Stopping the bike and jumping off, I let it drop to the floor with a thud. Eyes fixed on the doorway, dodging the fallen bodies of the Mechs, I ran. Yet my heart sunk as I came to a halt outside the solid, metal doors.

"No!" I yelled, kicking the nearest Mech as hard as I could.

The surge of anger evaporated, leaving me cold and trembling as I slumped against the door, head in my hands. I had forgotten the codes for the doors. I was so bloody close. I looked down at my watch: three minutes. The squeal of metal being ripped from metal made me peel my head from my hands and look up. Jackson stood tearing the outer skin off the nearest Mech's face, his fingers ripping out reams of colourful wires.

"They're powered down," I told him. "It's no use."

He ignored me and carried on until he found what he was looking for; a small sphere attached to more wires not dissimilar to a human eyeball.

"Get the bike," he said.

Hurrying to my feet, I pushed the bike over to the door, where Jackson pulled off the panel to the battery.

"Hold this on the terminals when I say," he instructed, handing me the nerve-like wires, then he lined up the eye with the scanner to the door.

"Now!" he shouted.

As I pushed the wires against the battery terminals, a spark flashed across the wires and the eye in his hand lit up. The scanner on the door beeped and the panels slid apart to let us in. Discarding the wires, I pushed past Jackson, pulling him with me into the brightly lit room within. The doors shut quickly behind us and my head was filled with a loud humming, even louder than it had been outside.

"Mechs don't use codes, do they," he explained, breathlessly, pre-empting my question. "Come on!"

Jackson started to run, wincing with each foot fall. To my amazement, he seemed to know where he was going as I followed him unquestioningly through the sterile corridors, leaping over the robotic bodies of the Mechs until we reached the inner sanctum. Jackson opened the door labelled Control Room and we were faced with an array of flashing lights and wires, hard drives stacked high on top of each other.

"Memory stick time," he said, pulling it out of his pocket.

As he smiled, the timer on my watch let out a beep that filled me with a cold terror. The inactive Mech who was slumped over at the desk began to twitch, processors whirring back into life.

"Hurry," I whispered, as if speaking quietly might save us.

Jackson reacted instinctively, pushing the memory stick into the nearest USB port. He shoved the stirring Mech off of its chair and punched a few keys on the console. The humming that filled the air began to fade and Jackson grabbed my wrist. He barely looked at me as we flew from the room, barrelling out of the door into a drowsy-looking Mech and sending it clattering to the floor; yet there were others congregating behind it. They seemed confused and unsteady but it wouldn't take long for them to regain control. They had scanned me as Ava; they would know my face now. I was an anomaly.

As we ran, I flicked up four minutes on my watch and started the countdown. Heads down, we made for the front doors and I pressed the release button. They slid back to reveal the Mech we had disarmed wandering around with half its face trailing after it. It turned as we emerged breathing heavily, the sound of Mech footsteps echoing behind us.

"Where now?" Jackson asked.

It was my turn to lead him. I turned left and headed for the back of the generation terminal. I glanced down at my watch: two minutes left. *Come on, come on!* I egged myself on, pushing harder and harder until my legs burned, but suddenly I could see it. I could see the outside, I could see the world beyond, and I almost stopped. Jackson blundered into the back of me and we tumbled across the border of our small world and into the next. I heard the beep of my watch as we fell, heard the instantaneous drone of the Barrier. There was a searing pain in my arm and then it went dark.

Chapter 10

The darkness that enveloped me was all-consuming and deep; it was all around me, above me and below me, covering my mouth and nose so I couldn't speak or breathe – suffocating me. I had no control of my body but I could hear desperate voices in the blackness; at first painfully loud, drumming on my ears, and then barely a whisper. I tried to tell them I was here in the darkness, that they needed to find me, but they didn't seem to hear me.

Suddenly there was a scream so loud and so terrifying that it frightened me, and for a moment I didn't want to be found; I wanted to stay away from the screaming, safe in the darkness. And then I was back, blinded by the light of the sun, pain coursing through my arm and my head. I could see Jackson crouched down with his back to me, peering over a large fallen tree. He turned to me and covered my mouth. It was in that moment that I realised the screaming was me. I stared at him, my eyes desperately trying to convey my fear and pain. The smell of his skin and sweat filled my nose and I could taste the saltiness of him on my lips. The dampness of the ground seeped through my skin and my body trembled as the cold perpetrated my awareness. As quickly as he had appeared, he began to fade into the darkness again, and as hard as I tried to fight, I couldn't stop it encroaching on me once more. As it swallowed me, I thought I felt hands lifting me up.

****

I lay there, pretending to be asleep, my head pounding, silently listening as they moved around me;

unable to bring myself to open my eyes and see what prison they had me in. I had been caught. I had tried and I had failed – but at least I had tried. I had tasted freedom before being dragged back into my pointless existence. A noise that I hadn't heard in years drifted into my consciousness, something that I had almost forgotten: the sound of children playing, of running and laughing – the sound of joy. It was so sweet and so pure that I opened my eyes, desperate to see them, tears welling up in the corners. Turning my head, I searched for them but I was in a small, shabby room and all I could see was the bed I was lying on, and pair of wooden chairs.

Taking a breath, I tried to move but as I did, pain, temporarily blocked by unconsciousness, welled up in my left wrist. I reached over with my other hand and felt for it, desperately searching the place where my hand should have been.

"No!" the words were barely a murmur.

I sat up; a cold sweat gathered on my face, dripping down my back as I gazed down in horror at the bloody, bandaged stump where my hand should have been – where my chip should have been and where my watch should have sat. My watch, how would I wear it? A stupid question – but it was all I could think about as I sat and stared at it like it was someone else's arm. I wanted to wiggle my fingers, to brush the hair from my eyes but I couldn't. My head span, vision blurring and my breathing became ragged gasps as panic gripped me.

There was a gentle knock on the door and I tore my eyes away from the stump. The door opened slowly and Jackson's big frame came into the small room. He stayed in the doorway for a moment, his eyes on me, on my arm, taking it all in. My stomach gave a flip as he looked at me as a woman, not through the blur of head wounds and car chases, but with clarity. He was the first man to look at me and see Ava, not Alec. I held my breath. Eventually, he came over to the bed and sat down heavily. He, too, had recently had medical treatment. His wounds looked clean and sterile, and were beginning to heal.

"I'm sorry," he said, and left it at that, his words hanging in the air.

I didn't say anything. Instead, I turned my gaze back to my arm and then, unable to look at it anymore, scanned the room, my eyes searching for something else, anything else, to look at. My gaze stopped at the window, which was slightly ajar, I could still hear the sound of children playing outside and feel the gentle current of cool air seeping into the room.

"What happened?" I asked Jackson, my own voice, Ava's voice, sounding strange to me.

Refusing to meet his eye, I continued to stare at the window. He shuffled around at the foot of the bed; then he stood up, and paced the room a couple of times, running his hand over his head before he stood with his back to me. His shoulders rose and fell as he took a deep breath. When he spoke, his voice was as quiet and sad as it was deep.

"What's your name?" he asked.

I looked down at myself; my underdeveloped breasts were visible through a grey cotton nightie, and it clung to the straight lines of my boyish body. I reached up to the back of my neck – the implant was still there, and for a moment I wanted to turn it on and hide behind it but I didn't. I looked down at my feet, shuffling them under the thin woollen blanket.

"Ava," I said.

"Ava," replied Jackson.

I wanted to hear him say it over and over. *Ava. Ava. Ava.* It was mine, my name. I looked up at him and he gave me a gentle smile while I stared at him blankly, my thoughts too many to show on my face.

"It's nice to meet you, Ava," he continued. "I do think we've met before."

I raised my eyebrows as he stretched out his hand but I ignored it, leaving him clasping air. After an awkward moment, he withdrew it and began to talk.

"When I spoke with Cain, I thought I recognised the surname. Scott. But I wasn't completely sure. Your father came to me when you were a child, wanted to make you 'Alec'," he said.

My mouth fell open; I could hardly process what he was saying. It was *him*: the tall, dark man with the broad shoulders. My father's friend!

I shook my head. "I don't get it."

"I'm a tech," he said with a shrug. "I worked with the government and your Dad was a friend. I helped out a colleague. Always wondered what happened to you."

"Well, now you know," I told him.

I didn't want to talk about Dad; it was an invasion of my privacy, him knowing about my private life.

"What happened after the Barrier?" I asked, changing the topic.

"We made it – we got out!"

"Almost," I said, dragging my eyes back to my arm.

"I know," he paused, deliberately not looking at it. "Look, as we crossed over the Barrier, our time ran out. It reactivated. Your hand was on the other side, Ava," Jackson told me.

Ava! It had been so long since I had been called that by anyone other than Cain, that it felt alien, even on my own lips. Then I remembered: Cain. Stupid, dead, traitorous Cain! I could feel the rumblings of anger in my stomach, bubbling up in my throat, clenching at my insides with poisonous claws. For a moment, I could still see him straddling me and feel the weight of him crushing me. I shook my head, focusing on Jackson's face.

"Where are we?" I said.

"Outside."

"Yeah, I get that. I lost a hand, not my mind!" I said cruelly.

Jackson pulled a face like I had just slapped him. I had gotten him out of that hole – why did *he* look so hurt? If he hadn't bulldozed into the back of me, I would have gotten through cleanly; in fact, the bloody mess at the end of my arm was more or less his fault. I clenched my teeth.

"I know," he replied, regaining his composure once again. "We're about a mile from the Barrier. Heading south, towards the coast. This was a nursing home. They use it because it still has basic medical facilities."

As I pushed myself up from the bed, my head still a little groggy, my feet stumbled and I felt Jackson's hands on my shoulders but he drew back quickly as I pushed against him, avoiding his worried eyes, and headed for the window, pushing it wide open. It appeared to be early evening and a group of kids were playing outside in the street, amongst the abandoned cars and empty-looking houses. Beyond the houses, there was a large field and I wondered why the children weren't playing there. They stopped and looked at me as I threw back the window, then one of them shouted something and they carried on with their game. Childhood: something that had been

132

stolen from me, and now I envied them playing in the wake of our devastation. I watched them for a moment, and I guess Jackson watched me, unsure of what to say, maybe; or scared of what I might say to him. Eventually, I turned round and flopped down on the bed, staring straight up at the ceiling, my hand under my head.

"So tell me, what now?" I asked Jackson.

"You and your friends were right. There's a whole community of people here. People survived the bombs and the radiation; they found us as we came through. Took out the Mechs that followed us. Look, Ava – there is someone you need to meet, but I need to tell you something first," he paused and stood up again.

"What?"

It was rude, but I was prickly, exhausted.

"The Mechs, the Barrier, it was my tech. I wrote the founding software, but they..." he began.

"But what? What lies are you about to give me, Jackson?" I shouted, feeling a spurt of anger frothing up inside me once more. "This whole crappy mess is your fault. Is that what you're telling me?"

"No! It was never intended for this. Look, I had my reasons...I," he tried again.

"Ha! What possible reason could you have for trapping us all in that bloody dome, creating those creatures that stalked us? That killed my friends? What possible reason have you got?"

The fire was uncontrollable; it rattled through my bones and radiated out of my skin, but I didn't care.

"Ava," he raised his voice to combat mine, and grabbed my good wrist.

I tried to push him away, expecting him to hold on to me even tighter, to slap me around a bit, just like Cain but he just let go and backed away.

"I thought someone like you would understand," he said bitterly. "If you would shut up for a minute and let me explain."

There was a knock on the door and we both fell silent; my nails dug into my hand. After a short pause, the door opened and a woman in her early twenties walked in. She wore jeans and an off-white t-shirt, brought together with a thick, khaki-green army shirt that swamped her small, boyish frame. I stood there staring at her, unable to move or speak. It felt like I had been punched in the stomach; all the breath was knocked out of me. The woman stayed in the doorway, taking me in as well – her eyes travelling up and down my body. They filled with sadness as she came to my hand and then to my battered face. Suddenly, she was wrapping her arms around me, pulling me into her, enveloping me with her scent, covering me in her softness. I stood there, unable to hold her – static as my head scrambled to make sense of it all.

"Ava," she murmured in my ear with a voice I never thought I would hear again. "Ava!"

"Anna?" I replied.

Over Anna's shoulder, I saw Jackson disappear out of the room, silently closing the door behind him. Our eyes met for a moment and he shook his head, his dark, soulful eyes full of things unsaid. Eventually, Anna released me from her grasp and I stepped back, still not sure if I could believe my eyes. I reached my good hand out to her face and she stepped towards it, brushing her cheek against my fingers, her eyes fixed on mine. In her, I saw a reflection of how I should have looked: dark hair and dark eyes, still feminine and gentle. With one finger, I traced the small shape of her mouth, the tilt of her nose, the powdery lids of her eyes and the deep scar across her cheek. I let my finger linger there for a moment.

"Shrapnel," she said, knowing what I was about to say before even I did.

She had always been like that. I nodded and let my hand drop. But she quickly reached for it and entwined her fingers in mine and smiled at me. It felt uncomfortable, awkward.

"Oh, Ava," she murmured softly, "what did they do to you?"

I pulled away, unable to return her smile; I couldn't look at her. I was so different from how I was when we last saw each other, more Alec than Ava. Ava was a ghost I thought I would find when I got out of the Barrier. She would be there, waiting for me on the other side, like a long-lost friend, and our souls would be one once more; I would be Ava again. But it hadn't happened; the shell Alec had created was hard to shed. It clung to me like a second skin, tight and restrictive, yet safe and familiar. Stubborn, hard-faced Alec reared his ugly head; I was still fighting for my life – to get out. The wait for the outside was over yet somehow I still felt incomplete, still as alone and lost. It tainted my joy with disappointment, sucking the colour from it.

"Nothing," I told Anna.

She let my hand go and brushed the loose bits of dark hair from her face, wrapping them tightly around one finger. She sighed and grabbed one of the chairs, dragging it over to the side of the bed and beckoning me to sit down with her. I obliged.

"What about Dad and Cain? Did they make it out?" she asked.

I shook my head, unable to meet her concerned eyes.

"What about Mum?" I asked quietly.

Anna shook her head, and I felt another pang of pain like I had lost Mum all over again.

"Look," she said softly, "I don't know what happened to you in there, but you're out now. I can't tell you it's better out here than it was in there but we're together again. I never thought that would happen."

I nodded.

"Clearly you have some stuff to deal with, but we'll get through that. I can tell you about Mum when you're feeling up to it," she continued, rubbing my arm, but I shrugged her off.

Anna didn't say anything else, just looked at me sadly. I had dreamed about this moment – perhaps she had too – but it felt like an anti-climax. Was I a disappointment? I didn't blame her for feeling that way; there was no Cain, no Dad – no one that mattered.

"Ava…" she began, but was interrupted by a knock at the door.

"Yep?" she called, looking over her shoulder.

A man with a pleasant face and a touch of grey in his beard and mousy hair, no more than thirty years old, peered around the door. He was tall and had an air of authority about him. He, too, wore a thick army shirt buttoned up with a grey t-shirt underneath, cargo trousers and boots. He smiled at Anna, his face lighting up, then a more reserved smile for me. I stared at him.

"Time check. It's just gone five, so three hours until sunset, okay?" he told Anna.

"Thanks, Seb, can you start the lockdown without me?" she replied, checking her own watch, and he nodded then disappeared, closing the door once more.

"Lockdown?" I asked, quickly getting to my feet.

"Yeah, we have to make sure everything we need and, more importantly, everyone is safely inside and locked down before nightfall," she replied, checking her watch.

"That doesn't really answer my question, does it? What are you hiding from? What's out here, Anna?"
My skin prickled and the headache pierced my skull like a hot needle. I sunk down onto the bed.

"Look, you won't believe me until you see it – and I have a lot to do before the sun sets. Floodlights to check, alarms to test…you know the drill," she said jovially, standing up and shifting the chair back against the wall again.

I didn't know the drill, but she had sparked my interest. The anger subsided a little as I put it on the back burner, still simmering gently.

"I'll come with you," I said, looking up at her.

She smiled and took me gently by the shoulders, shaking her head, and I felt all of my ten minutes younger than her.

"It's better if you just stay here. Get some rest. There's plenty of time for you to help out. I'm sure we'll be able to help each other out soon enough. Just focus on feeling better, yeah? Sort things out with *you* for now, Ava, okay? I'll be back later," she told me.
Her words were kind but they carried authority, as if she were used to giving people instructions. With that she gave me one last squeeze and left the room.

A wave of relief swept over me as she left, shortly followed by tiredness. My arm throbbed and my body ached; whatever painkillers they had given me were starting to wear off. I slumped down on the bed, my body crying out for sleep, but I knew it wouldn't come. I had so many questions, so much emotion pent up inside of me that I had no idea how I really felt. A mixture of joy, relief, disappointment, and anger swelled through my body, each emotion coming and going in waves until I felt like driftwood, floating away on an endless ocean of confusion, so overwhelming it felt like a physical force pushing me down into the mattress – so I pushed back, locked it all up and put on my mask once more. In my mind, I felt Alec slip back into control. I lay there with my eyes screwed shut, listening to the noise of people busy outside my window, footsteps and voices back and forth, back and forth.

The sound must have lulled me to sleep. I woke again with a start to the deafeningly loud wail of what sounded like an air raid siren. The sound cut through the walls of my room, shaking me to the core. Wrapping the blanket around myself, I climbed out of bed. Peering out of the window, I was fooled for a moment into thinking I had slept until the next morning. Blindingly bright floodlights lit the street outside, illuminating the dilapidated houses I had previously thought were whole. I craned my neck to look out but there was no one about. There was another blast from the siren and then everything fell silent again. Beyond the glare of the floodlights was the inky blackness of night. The empty field stretched out past the houses and I could see the shadow cast by a barbwire fence that skirted the edge of it, invisible to my foggy mind in the earlier rosy light of the sunset.

"What's going on?" I murmured, taking a few steps back and pulling the blanket tighter around my shoulders.

I took a step towards the door then hesitated. *What if they come back for me and I'm not here?* But they'd left me – for all I knew they'd never return. I pulled open the door, determined not to wait to be snatched away by whatever they were so desperate to keep out, and stepped out into another small room which looked like a kitchenette-cum-sitting room. It was bare, apart from rows of padlocked cupboards. The Lino tiles squeaked under my bare feet as I headed for the way out on the other side of the room. There was a peephole in the door there and I pressed my eye against it, trying to see what was on the other side. Beyond was an empty corridor lined with a couple of other doors like mine, numbered 'two' and 'three', as well as a door labelled 'Warden'. There was a fourth door made up of two panels of fogged glass; it had to be the way out. I jiggled the door handle but it was locked. My chest tightened and I fought to get enough oxygen into my lungs; I would die here, alone and forgotten.

Taking a few steps back, I barrelled into the door. It was cheaply made, flexing as I slammed into it. Although pain coursed through my shoulder, I stepped back again and charged into the door once more. The flimsy chipboard caved, splintering nastily. Pain swam in front of my eyes, a dark mist that made me stop; I scanned the room desperately for something to use as a battering ram. Scrambling over to the kitchenette, I pulled at the cupboards wildly. Suddenly it seemed urgent that I got out of that room. Finding nothing, I headed for the bedroom again, grabbing a chair. I picked it up, one-handed; then I spotted the open window and the darkness that lay beyond it. Something was moving, stalking the perimeter out in the blackness, just beyond the reach of the floodlights; something big, which moved like an animal on all fours, pacing, stalking, but I couldn't quite make it out. I dropped the chair and edged closer, heart pounding.

Suddenly, a powerful beam of light swung over the fenced area and there was a blood-curdling cry. The siren sounded again but at a pitch that made my skin crawl and my eardrums tighten. I covered my ears with my hand and arm, unable to tear my eyes away from the window. A creature the height of a building was writhing around, trying to get away from the blare of the siren and the searing light which somehow pinned it to the ground. It was like nothing I had ever seen before; tall enough to be able to look into second-storey windows easily, with legs and arms like splinters strung together with sinewy muscles and skin stretched taut over an elongated skull. Its bare eye sockets were sunk deep into the side of its head like an animal and its nose was two large slits that gaped as it breathed. Its lips receded to reveal rows of glisteningly sharp teeth and its hands were adorned with talon-like fingers. It thrashed about, clawing at its own head, tugging at its skin and wailing.

The siren continued as I watched the creature slump to the floor. Its skin appeared to smoulder and its flesh began to shrivel, sticking to its bones. Petrified, I wanted to stop watching, but couldn't. A scream had stuck in my throat and my feet were rooted to the floor.

In a last desperate attempt to get out of the light, the beast pulled itself up, lifting its head, and for a moment it fixed on me. Even though it was void of eyes, I knew it was looking at me. Hunger, sadness, and anger surged through my body, followed by a darkness that was so overwhelming I broke down and sobbed. I crumpled to the floor, pulling at my head and wailing.

"No, stop! Please," I cried, my voice sounding distant and odd.

Shadowy images appeared in front of me, distorted as if I were looking through an out-of-focus lens. A rapid fire of gunshots made me convulse as if I, too, had been shot. The siren stopped and there was a loud bang as the door to the front room crashed open, breaking my trance. Arms wrapped around my waist, pulling me back from the window I was somehow half hanging out of, filling me with warmth again. The room came back to life, colours saturating the world once more.

"No!" came Anna's voice. "How could I be so stupid?"

My body shook and my throat felt tight; I stood there staring at her, dumbfounded and disorientated. The windowsill, the darkness, that creature; nothing made sense.

"Come on, come on," she said, throwing the blanket around me again and pulling me into her before we bundled out of the front door and down the corridor.

"Anna…" I managed at last.

"I'm so sorry," she murmured, more to herself than me.

As we emerged from the glass-panelled door and out into a courtyard edged with flats, Anna picked up the pace. I could feel her next to me, her body tense as she led me away from the nursing home and away from the floodlights. I bumbled along next to her, not sure if I was walking or being dragged. I couldn't feel my body or the ground beneath my feet; my bones were cold and I tried not to shiver but despite the thick blanket my skin still crawled. An unpleasant feeling lingered and I felt like I had seen something I shouldn't; been caught between two worlds. I took a last look over my shoulder before we disappeared between the blocks of flats and out onto a narrow path that ran along the back of a row of houses, but I couldn't see anything – just darkness. We rushed along the streets until we arrived at the base of a road leading up to a large, fenced building that had its own floodlights, unlike the other dimly lit roads that were illuminated only by street lamps. Anna made a beeline for the building and I followed; her arm was still tight around my shoulders. A man sat waiting outside, bathed in the white glow of the floodlights. A machine gun was strapped to his body and there was a box at his feet. He stood as we arrived. I recognised him from earlier; it was Seb.

"Anna!" he called as we got within hearing distance.

"Open the door, Seb, we need to get her in!" Anna called back, and Seb hurriedly pulled a bunch of keys from his pocket, unlocking the door.

The wood sounded heavy and solid as he pushed it back, and I was hit with a mixture of smells that reminded me of being at school: cabbage, books, and that odd, rubbery smell that sports halls have. Anna paused to speak to Seb as he shut the door behind us and as she finally let go of me, I took a moment to catch my breath and look around. Rows of lockers lined the walls of a wide, linoleum-floored corridor. There were doors leading off into other rooms, which were labelled with the names of different types of trees, and I could hear voices coming from somewhere nearby. As my senses returned, I felt pain in the soles of my feet and looked down; I wasn't wearing any shoes and I was still wearing the stupid nightie I had on from earlier. The colour rose in my face and I pulled the blanket tighter around my shoulders.

"Did she see it?" I heard Seb ask Anna, despite the low tone he had adopted.

"I think so," replied Anna.

Turning to look at them, I saw Seb's hand go to his gun. They stopped talking immediately.

"I can hear you, you know," I said.

Anna placed a reassuring hand on Seb's arm and turned to me. "Sorry, Ava – of course."

"What's going on here?" I said. "What the hell did I just see?"

"Let's get inside properly, Ava, yeah?" said Anna softly, placing a hand on my shoulder.

"No!" I shouted, shrugging her off. "Don't bloody well fob me off again with your softly-softly crap. What is out there? What are you hiding from?"

Anna looked surprised for a moment, then regained control. As I stared at her, I realised she too had a gun strapped to her body. She adjusted it then took it off and gave it to Seb with a resigned sigh.

"Sure, follow me," she said, trying to take my hand. I dodged her, staying where I was.

"Do you want to stay in that nightie for the rest of the evening?" she retorted.

I rolled my eyes in the same way Cain had always done to me; maybe I was more like him than I'd realised. I still needed to tell her about Cain. My skin prickled and my stomach clenched once more, as if he were there, touching me all over again. I had to tell her about all the crap that had happened before we got out: the blood and the mess and the dying. And Dad, oh Dad! That would be a bitter pill to swallow; it still choked me all these years later.

I followed Anna down the corridor, peering into each room as I went. Most were empty, and those that weren't were being used for storage. Long gone were the students who sat at their desks, although in some rooms I could still see kids' paintings and scribbly spider writing adorning the faded displays. I wondered how many of those children had survived? Had been able to experience the awkward strivings of puberty and the misery of adulthood? We reached the end of the corridor and turned right. I could hear voices more clearly here, but we didn't head towards them; instead, I followed Anna a little further, past a door with a female figure on it and into a room labelled 'Staff Room'.

The room was much the same as the others we had passed, half-filled with boxes, but some of the sofas remained. Anna gestured for me to sit but I refused and she rolled her eyes and began rummaging through one of the cardboard storage boxes. After a moment or two, she produced a pair of slim-legged cargo trousers and a black racer-backed vest top. She held them out to me and I took them. They were clean but musty from being stored.

"Bra?" said Anna,

"What?" I said.

"Want one?"

I looked at her and shook my head. I had nothing to fill it, surely she could see that – even without the implant, I still looked more like a teenage boy than a twenty-three-year-old woman. Anna opened the box underneath.

"We've got masses of these," she said, handing me a green army shirt similar to hers, "Not very flattering, but it's another layer."

As I took it, she returned to her rummaging until she found a packet of socks and another pair of pants in an unopened box.

"Here," she said, "you get changed in here. I'll go find you some boots and then we can talk."

"Umm…can I wash?" I asked.

"Oh yeah…it's only rain water so it's not very warm but it has had the sun on it most of the day," she told me.

She walked over to the door and I followed again. We stood in the middle of the corridor and she directed me back the way we had come, towards a large set of double doors labelled 'Sports Hall' where I found the door to a female changing room. Inside, it was just as I remembered the changing rooms at school: rows of benches and hooks lined the tiled walls, and at the very end of the room was a run of drains hemming in a three-shower cubicle.

Sticking my clothes on one of the benches, I shed the nightie onto the floor, then made a beeline for the middle cubicle. I half expected to hear the noise of people screwing in the cubicles next to me as I turned on the shower, but it was quiet; all I could hear was the drum of the water on the floor. Cautiously, I stepped into the flow of water but it was pleasantly warm. I washed the dirt from my skin with my good hand, attempting to keep the bandaged stump dry. Every part of me stung under the gentle stream of water as it washed away the dirt but left the bruises. Since running into those thugs on the inside, I had been beaten, battered, and bruised, and now I had finally stopped everything hurt. And then there was my hand and the sorry mess that was left of my arm. I could barely look at it. If I ignored it, then it might not be real; I might wake up tomorrow and it would be there again. *Just a dream.* I laughed to myself, at the ridiculousness of it all.

Glancing around I spotted a bar of soap sitting on a tray fixed to the cubicle wall. I grabbed it, trying to rub it into my hair, but it slipped from my one-handed grasp, bouncing across the cubicle floor and collecting with the dirty water in the drain. As I bent to pick it up, my feet went from under me and I put my hand out to the cubicle wall to stop my fall. But it wasn't there. Missing the wall, I landed on my backside in the pool of water. I sat there, unable to move, not wanting to carry on or to look at my mutilated arm. Leaning my head back against the wall, I let the water fall onto my face.

I don't know how long I sat there sulking, feuding, but eventually, the steady stream of water turned to a trickle and stopped. My skin puckered with the cold but I didn't move. There was a gentle knock and the door of the changing room opened. A cold draft blew in, followed by Anna's voice echoing around the tiled room.

"Hey, Ava, you okay? I forgot to give you a towel," she called.

When I didn't reply, her footsteps quickened and drew closer to my cubicle.

"Ava?"

"I'm here," I said quietly; I could see her boots under the cubicle door. "Just pass me the towel, would you?"

A large, well used, cream towel appeared over the top of the door and I took it, wrapped it around myself and opened the door. Anna stood there, worry all over her face. I felt her eyes follow me up and down before I pushed past her to my clothes.

"Do you mind?" I said and she hurriedly turned round.

"What happened, Ava?" she asked me. "Your body…"

I finished getting dressed before I answered her; I needed that time to think of a reply. There were still things I didn't

146

want to tell her, not yet – she was still a stranger to me. If we didn't look so much alike there would have been no way of connecting us, except now that I looked at her, I noticed that her face was rounder and her body curvier and fuller than mine. She had a little tummy, which suited her. She was a better, healthier version of me.

"Look, I think we both have a lot of questions. Let's go talk," I said.

Anna stared at me hard.

"Okay, come on. We can head back to the staff room, it's quiet there," she told me.

We walked in silence back through the corridors as I tried to but left work out where I would start. Maybe I would let Anna start? Maybe we would sit there in awkward silence?

I perched on the edge of the sofa and watched Anna get comfy against the arm, tucking her legs underneath her as if we were at home having a chat over a cup of tea. She brushed her hair from her face and smiled at me.

"So," she said, "I've got a lot of talking to do, so maybe just listen for a bit? Don't worry about asking questions for now. Let me get to the end first, okay? You want anything to eat? Or a glass of water? Don't worry, it's not rain water!"

I nodded. "Water, please."

She got up and disappeared out of the room, returning a few minutes later with a glass of water and a pack of biscuits. She handed me the glass and I took a long, refreshing gulp.

"Okay, well I guess we begin with the bombs," she began.

I listened as Anna explained how the same day Dad, Cain, and I left for the city she had been playing in the back

147

garden with our dog Zumba when there had been a massive power surge; sparks had flown from the electricity pylons on the hill near our house. Then it went dark. The sky had filled with aircraft like something out of Star Trek. Anna told me how she could see a blue light from the engines; the air around them trembled with the heat.

Questions pressed against the back of my teeth and I opened my mouth to speak, but she shushed me and carried on. She had watched as some aircraft turned nose down and dived into the ground, others began firing on the surrounding houses. Then the bombs had come, sent from our own government to destroy the alien invaders and whatever happened to be nearby, but the aliens had simply emerged from their ships, like giant, pale ghosts, and absorbed the radiation from the bombs as they exploded, carrying on with their demolition and destruction.

"The government aided them, if anything, and then abandoned us when they saw that they weren't going to win. Left us outsiders – those of us who weren't worthy of a place of safety – to fend for ourselves. They all went and hid behind the Barrier, safe from the bombs and the radiation, and the gnashing teeth of the Ghosts. They knew it was coming. They pummelled the Ghosts with all they had and it just made them stronger, so they went with plan B," she paused and took a bite of her biscuit. "I remember Mum coming running out of the house when she heard the Ghosts' ships appear, and then she just stopped; she just stood there watching. And then she was gone. I don't know where she went but Zumba and I hid in the chicken coop…you remember it, Ava? The one you could stand up in with all the shelves for the chickens to perch on, but they all bundled on the same one?"

I nodded. I remembered the chicken coop. I'd always loved going out to find the eggs, still warm from the chicken's bodies.

"The chicken coop wasn't a lot of protection. The Ghosts dug a hole right next to our house. Cut off the power, the water, the gas, everything. Stuff went flying," Anna pointed to the scar on her face, "that's how I got this. Anyway, when it finally went quiet, Zumba and I snuck out from under the coop and it was like an apocalypse, like out of those zombie movies we always bugged Dad to let us watch. The house was half-collapsed, others down the street were rubble. There were huge craters everywhere that seemed to go down for miles, couldn't see the bottom. I don't know what did more damage: the bombs or the Ghosts. Those of us that were left rallied together. Mrs Rogers who lived next door had survived by hiding in the basement with Sebastian their son, remember him? Mr Roger was taken, like so many others, but Mrs Rogers took me under her wing and we survived somehow."

Here she got up and walked around the room a bit; I watched her twist her hair around her finger, the way she had done as a child when she was thinking.

"I didn't really understand what was going on for a while, I just knew I was scared all the time – that every day more of the survivors disappeared. In the dark sometimes I can still hear the screams."

A strange look came over her and I reached out to take her hand. After a moment she began recounting her story again. "Took us a while to work out that the Ghosts were blind and that they have sensitive skin and hearing, which means they don't like the light or that siren you heard. That's why they live underground in tunnels and only come out at night."

"Like ghosts," I interjected.

My stomach growled and I took a biscuit.

"Exactly," she smiled, but it was a sad smile. "Just a shame it took us so long to work that out. They took so many of us, Ava; no-one's come back either. I still don't know what they do down there, but they come in the cover of night, looking for us, hunting us. That's why we have the floodlights and the sirens and the fences. But as you know, it's been fourteen years and, well, there hasn't been anyone to run the power plants, pump water, import food. We've almost used up the power we have to keep the floodlights going – our old fuel generators and solar generators just don't cut it. We need a bigger power source, a permanent power source…like the Barrier."

"The Barrier?" I said, shifting in my seat, poised to take a bite of my biscuit.

"The Ghosts are heading for the Barrier anyway; they've taken everyone they can and they can hear the drone of the Barrier. They can smell the people hiding under it. It's like a deadly migration. But it means they'll all be in one place soon, and then if we can harness the power of the Barrier, we could drown them in light – drive out the darkness," she paused to take a breath, "but we haven't found a way in, not yet anyway…but you, Ava, you found a way out."

I sat there quietly, contemplating everything she had just told me. I wouldn't have believed her if I hadn't seen that creature, that thing she called a Ghost. It was like an outline for the latest sci-fi movie – and I couldn't be their hero.

"It wasn't me," I said. "You need to speak to Jackson Quinn. He invented that tech."

Anna looked surprised. "But I thought you were working together?"

"It was a partnership of convenience, Anna. We only met because Cain hired Jackson to kill me," I told her, "and something about Jackson knowing Dad back in the day."

"What?" her face was a picture.

"Yeah, Cain, our big brother, the one who was supposed to look after me when Dad died," I paused. "Oh…yeah…sorry, Dad died."

She shook her head, "I had guessed that was what you had meant before."

I hadn't meant for it to come out so abruptly, but it had and there was nothing I could do about it now.

"Alcohol and a broken heart," I said.

Anna took a deep breath and nodded for me to carry on.

"And Cain wasn't really Cain, something happened," I couldn't help but shudder a little; I crossed my arms over my chest. "MTech turned him into some kind of super-Mech. I didn't realise he was working with the government to stop anyone getting out of the Barrier, finding out the truth, and letting the outside back in.

After the Barrier appeared, MTech, the company Dad worked for, took over. They controlled everything, from your name, to your gender. And they policed their dictatorship with machines. We lost people too, Anna – anyone who spoke up or who was considered a drain on what resources we had, disappeared. They wiped out the older generation - killed our free will.

But Dad saved me. He saw the future and guarded me from it. It's thanks to him I got out. But it wasn't just me – there was a group of us trying to find a way out, but we were betrayed - by Cain."

By me.

The bitter taste of that evening filled my mouth and felt my resolve waver. My skin puckered, a wave of cold spread through my flesh; the betrayal was not forgotten, the loss still raw. I hurried my words, not wanting to revisit the image of Lucy sprawled in the rubbish, blood, and brains everywhere. "The Mechs came and killed everyone, then Cain tried to kill me. Jackson saved me and I killed Cain. Then Jackson and I got out."

Anna opened her mouth to speak but was interrupted by a knock at the door and I looked up to see a little figure at the frosted glass window. Anna stood up and opened the door.

"Why are you not asleep?" I heard her say to the person at the door.

"I'm scared, Mummy," said a small childish voice.

"Of what sweetheart?" she asked.

"The dark."

"Daddy's there."

"But I want *you*, Mummy."

I couldn't remember the last time I had heard anyone use the word 'mummy'. Anna stepped out of the staffroom and closed the door but I could still hear her voice and what sounded like Seb's. A moment later, she came back into the room with a small girl clutching her hand. Seb followed them in but hung back in the doorway. He bent down and handed the girl a well-loved rabbit toy before kissing her on the top of her head, then he kissed Anna on the cheek and gave me a long look before leaving. Fists clenched, I looked from Anna to the girl and back again. Suddenly it all made sense. Anna, Seb and this little girl: a little unit, a family. Anna had another family besides me.

"Ava, meet Eve," Anna said, brimming with pride.

I looked at the little girl presented to me. She had big hazel eyes like autumn leaves, the same as Anna and I, but fair, mousy curls like Seb. Loose curls that I remembered Sebastian Rogers having as he had leaned over our garden fence all those years ago and laughed with Anna. I felt replaced; after all those years of wondering if Anna and Mum had survived and were waiting for me, I had been replaced by this little girl. I instantly recoiled from her.

"Eve, this is, Ava, she's Mummy's sister. That makes her your Auntie," said Anna softly.

"I thought she was a long way away? Like Grandma and Grandad and Uncle Cain?" said the girl.

"She was but she found her way back," Anna told Eve.

Anna's little tummy made sense now, the fullness of her body; motherhood had been kind to her. Eve stepped forward, still clutching Anna's hand, giving it a tug when she didn't move with her. She popped herself down on the sofa and pulled Anna down next to her.

"This is Babit, Auntie Ava," she said, holding up the faded toy for me to see.

"I see," I said, unsure how to reply.

Eve looked at me, then at Anna and then at me again. She looked puzzled.

"Are you a boy?" Eve asked me.

"No, Eve, Ava is a girl," Anna interjected.

"But she's got short hair like a boy," continued Eve.

"Some girls have short hair, sweetie," replied Anna.

"You look like Mummy," said Eve.

"Ava is Mummy's sister; Grandma was her mummy and my mummy. We were in Grandma's tummy together. We're twins," said Anna.

"Twins?" said the girl.

Anna gathered Eve up onto her lap and the little girl snuggled into her chest. I gritted my teeth and attempted to ask something I thought I should ask.

"How old is she?" I asked.

"I'm four," exclaimed Eve. "I had a party and everything."

I nodded and Eve yawned. Anna hugged her tighter; she began to sway a little and as she did, I saw Eve's hazel eyes grow heavy, fighting sleep. Anna watched Eve's sleepy little face until she finally succumbed to sleep, still clutching Babit. I shifted a little in my seat, trying to get as far away from them as I could. I couldn't think of anything to say so I sat there watching them, mother and daughter, in a gentle embrace. After a moment Anna spoke quietly.

"Is there anyone back inside, you know…for you?" she asked.

"No," I said. "They sterilised all the women, froze the eggs, and sent us on our way. That's why Dad made the implant for me."

"Implant?"

"Yeah," I said reaching for the back of my neck and switching it on.

Screwing my eyes shut for a moment, I held my breath, waiting for the pain to stop as I became Alec once more. As I let out a breath, my shoulders dropped and my fists unclenched. As much as I had longed to be Ava, now I wasn't sure I wanted to be her after all; Alec felt much more like my own skin. I heard Anna catch her breath. She stared at me open-mouthed.

154

"And what about the rest of you?" she asked, gesturing downward, awkwardly.

"That's still Ava, sort of. I had a binding for my chest," I told her.

"Your voice?"

"Alec," I said, reaching out a hand to her.

She shook it in disbelief and I smiled at the look on her face. I had one up on her now; I became the unknown, the unexpected.

"And this is how you hid? From the sterilisation? From the authorities?" she said.

I nodded.

"This was what Dad was working on. This was the tech the military wanted and why we were on the inside."

Carefully, so as not to disturb Eve, Anna reached over until her fingers rested just millimetres from my face. She lingered there as I drew back, not touching me but not pulling away either. The warmth from her fingers hovered over my skin. Part of me wanted her to touch me, yet the louder part wanted her to leave me alone. After a moment, she let her hand fall and gave her caress to Eve. I reached up and turned the implant off again, and within a moment I was Ava again, uncomfortable and strange.

"So, did they find you?" Anna asked quietly.

"No."

One-word answers were all I wanted to give her.

"You can have kids then?"

"If I wanted to," I said then added, "but I don't. Look at how messed up this world is, why would you put that misery on someone else?"

"That's a sad thing to say, Ava," murmured Anna, her eyes flicking down towards Eve.

I gathered myself.

"Speak to Jackson, OK – he's the one you need."

"Ava, he left."

"What?"

"After you argued, he left. Went to look for his son," she said.

"He has a son?" This was news to me.

"Yeah, didn't he tell you? His wife and daughter were killed by MTech but he has a son who was with his parents when MTech came. They held them hostage, that's why he built the Mechs and helped with the Barrier," Anna explained.

It was like a punch in the face. I had been so quick to judge Jackson; but then, he hadn't told me about his family. Standing up, I ran a hand through my hair, my head whirling. Then I decided. He had had plenty of chances to tell me; it was just another lie, from another liar. *It wasn't my fault; none of it was.*

I stood up and walked over to the boxes, then back to the sofa, and sat down again. *Now what?*

"I tried to persuade him not to go but he was adamant, and he's a big guy – I wasn't going to argue with him. Strong and silent type. But you're still here, Ava, will you help us?" Anna asked.

I couldn't look at her; if I did, I wouldn't be able to just leave and go my own way. There was a gentle thud as Babit slipped from Eve's hand, and I automatically reached down to pick it up. I handed it to Anna and she smiled at me pleadingly. My eyes darted from the sleeping girl to my twin sister and back again. As much as I didn't want to help – wanted to go back to just worrying about myself and what I wanted – I couldn't leave them like this.

"Fine," I said. "Jackson said something about Mechs that came through?"

"Yeah, we took out the two that followed you through. They seemed glitchy though, uncoordinated."

"I guess that will do," I shrugged, "when do I begin?"

Chapter 11

Anna put Eve back to bed and I spent the rest of the night being introduced to the rest of the people who were staying in the school. There were about twenty of them, including three children, who slept in the school at night under the protection of the floodlights. There was a mixture of people but no one older than sixty by my estimation; I guessed the Ghosts took the weak and the elderly first, just like the government had done inside the Barrier.

Then I met Sebastian Rogers, my sister's husband in all but paperwork. A little older than Anna and I, I could see why she had fallen in love with him. He doted on Eve, ruffling her hair and tickling her, adoration in his ocean-blue eyes. He saved the same look for Anna. For me, however, his face smiled and his conversation was friendly but his eyes moved across my face, taking me in; all the while his hand never left the gun slung over his shoulder.

Ignoring the sting of another rejection, I focused on Anna. Relearning her mannerisms, remembering the girl I had left behind. We were two halves reunited. Sebastian and Eve were my replacements, no matter how *nice* they were; I was only helping them for Anna – she was mine first.

Once I had met everyone, I took a seat at the long school dining table. I sat there, lost in the crowd for a moment, watching the men and women I had just met milling around, some in small groups talking, others sitting alone reading. This was a community of people who knew each other, who helped each other. They all had someone. Unlike where I had come from, they didn't ignore each other. I pictured the woman at the scanners again, huddled on the floor like a pile of rags – and I had walked away like everyone else. We chose not to see the pain. A lull in the chatter and the jangle of a small, tinny bell interrupted my thoughts, bringing me back to the school hall and a man I didn't know who presented me with a plate of bland tinned food.

As I chased the last elusive bit of food around my plate, Anna shifted down a place to make space for a woman in her thirties with skin like honey and rich, dark eyes, which smiled at me even though she didn't know me. Anna introduced her as DiDi, previously an Accident and Emergency nurse and the 'best medic she had ever met'. DiDi busied herself with redressing my arm as she talked merrily with Anna. I watched her work, her tight ringlets of mahogany hair fighting to break free of the black bandana she wore. She patted me on the arm when she was done, telling me she would keep an eye on me. I offered her a small nod and quickly returned to the lukewarm cup of tea that had been presented to me at the beginning of the evening as they filled me in on their plans.

A small group of them had left the safety of the main compound further north, where most of the population that was left were living, to get closer to the Barrier to use its power. They had found smaller groups along the way, recruiting some and leaving others. I watched the little red hands on the school clock tick slowly by as they relived the group's countless tales of devastation and escape. Every story seemed more tragic than the last, filled with grief and loss, yet the fire behind their eyes still burnt. They had all come here with a purpose: to put an end to the suffering. And then I had arrived – someone from the inside. The weight of their hope and anticipation was overwhelming. *I was not the answer.* My eyes flicked from one overly cheerful face to the next, until I couldn't bear it anymore. My skin grew hot and I struggled to breathe; their words were suffocating me. I stood up, knocking my cup onto the floor. Glancing down at it, I knew I should pick it up, but I had to get out of there; I couldn't be the solution to their problem.

Footsteps followed behind me and Anna's voice chased me as I flung open the hall doors and ran down the corridor. I ran blindly, trying to escape the stifling atmosphere in the school hall. Twisting round, I headed for the front door where a man I hadn't met yet was sitting, gun strapped to his chest, reading a book. He looked up at me in surprise as I dashed towards him, and stood up with a jerk. His hand went to his gun and I automatically prepared myself to fight.

"No, Daniel, it's OK," I heard Anna's voice shout from behind me. "Let her out. I'll go with her."

"But it's dangerous," he replied.

I reached the door and reluctantly Daniel took the key from a fob attached to his belt and unlocked it. He seemed to flinch as he opened the door, as if he were half expected something to rush in at him out of the dark, but only the night greeted him. Stepping into the outside world, the coolness of the night was a relief to my hot skin and tired body. I revelled in the smell of the evening air, so different to inside the Barrier; it seemed sweeter, richer, and more complex – not the same air recirculated and pumped around over and over, getting stale. It was easier to breathe out here, and I took a deep breath, letting it fill me up and infuse my body. I could feel Anna's eyes on me as I stood there, eyes closed just breathing. I was sure she thought I was an idiot, ruined by what happened on the inside but she didn't say anything; she just stood there, waiting patiently for me.

"I've done awful things, Anna," I said turning to her. "I'm not the kind of person you want around."

"Let me be the judge of that," she said.

My body tensed as I waited for her to try and hug me but she didn't.

"I think I just need to sleep, it's been one hell of a day," I told her, almost letting myself smile.

"Sure," she said.

With one final lung-full of air, I followed her back inside and away from the inky night but we didn't go into the hall again. Instead, Anna took me upstairs to where there were more classrooms which all housed at least three or four beds. Some beds had bags next to them, clothes strewn on the floor and books piled up beside them; others were neat and kempt. Heavy black paint on the windows stifled the brilliant glare of the floodlights.

"Here," said Anna, stopping at what looked like a small office and opening the door. She flicked the light switch on the wall and illuminated the cramped room.

I peered inside. It had been gutted like the other rooms and repurposed as a bedroom. It housed two narrow camping-beds, both neatly made and unslept in. I stepped into the room.

"It's basic, I know," Anna sighed.

"It's fine," I told her.

I wanted her to leave and to be left alone to process everything I'd heard but she hung around, shuffling her feet in the doorway and inspecting the door frame. The bed creaked under my weight as I slumped down onto it, letting my breath out through my teeth.

"OK, well there are toilets on this floor, two doors down, and Seb and I are next door," she paused. "Need anything?"

"Night!"

Anna opened her mouth and then shut it again, then turned and left. I rummaged in my pockets for my phone before remembering I hadn't seen it since we were running towards the edge of the Barrier yesterday, Mechs pounding behind us.

"Anna," I called, "do you guys have my phone and watch?"

Not that I could wear my watch anymore. Anna reappeared in the doorway, quicker than I expected.

"Yeah, sorry. It's all back at the nursing home by the playing field. We can get it in the morning although I don't know if the signal goes through the Barrier. Did you need to get in contact with someone?" she asked.

Shaking my head, I lay down on the bed, still fully dressed, and stared up at the unshaded bulb. I could still see Anna's frame in the doorway out of the corner of my eye, so I closed my eyes until her footsteps crept away resignedly. Who did I have to contact? I thought about Lucy and the others; I had finally come to a standstill and it all came flooding back. In painful play-by-play I saw the terror in my friends' faces as the Mechs filled that small back room with lead. I saw the tears fall from Lucy's eyes and her body, limp and bloody. Then Cain, face down in the dirt of that alley: the alley where I killed my brother. My brother, who wasn't really my brother, who had tried to kill me. I saw Jackson, bruised and bleeding from the beating Cain had given him; he was the man who was sent to kill me, yet he had set me free…and then left me. I

162

clearly wasn't worth sticking around for. Too damaged. I didn't blame him either.

A strange noise, like moths frying against a moth trap, made me flick my eyes open once more and as I watched the light bulb, it flickered and the bed started to shake. Scrambling to my feet, I threw open the door. Darkness swallowed up the corridor beyond. A frightened cry escaped my throat as I called out to Anna but there was no answer. How could no one hear me? There were twenty or so people asleep in these rooms, and yet no one was awake. The floor continued to shake, my heart matching its turbulence, as I steadied myself on the door frame, then it stopped. I tried the light switch. Nothing. Opening my mouth to call out again, something stopped me. A tingling sensation seemed to engulf my whole body. There was something out there in the blackness; something waiting for me. Scanning the corridor, I tried desperately to see what was out there, not daring to leave the false safety of my bedroom. An overwhelming sadness, pain, and darkness hit me like a wave of ice-cold water, and I wanted to scream but the sound was lost somewhere between my throat and my lips. Instead, a light at the end of the corridor flickered on, illuminating a starved woman crouched naked on the floor. Her crying filled the air, soft and weak. My stomach lurched.

"Anna!" I cried.

Anna didn't look up, instead, she hugged her knees tighter and wailed louder. I forced myself to run towards her but didn't seem to get any closer. The further I ran down that dark corridor, the further she moved away. She couldn't hear my desperate cries, instead rocking back and forth on bony haunches. My legs were heavy. Breathless, I slumped against the wall, watching her cry, helpless to save her. Then she began to fade away, her thin form getting smaller and smaller.

"No!" I cried. "No, don't take her!"

I tried to stand, clawing at the walls to get up, but couldn't. Suddenly, I was blinded by a bright light. There were voices in the distance. Covering my eyes with my good hand, I tried to protect myself from whatever was coming for me now. Slowly, the light faded and I could see Anna and Seb standing over me, as well as the barrel of Daniel's gun dangerously close to my face. Pushing the gun away, I sluggishly rose to my feet. My head was spinning and my hand hurt; pain throbbed down my arm and I clutched my wrist to my body, still dazed. I was at the front door of the school. Daniel was trembling ever so slightly next to me, his gun still ready. Anna's eyes were wide with concern. Seb had a look of fire about him.

"What's going on?" I asked.

Anna simply shook her head. "Are you OK?"

"What happened? I was in my room and then there was a power cut and an earthquake and I saw you, Anna, and you were…" I couldn't say the last part.

"You saw it didn't you?" Seb said.

"Saw what?" I asked.

"A Ghost! And it saw you…"

"You mean that thing out there, that creature?" I shuddered.

Seb nodded and ran his hand through his hair. He turned and cursed under his breath.

"She's a liability now, Anna," he said bluntly, his back to me. His words were for her, not me, yet they filled me with a cold dread.

"What?" I shouted.

164

Seb grabbed the gun from Daniel and pointed it at me. I stepped back quickly, feeling the door solid behind me, walls on either side.

"Seb, no wait!" shouted Anna, throwing herself in front of me.

Her body felt so alive against mine, still warm from her bed. Both hands reached behind, hunting for mine as she made a shield for me with her body. I took her hands. I knew she would finally choose me.

"Get out of the way, Anna, you know she'll go to them. She'll lead them to us," said Seb, lining up his shot.

"No, Seb, she's my sister. We can find a way around this," Anna pleaded.

I could feel her heart drumming through her back.

"Think of the rest of us – think of Eve! We can't put her in danger. She's not your sister, she's a stranger, Anna."

"I am thinking of Eve. We need Ava, she's our way in…our way to end this all," Anna said, and I saw the gun lower a little. "She's how we make a safe future for Eve."

Anna stepped away from me and held out her hand to Seb. He looked from Anna to me and back again, as sweat gathered on my back and forehead with a rush of adrenaline. His fingers twitched and then he handed Anna the gun. The breath I had been holding rushed out between my teeth as Anna put the gun on the floor and rushed towards him, gathering Seb into her arms just as she had done with Eve. After a moment, he released her and turned to me.

"Don't let me regret not killing you tonight," he said, and then to Anna, "all yours!"

I watched him and Daniel walk away, my head spinning; the images of what I'd seen still vivid. The beat of my pounding heart banged in my ears and I shivered.

Anna turned to me but couldn't meet my eyes. Her soft face was full of sadness.

"I'd hoped this wouldn't happen. I'm sorry, Ava, it's all my fault. I didn't come for you in time," she said, gazing at the ground.

For a moment, I was transported back to our childhood, with her saying sorry for taking my stuffed toy dog, unable to look me in the face. There was a pang in my chest as I remembered our past, and an affection for her began to surface again. Anna, my ten-minute-older-wont-let-me-forget-it womb-wrestler. My mirror image – except she was different now; I was different. I shuffled my feet and shoved my hands in my pockets. The last person that had shown me affection had ended up dead. What Lucy had loved about me was a lie; she hadn't liked me for me – no one did really. But here was Anna, someone who knew only Ava and not Alec. It felt good.

Anna slid past me and sat down, resting her head against the wall, then closed her eyes. I stood there, unsure of what to do. I gave her a moment but she didn't open her eyes so I sat down quietly next to her. As I got closer, I could see tears in the corners of her eyes, hanging onto her eyelashes. I cleared my throat. Anna turned and gave me a gentle smile.

"I'm sorry," she said, "that I didn't come sooner."

My hand moved at my side, wanting to wipe her tears away but I couldn't; I sat there, stiff and awkward. She dried her eyes with her sleeve as I looked down at the floor.

"Like I said before, the Ghosts are virtually blind. They see with their other senses. I've heard that they see in shadows, like a bat with sonar. They must communicate telepathically because they're usually silent. That's why we use the lights and sirens to stop them; they're more sensitive to high-frequency noise and bright lights. So much so, it can kill them," Anna said quietly, her voice slow and heavy. "But if they see you and you see them in their dying moments, they make a link with you and get inside your head, Ava. A little part of them is left behind and it's like a homing beacon and a distress call all in one; it calls to the others and it draws you to them."

"That thing – that Ghost did this to me? That's why I had the nightmare? Why I woke up here?" I asked, trying to understand what I was hearing.

Anna nodded, "You were trying to get out."

"I was trying to save you," I replied.
Her eyes filled with tears again.

"We have a rule," she swallowed. "Anyone who gets linked…"
She didn't finish her sentence but I understood. Now I knew why Seb wanted to kill me, and I didn't blame him; I would have done the same. I wouldn't have hesitated.

"Thank you for not letting him shoot me," I said.
Anna nodded and gave me another smile. "You're my sister!"

"Yeah we share the same genes, same DNA, but that's just numbers and letters. Seb's right. I'm a stranger," I told her, taking a deep breath. "You should've just let him kill me."

"No, Ava, I just got you back. I'm not letting you go again. I never thought I'd see you again," Anna said, wiping her face with the back of her sleeve.

"Anna, I'll help you like I said I would, and then I'm gone. I'm not the kind of person you want around, especially if it puts you in danger."

167

Anna said nothing, suddenly fascinated by a damp mark on the cuff of her sleeve. Inner turmoil showed in the thin lines that had appeared across her forehead and the distant look in her eyes; her loyalty to her family had been turned on its head by my arrival. As angry as I was at her for moving on and having a family that wasn't me, I couldn't make her choose. There was no question about it.

"Let me make this easy for you, Anna, let me do something good, for once, that isn't about me," I said quietly.

Standing up, I held out my hand to her. She took it and I helped her to her feet. I thought she was going to hug me but she didn't. Maybe it was her way of distancing herself from me again.

"Those Mechs you took down, where are they?" I asked.

"They're in one of the warehouses. There's an industrial part to this town, which is why we chose it as a base," nodded Anna. "It's nearly sun up, let's have a cup of coffee and then we'll go?"

"Sure."

We walked side by side to the sports hall. I followed her into the kitchen, grabbing two cheap ceramic mugs from the cupboard Anna pointed out to me, while she found the coffee. It didn't take long for the canteen to heat up and we were soon sipping sweet, black coffee together. We sat there in silence, both lost in our own thoughts. I wasn't sure how I was going to help Anna and her family through the Barrier. I knew about my implant and about the ID chips, a little about the Mechs and some computer know-how from Dad, but that was the limit of my knowledge – that's why I had Chris and the others, and why I needed Jackson.

There was a loud clunk and the floodlights turned off, signalling the start of the day. I looked up to the ceiling where there was a row of narrow, rectangular windows and saw the dusty pink of the sunrise.

"Can we go outside?" I asked Anna.

"Yeah sure," she said, her chair squeaking across the polished floor as she stood up.

We headed back to the front door, where Daniel had returned to his post; he was sitting reading a book but looked up as we approached. There was a mixture of fear and anger in his eyes, so I looked away and followed Anna wordlessly as she unlocked the front door and led me out.

The world seemed much bigger in the daylight. I lifted my face to the sky and felt the rays of the real sun on my skin. It was still cool from the night, but it was real: the air was real, the sky, real. In the daylight, the rows of houses that lined the street became clear, all empty, some collapsing, the odd one used for storage. The front gardens were overgrown and wild, spreading out onto the street and through the doors into the houses themselves: nature retaking what was rightfully hers. Front doors hung off hinges and most of the windows were smashed in. Furniture and belongings still sat where their former owners had left them, while other homes had spewed their contents out onto the street so Anna and I had to pick our way between a sofa or television.

There were empty, dusty cars with smashed windows and crushed body panels; most of them had their bonnets up like gaping mouths, and the batteries had been removed. It was eerily quiet – a town lost in a strange state of half abandonment. I was used to the busyness of the city, with its lights and noises, and to sleeping with the noise of the clubs and bars, and people milling about the streets at all hours of the day and night. This quiet peacefulness was strange to me but not unwelcome, although I knew it was a false pretence; there was something out there more terrifying and more deadly even than the Mechs. As I gazed around at my post-apocalyptic surroundings, I realised I'd exchanged one evil for another

"This way," said Anna.

As we walked, we passed a small convenience store, its shopping trolleys still lined up in their bay. Old signs peeling from the windows advertised fresh fruit and vegetables. Out-of-date newspapers and magazines littered the street and I saw glimpses of famous faces I half recognised. I stopped for a moment and picked up one of the loose newspaper sheets. It was dated fourteen years ago, the day after the bombs. They had run one last edition; there was a single headline, that brought everything into reality: *Have We Been Forsaken?*

Anna didn't stop. She didn't need to read the headlines, she had seen it first hand; she was the forsaken. I had been the chosen one. Letting the wind snatch the paper from my hand, I hurried to catch up with her. The warehouse was only a mile from the school. It took us less than twenty minutes to get there. It loomed up out of the rows of houses, odd and out of place, sitting at the end of a street of garages, most of which had been looted. I couldn't help but wonder if this was what it was like in other countries.

"What about the rest of the world, Anna?" I asked as we approached the warehouse.

She turned, her finger twisting into her hair, and gave me a little shrug. "We've heard some chatter on the radios, but nothing solid. I can only pray that they've had better luck than we have."

170

Her tone was light, but there was a hopelessness in her voice. She shifted on the spot then turned and rapped on the warehouse door.

"Here we are then," she said, changing the subject.

I gazed up at the tall windows and sheet metal walls; it was like a tin box with a roof. However, it looked clean and sturdy, despite being abandoned for so long. Anna slid back the bolt and opened the door. Inside was grey and dark, and I coughed as the musty smell of things unused accosted me. Dust particles caught in the thin rays of the morning sun, which slipped through the shuttered windows and stacked storage boxes. Tool boxes lay on disused work benches.

"It used to be a workshop. Metal work, I think. Maybe vehicles? I'm not really sure, most stuff was stolen in the first few months after the Ghosts appeared, when people thought things would pass. I saw people taking TVs and laptops...we did strange things in the chaos," Anna appeared to be talking more to herself than me.

I listened without saying anything, looking around for the hook to undo the shutters and let some light in. It was propped next to the door and as I lifted the shutters, the large room gradually filled with light, illuminating the Mechs that had followed us out of the Barrier, slumped in a pile on the floor. I knelt down next to them, running my hand over the metal corpses – three of them – in total disrepair, and riddled with bullet holes.

"Give me a hand, Anna," I called. *A hand, yep, because I only have one*, I almost laughed to myself.

We hauled the large robots into a space on the floor and stood peering down at their lifeless faces. I had never seen one close up that wasn't trying to scan me or kill me. A familiar nervousness bubbled in the pit of my stomach;

I half expected them to return to life and haul me off to some government facility, where I would be terminated. I kicked one, just to make sure, but nothing happened; it lay there, silent and unresponsive. Two out of the three Mechs had multiple bullet holes to the head, destroying the main processor, but the third was relatively intact. There was a brilliant shot to its neck that must have severed the mainframe, its brain, from the rest of its body, causing it to shut down. This was the one. I stood up and stretched, my body still aching, not yet healed. I could feel Anna watching me.

"You go back," I said. "I'll stay here and work on this. I'll sleep here too, if you can spare a floodlight? Then I won't be a danger to anyone."

"I can't leave you here," Anna said, her finger was knotted in her hair again.

"You can, it's OK," I replied, turning my back on her, and headed for the tool boxes to rummage through the abandoned tools.

There was a long pause before Anna spoke again.

"I'll bring you some food and a bed," she said, "oh, and your things too."

"OK," I called out, not looking up from the box.

My heart sank a little at her words, but I knew it was the best option – and so did she. After a moment, the door to the warehouse banged open and closed again. I was alone: just me and the Mechs.

Chapter 12

Once Anna had gone, I put the tools down and took a wander around the warehouse. There were partitioned workbenches numbered one to eight. I drifted slowly from one to the other, peering into each one. Most were empty; some still had coffee mugs that had sat untouched for the last fourteen years, others had tools scattered around them. When I got to number eight, I froze. The bench was neat and orderly; the owner had tidied it up before they left and in pride of place on the top was a framed photo. I reached down and picked it up, brushing a heavy layer of dust off it with my sleeve. A woman and two children smiled up at me from behind a sheet of broken glass. Balancing it in the crook of my bad arm, I traced the happy faces with the fingers I had left. I didn't know them but I felt sad that something so precious was left here in this dark, dank place; no one saw their smiles anymore. Turning it over, shaking the broken glass from the frame, I placed it carefully back on the workbench. This would be my bench; they could smile at *me*. Grabbing one end of the bench, I dragged it awkwardly, in stops and starts, back into the middle of the warehouse. Apart from the work benches, storage boxes, and Mechs, the place was relatively empty: no machinery, no office, just a small room at the back, which I discovered was a toilet.

The Mech stared up at me, solid and unmoving, as I wondered how I was going to get it onto the bench. Bending down, I lifted one arm and dug my heels into the floor as I pulled with all the force I could muster. Twinges of pain radiated down my arm and my legs burnt as the machine inched its way up off of the ground, scraping on the concrete floor. Just as it seemed my eyes would burst out of their sockets, I gave up, heading instead to the toolbox and returning with a selection of tools.

Hole punch in hand and hammer at my side, I hovered over its metal arm, trying to decide where to make the hole. Reaching back into my memory hunting for the diagram Dad had shown me once, rough and drawn on four bits of paper stuck together, the image of the machines' insides returned. It had scared me as a child. But Dad's insistence came into its own now. Placing the punch at the shoulder, I pictured the weaker, rotating joint and subconsciously reached for the hammer – but couldn't feel its smooth, wooden handle, nor the cold, concrete floor. My arm swatted the air and I let out a small moan. I let the punch fall out of my good hand, clattering against the ground and rolling away, then stood up, drew my leg back and kicked the Mech as hard as I could, as a roar escaped my chest. I was useless and broken. I couldn't even save myself. How could I save these people? I needed that Mech to fix my arm – but I needed my other hand to take the Mech apart. Anger filled me up, spreading like a wave and burning in the back of my eyes as my muscles tensed. I picked up the solid metal hole punch, about to lob it across the room as hard as I could, when a vehicle pulled up outside. There was a bang on the warehouse door.

"What?" I shouted, the punch still raised above my head.

The door opened and Eve's face appeared around the door. I must have looked wild because the smile dropped from her face and she retracted back from the door. I groaned inwardly and let my hand drop to my side; I didn't know how to handle this little girl – my niece. She watched me for a moment and then called out to her mum. There were voices outside and Eve strolled in with Anna in tow, followed shortly by DiDi and another guy whose name I couldn't remember. The man was carrying a folded-up camping-bed, and DiDi was carrying a pillow and duvet. They set them up for me and then left; the guy looked wary but DiDi gave a smile as she went.

"What are those, Auntie Ava?" asked Eve, hovering around the machines on the floor with a morbid fascination.

"Mechs," I told her.

"Oh, what do they do?"

"They're like policemen," I said.

"Policemen?" Eve asked. "Are they goodies?"

"No."

Anna handed me a backpack. Inside was my phone and watch and a few other bits that had been in my pockets when we dived through the Barrier.

"I've set up a light outside and there's all the food we could spare on your bed but it's not much. You'll come back for dinner at least?" she said.

Eve appeared at her side, bored of the Mechs, and Anna instinctively reached down for her hand and squeezed it.

I nodded. "Sure, sure. I don't suppose my holdall made it through?"

She shook her head. "Sorry, we didn't find it – just you and Jackson."

She turned to leave, taking a waving Eve with her, and headed for the door.

"Anna," I said, and she looked round, "I need some help."

I hated to admit defeat but I couldn't do the things I needed to do without both hands. I didn't have time to adapt – I had to find Jackson soon if I stood any chance of finding a way to take down the Barrier for Anna…or of him still being alive.

"Sure, what can I do?" she asked, while Eve hopped up and down impatiently.

"I need another pair of hands – literally," I said, holding the punch out towards her.

Instead of taking it as I thought she would, she nodded and disappeared out of the door. Eve gave me another wave as she went but I gritted my teeth and turned away, Eve's confused face filling me with a mix of guilt and anger. Anna soon returned with DiDi, who beamed from ear to ear. She ushered Anna out of the door, muttering something about dinner at six, then strode over to me and grabbed the punch from my hand.

"How can I help?" she asked.

I looked at her, astounded. I was tainted now, something to fear, yet she acted as if she had been asked to help a friend choose a new jacket.

"You know, right?" I asked her.

"Yup."

"And you don't want to shoot me?"

"Nope, the Ghosts only call you at night. Don't worry. I'm sick of being stuck here in this nothingness, eking out the power until finally we won't have any – and then we're all dead anyway," she said with a shrug. "So how can I help?"

I pointed towards the Mech.

"I need to get the arm off at the shoulder."

"Sure," she said kneeling down and picking up the hammer.

The sound of metal on metal clanged around the echoey warehouse but within five minutes, the Mech arm was lying on my workbench, its wires hanging out like veins. I shuddered as I looked at it; the very thing I hated, was going to be my saviour. As I ran my hand through my hair, wondering how to attach it, a loud beeping emanated from the new backpack. Diving at it, I pulled out my phone, searching the screen for the name of someone I knew from the inside but it was just my alarm to get up for work. The glimmer of false hope evaporated, leaving me cold as I silenced the reminder of my old life and friends. As I cast it back onto the bed it hit the backpack, knocking it over and it spewing its contents onto the floor.

There it was: the chip I had taken from Cain – the one with half the virus on it. This was it – a flash of hope in the gloom. Grabbing the chip, I turned to DiDi.

"This is it!" I told her.

She looked at the chip, confused.

"I took this from my brother after he died. He was half-Mech," I added. "There must be software on this that let his human parts talk to his Mech parts."

The words bubbled up, flowing out in a gabbled monologue, as I forgot that DiDi had no idea who my brother was or even what a Mech was. I headed for the toolbox and rummaged for something to cut open the arm without damaging the inside of it. The lack of power rendered most tools useless but after a moment, I found a small handsaw. DiDi held the arm steady on the workbench as I carefully sawed just next to its neatly welded joint until the wires were exposed.

"Get me a chair, would you? And a clamp," I ordered DiDi.

She nodded and went to find one.

I rummaged in the drawers of the bench for more tools. Inside was a strap holding a selection of small pliers and screwdrivers, all neatly ordered by size – Dad would've been proud of this man's organisation. Reaching in, I picked up a small pair of pliers and picked up the chip.

"This OK?" called DiDi from one of the other workbenches, holding up a small clamp.

"Yes, thanks. Put it carefully in the gap I've made and open it just enough so I can get my fingers in," I instructed.

If there was one thing I knew, it was how to put these chips in and take them out; Dad had spent hours with me, showing me how to wire and adjust them, so if he were no longer around then I would be able to deal with the updates and figure it out if the hardware went wrong. My excitement ebbed for a moment as I thought of him. I'd loved those times with Dad: the smell of solder and his aftershave mingled together, the close proximity to him – the way he didn't drink on the days he was teaching me. Maybe that was why Cain hated me so much; he never had that time with Dad. Yet Dad had so much to teach him if only he'd wanted to. I'd often hear them arguing late in the evening when they thought I was asleep. Cain would tell Dad that he wasn't really his father, that they didn't want him once the girls came along. I'd hear the front door slam and the screw top on the vodka, and I'd cry silently until I fell asleep. *But that was then: this is now.* I rallied.

DiDi carefully positioned the clamp and wound it open just enough for me to reach the wires. Placing the chip on the bench, I removed the cables from the connectors at the bottom, laying them out on the table. Dad's lessons echoed in my mind about the ID chips having their own power source. They were charged by the electricity that ran through the human body, as well as from movement and the scanners. I smiled; Dad was still here, even though a vodka bottle had claimed his frail body all those years ago.

As I fiddled and dismantled it, I was surprised to see that Cain's chip had a larger cell than mine ever had. Turning my attention to the Mech arm, I grabbed the pliers and pulled out the wires I needed; the ones that controlled movement. There was a gun and a torch built into the Mech's palm. The hours passed quickly as we worked together, stripping wires and rewiring them. DiDi sat patiently with me, fetching all the things I needed. She never asked questions and didn't seem scared of me. She chatted merrily about this and that: her family, her sister, her husband, all of them gone but she never stopped smiling or hunted out pity. I listened to her with a jealous admiration. I had nothing but anger for those who had wronged me: every time I thought of Cain, there was nothing but deep loathing and betrayal. The prospect of having to speak to Jackson, facing him again after what he did and what I said, filled me with dread; yet here was a woman who had lost everything, and she was still smiling, happy to help others – she seemed to be undeterred by it all. As I worked and listened to DiDi, my stomach grumbled. It must have been audible, as DiDi stopped talking and gave me a sideways smile.

"Hungry?" she said.

"Yeah, I guess I must be. Sorry – I've been so involved, time slipped by. You go and eat. I'll be there soon, okay? Tell Anna I won't be long."

"If you're sure? Don't be long, okay. I'll tell Anna but you know what she's like, worries about everyone."

No – I didn't know what Anna was like, but I'd have time to learn again. I waved her off as she stood up and headed for the door, leaving me alone with the smell of

179

solder. As the door opened, DiDi gasped. The door opened wide to reveal Eve standing there, her hand raised to knock. The little girl beamed at me and bounded in like a puppy. She peered at the Mech arm and her hand reached out to touch the wires, her eyes wide with curiosity.

"No!" I said before I could stop myself, my voice echoing loudly around the room.

Eve jumped back and looked at me, the smile dropping from her face; she sniffed and bit her lip. The smile slipped from DiDi's face, too, for a moment.

"You'll break it," I told Eve more softly. "You can look but don't touch!"

Eve nodded and scrambled over to the workbench again while the softness returned to Didi's face once more.

"What are you doing, Auntie Ava?" she asked.

"Just 'Ava' is fine," I said.

"But Mummy said you're 'Auntie Ava'?" she looked at me quizzically.

"I prefer Ava… It's a new arm, to replace the one I lost."

"Oh, okay. That's a good idea. Where did your arm go? Mummy said not to ask," Eve said.

I looked over at DiDi, who was laughing to herself. I raised my eyebrows in a hope that she would rescue me from the curious kid but she didn't; instead, she turned to leave – and walked straight into Seb.

"Eve," he shouted storming in, his face red and contorted with anger. "Eve!"

His voice reverberated off of every wall and Eve jumped away from me. She stared up at her dad as he strode across the room. I pushed my chair back and got to my feet. Adrenaline pounded in my chest and my stomach clenched, but he didn't come for me; instead, he rounded on Eve, grabbing her by the arm and pulling her into his chest. She stood ensnared in his arms like a frightened rabbit, her small frame trembling.

"What the hell was she doing here?" he shouted, spittle flying from his mouth.

"I didn't ask her to come; she just turned up. DiDi will tell you," I retorted.

I turned and sat down. There wasn't time for a slanging match: I had things to do, and I didn't want to be an imposter in his life any more than he wanted me in it. His hand pressed into my shoulder, hard and strong, and the heat of his breath brushed my cheek as he brought his face close to mine. I could smell sweat and adrenaline on his skin.

"Stay away from my daughter," he snarled in my ear. I clenched my fist; days ago, I could have taken him, floored him in two swift moves and left him a mess at my feet but I was a left-hook down – and also Eve was there watching. I couldn't destroy a father in front of his daughter. Perhaps I wasn't the monster he thought I was. Satisfied with his threat, Seb let go of me. My jaw relaxed as he walked away; the heat of his hand still lingered on my shoulder. I placed the wire cutters I had instinctively picked up back down and stared at the arm. The door slammed and I glanced over my shoulder; DiDi had gone, too. I was alone again. Closing my eyes against the tears that threatened, I breathed deeply, pushing the anger away before finally crumbling onto the workbench. By the time I had regained my composure, I had vowed to stay as far away from Seb and Eve as I could. I was only here for Anna – she was the one I'd been waiting for. For her I'd push on.

Taking a deep breath, I stood back up and went on the hunt for a knife: something small and sharp that would cut through skin and flesh without tearing it. There was a scalpel buried in one of the toolboxes. It was almost blunt, but there was sure to be a knife sharpener in the kitchen. Shoving the scalpel into my backpack, I headed for the warehouse door; the prospect of what I was about to do made my palms slick and my shoulders tense.

The light was beginning to fade as I emerged into the cool air, and the drone of the siren greeted me as I wandered down the empty street back to the school. Outside the safehouse, a group of people milled about waiting to be let in. I could hear their happy hum of voices from a street back but they fell silent as I approached. *Ava the Hunted - The Infected.* I knew what they were thinking. I stepped into the crowd and shuffled my way to the front door. The whisper of rumours spread behind me but I kept my eyes forward, unwilling to give them the satisfaction of a reaction.

Anna answered the door and everyone poured in. Slipping inside first, I hung back, waiting until the crowd had passed, and only Anna and I remained.

"You okay, Ava?" she asked, pushing the door shut again with a clunk.

"Yeah, I just don't think many people want me around here," I laughed, brushing my hair off of my damp forehead.

"That's not true," she said, but wasn't able to look me in the eye.

I raised my eyebrows at her and she changed the subject. "Want some dinner?"

Nodding, I followed her back to the sports hall. Inside, the tables had been lined up in rows and most of

182

the seats were taken. There were two spaces next to Seb and Eve, and Anna made a beeline for them. I caught her sleeve before she got there and gestured to a space at the other end of the table.

"I'll sit here," I said.

"I'll join you then," she smiled.

"No – sit with your family," I said.

"But you're *all* my family," she pleaded.

With a small shrug, I turned and headed the opposite way. No one acknowledged me as I sat down, but I didn't care; all I could think of was the scalpel in my backpack. The smell of jacket potatoes and baked beans drifted out of the kitchen. It was basic food but it smelt so good. It was better than the crap we ate on the inside – it was homemade and unadulterated. I took a deep breath, suddenly aware that my insides were screaming at me for sustenance. As I ate, I savoured the taste of the first proper meal I'd had in ages. And then I waited for the others to finish. The time seemed to drag its heels, hanging onto each second that passed. My eyes flicked back and forth to the clock as I waited, the scalpel heavy in my bag. Once most of the other plates were clean, I got up and began gathering up the dishes. No one stopped me, happy for me to do this menial task for them; when everyone had finished, they began exiting the hall in dribs and drabs. Anna offered to walk back with me but I brushed her aside. Finally, the large dishwashers were churning away loudly in the corner and the others on clean-up duty had swept the hall and cleared the tables. I dipped into the kitchen once more and slung my bag on the side, taking out the scalpel stealthily. I couldn't be seen with a blade, especially not Seb; I was sure he would pin me to the floor and slit my throat with it.

A large knife sharpener was fixed to the work surface in the larder, and I drew the scalpel quickly through it. The feel of the metal against the abrasive surface of the sharpening steels made me shudder a little; it reminded me of cutting through Cain's skin as he lay in a pool of his own piss, or robotic fluids, or whatever that crap was? I pushed the thought away. The sharpened blade gleamed in the lights and I went to the hob and turned on the gas bottle, taking with me a packet of disinfectant wipes and a first aid kit I'd spotted on the shelf. There was a hiss as the gas flooded the system, and I pushed down on the ignition. A circle of blue flames appeared on the ring of the stove and wrapping my shirt around the handle of the scalpel, I held it in the heat, waiting for the metal to glow red. As the metal changed from silver to yellow to red, I scanned the room. Spotting a short wooden spoon, I grabbed it and shoved it between my teeth. The blade now glowing, I felt my resolve waver. *I could stop now, I could walk away.* I tried to swallow, to wet my desert-dry throat. Taking a deep breath, I whipped the scalpel from the flames and drew it across my forearm before I could dwell on it anymore. An involuntary grunt rumbled in my throat as I bit down hard on the spoon to stop myself from screaming. A searing pain coursed up my arm. The nauseating smell of burning flesh turned my stomach. It was over in a matter of seconds but my legs swayed underneath me. Holding onto the counter, I fought desperately to stand. I collapsed forward as the world spun and my head pressed on the cold, bleachy-smelling worktop as I waited with my eyes closed for the agony to subside. Trembling, I fixated on my breathing, counting each breath: in and out, in and out, until the haze in front of my eyes slowly receded.

After a few minutes I straightened up, glancing down at the wound: it was about five centimetres across, and bleeding. A thin trickle of blood ran down my arm and onto the counter top, pooling around the packet of wipes. The pain had dulled to a sharp stinging as I readied myself for round two; I still had to make a pocket for the chip. I pushed the scalpel back into the wound and cut through my flesh, releasing a small pocket of skin. The pain still took my breath away. Again, the spoon took the brunt of it as I sunk my teeth into it, deeper this time. Once it was done, took the chip and carefully wiped it with one of the disinfectant wipes. Gritting my teeth, I pushed it under the skin. My head screamed at me to stop; the feel of my flesh against my finger made me retch but I still had to secure it into the pocket. By the time I was done, a film of cold, clammy sweat drenched my clothes and my heart sounded loud in my ears. My vision wafted in and out as a dark cloud began to cover my senses, and I stopped, grabbing hold of the counter once more. As my legs gave way, I sat down heavily on the tiled floor to stop myself from falling and smashing my head open. *Jackson had better still be out there after all this.*

Although my arm throbbed and my vision was hazy, I knew couldn't be found here on the floor. I tried to move but everything started to spin. A light tap of feet on the floor sent a rush of panic through me and I rolled onto my side. A door opened nearby, I wasn't sure where; shock had drained me of spacial awareness. A little hand touched my head. I opened my eyes and through the bleariness could make out Eve's round face hovering over me. I groaned; she was the last person I wanted to see right now. Anna or Seb were sure to be close behind.

"You OK, Auntie Ava?" she asked.

Shuffling uncomfortably under her hand, I attempted to sit up. The world was starting to slow down again, and I managed to heave myself over to lean against a cupboard. My eyes searched the floor for my bag as Eve chatted her meaningless prattle at me; I reached out for it, hauling myself off the floor and grabbing the first-aid box. Shoving it in my bag I pushed past Eve, clutching my forearm, and headed out of the kitchen into the sports hall. The sadness in Eve's eyes caught me off guard and I hesitated, feeling a prick of guilt in my chest. But it was too late – I couldn't let her in now; I wasn't even sure if I could even if I wanted to.

On the other side of the doors, Anna was talking with DiDi and both women looked up as I flew out of the kitchen. Ignoring them, I let their concerned voices get caught by the sports hall doors. I had no problem getting out of the school; they were happy to let me go. Leaving the brightly lit school behind me, I wandered back to the warehouse as darkness fell. The cool of the night air brought me back to my senses. My arm throbbed but it hardly registered – my body only able to focus on one discomfort at a time. I looked down at the wound as I walked, carefully prizing my fingers away so as not to disturb the blood clots that were forming. The incision was surprisingly neat, and the chip fitted snuggly in its new home. I was quite impressed with myself.

As I reached the warehouse, my eyelids felt heavy and my feet dragged with each forced step. I was overwhelmed by the urge to lie down and sleep. Flicking on the floodlight – my only protection out here on my own – I entered the warehouse. My bed waited silently for me. Wandering over, I slung my bag down on the floor, and by the light of the floodlight outside, fixed myself up using the first aid kit. Afterwards, exhausted, I flopped down on the bed and fell asleep instantly.

Chapter 13

The sound of the earth tearing in two, wrenched me from my sleep as my bed walked across the floor taking on a life of its own. I held on to the frame with both hands as tight as I could. The tremors ceased and the feel of the cotton bedsheet gripped in *both* hands, drew my attention. A silent cry escaped my dry lips as I stared down at a pair of white-knuckled hands. Astonished, I traced the rematerialised left hand with the other; flexing the fingers and touching my face. Like a salamander, I had managed to regrow a limb. Still sitting there in disbelief, I heard the cry of a child, softly at first, barely more than a murmur. I climbed off the bed and looked around but seemed to be alone. A cascade of deep darkness swamped me as I stood, listening, blotting out my hands in front of my face.

"Hello?"

My skin puckered with a deep penetrating cold that seemed to needle into my very bones like fingers of ice. Something moved; a shuffling in the inky black. I wrapped my arms around myself as the crying got slowly louder. Frantic, I pivoted on the spot trying to work out where it was coming from. A bolt of illumination to my right almost blinded me and, pressing my hands to my eyes, I turned to face it. The bed stood in disarray, bedsheets hanging limply from the edge, pillow dented and crushed. A petite figure lay face down, crumpled within the bone-white sheets; outstretched fingers reaching for Babit. Eve's small frame was lifeless and still. A dark stain spread out from beneath her, leeching into the sheets. I shook my head. *No, it's not real.* Then multiple hands grabbed me from behind, fingers pressing sharply into my flesh, pinning me to the ground;

something hard and cold pressed against the back of my head.

"Run," I heard a voice whisper. "Get up and run!"

"I can't," I cried, struggling against the hands that held me; I couldn't see who they belonged to.

"Ava!" came a voice I recognised.

"DiDi?" I called out.

"Ava, stop fighting. Wake up!"

As I blinked heavily DiDi emerged from the darkness. Her face, crowned with dark, tightly curled hair, came closer to mine as the darkness retreated and the sky came into view, brilliantly blue, so different from the blackness I had been lost in moments before. Lifting my hands to shield my eyes from the morning sun, only one appendage hovered in front of my face and I was plunged back into bitter darkness. As DiDi helped me up, I spotted the ridged perimeter fence towering above me curls of razor wire meant to keep the bad things out – except that now it was keeping the danger in. I turned to DiDi, who shrugged.

"I guess you were trying to get back to them," she said.

Scraps of my clothing appeared to be snagged on some of the verticals on the six-metre-high fence, while my oversized army shirt looked like it had been attacked with a pair of scissors and my arms were covered in cuts and scrapes. All I could do was stare at the strands of thread caught on the razor wire fluttering gently in the breeze.

"How did I get up there?" I stuttered.

DiDi shrugged again. "Beats me. Those that get linked either get taken or umm…dealt with."

Our eyes met and she looked away.

"It's OK, Seb and I already had that conversation," I told her.

"Oh."

"I'm surprised you're here," I said.

"Yeah, I volunteered. We're all in this together, right? I don't judge. It's not your fault what happened," she smiled at me. "Breakfast?"

There was a lingering bitterness in my mouth, I didn't want to eat; I was desperate to get back to secure the warehouse; I couldn't put the others in danger for my sake. As much as I hated to admit it, Seb was right. Maybe he should have shot me, I thought; it might have been a better death than whatever the Ghosts wanted with me. I shook my head.

"I won't come back to the school," I said. "I've got some food at the warehouse."

"Then I'll bring something to you," said DiDi.
Her arms, folded tightly across her chest, told me she wasn't going to give in so I nodded and we walked slowly back to the warehouse together. Every inch of my body ached. The nightmare was fading and the sting of torn flesh and bruised knuckles was starting to follow in its wretched wake.

DiDi left me there to get more food, and I went inside and started hunting for things to make the door more secure. I spent the day with DiDi, letting her calming voice flow over me as she helped me fix bolts and locks to the outside of the door to lock me in when she left. Together we fashioned an ankle-cuff to fix me to the floor, a precaution that felt like a stone in my stomach; I had left one prison for another. When she left that evening, I knew that even when the Ghosts called me, the others would be safe.

The blare of sirens punctuated my fitful sleep that evening. I lay in the thin sheets, cold and clammy, swallowing hard against the dread that gurgled in my throat. Something in my blood could feel the Ghosts creeping closer and closer to the compound. Wave after wave of bleak, grief washed over me as I pressed my arm across my eyes and focused on my damp breath. They had come to gather the people were left – anyone that was a threat to them. They wanted to join us to their hive mind or destroy us. I could sense their indiscriminate disregard for us, an inferior species that was merely an inconvenience; a plague on the planet they needed for themselves. We were but a source of fuel for them.

Yet as I trembled in the darkness, something else drifted in with the Ghost's roaring; a sorrow and regret, which was so quiet I could barely feel it. It was a different note that didn't fit with the horrific melody that they played. I stayed where I was, unable to move, under their control once again. The warehouse filled with light and gunfire rattled in the distance as I screwed my eyes shut, fighting the Ghosts that were screaming inside my mind. I fought them until the sirens fell silent and the sun rose.

****

DiDi and I spent the next couple of days testing the Mech arm, connecting it to the chip to see if I could control it. Each day, I grew to like DiDi and her sunny, no-nonsense disposition even more; I almost considered her a friend. Despite the growing fear in my gut, I let myself smile at her stories and laugh at her sarcastic sense of humour. It seemed to push the darkness back a little, making the long, drawn-out nights easier to bear.

The nights that weren't punctuated by the wail of the sirens and rounds of gunfire were instead filled with the sound of the Ghosts in my head, making my senses explode: a long, low, drone that spoke a million words yet none at the same time. They called to me, luring me towards the precipice of my mind. When I slept, I entered their nightmare world of shadows; their minds linked with mine, taking me through miles of tunnels that twisted and turned, disorientating me. I hovered over vast control panels with no buttons, while the tall figures of Ghosts sat at them; their long elongated fingers seeming to merge with it. I endured screams that made my skin crawl and the smell of blood hung in the thick, stifling air. Yet I never left my bed.

As terrifying as the nights were, it was more tolerable knowing that DiDi would be there the next morning, treating me not as if I were a caged wild animal, but with a genuine concern for my welfare. It was a new and fragile thing to feel that someone truly cared. I knew I'd had Lucy and the others before – but that was when I was Alec, a liar and a fake. Now I was Ava again and that was becoming less and less strange. DiDi liked me for *me,* and for that I was deeply grateful. Between us, we put me back together, physically and mentally, until I almost resembled a person again.

****

DiDi stood up from our warm spot in the sunshine and repositioned the row of tin cans I was aiming at. She stepped back and watched as I adjusted my aim with the replacement Mech arm that was grafted onto my stump. After three days of tinkering, I was finally getting the hang of using it; the slim metal fingers curled into a fist, glinting in the bright sunlight. The stilted movements of the hand had become smooth and natural; no longer crushing objects I tried to pick up, instead twisting and turning them with ease. I was starting to have some fun with the added extras a Mech arm had to offer.

Holding my arm steady, with a whoosh the gun shot a pulse of energy at a baked bean tin. It popped delightfully, flying several metres back and clattering along the floor.

"Ava, I'm going to go, okay? I have some stuff to get ready at the school, but I will be back to lock up at dusk," DiDi informed me, shielding her eyes from the glare of the low afternoon sun.

"Yeah sure," I said looking up from my arm. "No rush."

DiDi smiled, "I hate leaving you here. It makes me feel sad that you're alone so much."

"It's OK, I don't mind. Other people don't like me much anyway…safer for them, too."

Didi shrugged, "You shouldn't think like that."

I raised my eyebrows at her and let out a grunt of a laugh. She ignored me, heading in the direction of the school, giving me a little wave as she left and pulling the door shut; she would be back later. My attention switched back to my arm; the metal skin that was grafted to my body glistened in the sunlight. Even though I was trapped in my little warehouse, I was freer than I'd ever been. I was nearly ready to move on and find Jackson, to bring him back to the compound and find a way back into the Barrier for Anna and her little army, to get rid of the Ghosts. Then I would be free to do as I pleased, away from those that kept me down trodden on the Inside and Outside. Another day or two would be all I needed to iron out the problems with the arm; occasionally the fingers clamped shut and wouldn't open again until I disconnected it, or the pulse gun wouldn't fire properly – but I was getting there.

I fired off another few rounds before the gun needed charging, and I stood up, leaving the cans scattered across the road ready for another round after dinner. The warehouse was quiet and still when I entered; the three dismembered Mechs lay sprawled on the floor where I had harvested them for parts – a bit like they had done to Cain. The thought of him still made me shudder with a strange anger mixed with sadness. He had been my brother once and I, his little sister.

Flopping down beside the workbench, there was a click and the metal skin of the Mech arm detached itself from me. I slipped it off and disconnected the wires attaching the chip to my stump. The wound was healing nicely now but it itched like hell; it took all I had not to scratch it until it bled. Taking off the arm was a blessed relief and the fresh air felt good against my hot skin. Leaning back in my chair, I stared at the arm and the new limb I'd crafted for myself – the one good thing MTech had done for me.

Picking up a small screw driver strewn on the bench, I began to unbolt the seam of the arm to get to its insides – there was enough time before DiDi came back with dinner to have a play and see if I could get the pulse gun working every time, cause maximum damage to the pale skin of the Ghosts. I'd added a siren, too, to bombard any aliens I came into contact with. If I was going to go out alone, I had to make sure I survived long enough to bring Jackson back.

I tinkered until the sun began to set and the light was fading. My stomach rumbled and I glanced up at the small clock I'd found a day or so ago cast aside in the corner of the warehouse. It was gone six – normally DiDi was back by now with a couple of plates of foil-covered food. Getting up, I paced the room. Maybe she had been distracted by something important? Perhaps she'd forgotten me – decided she'd had enough, that I was too dangerous.

I wandered over to the door and opened it, staring out across the hazy street and stepping over the threshold. Something in my chest held me back, an invisible rope that kept me securely in the warehouse. Stepping back into the shadow of the warehouse, I closed the door carefully behind me. As I pushed a desk against the door, unable to lock it myself from the inside, a panic tightened around my chest and I longed for DiDi's reassuring presence. Sitting down heavily on the camping-bed I rummaged underneath for a packet of biscuits I'd stashed there. I tore open the packet with my teeth, spitting the corner of the wrapper onto the floor. Sprawled on the bed with the biscuits on my chest to eat, I began to eat, staring up at the high-rafted ceiling and wondering where I would even begin to look for Jackson. Then my eyes grew heavy.

The next thing I knew, my whole body had jolted awake. I sat up. The sound of screaming, high and terrified, filled my every sense. It was nowhere and everywhere, filling up my ears and seeping into my head. But there was no one there. I was alone. I was always alone. The darkness of the warehouse seemed all-encompassing, pressing in on every side. The silver light of the moon was absent from the pitch-black sky and even the light of my flood light was gone. I was not asleep. Over the last few days, I had come to recognise the shadow world I entered in my sleep, and I knew to stay on my bed in the darkness and ignore everything I saw and heard. Something was different this time; the screaming was all too real. It was not some distant sobbing that lured me out of my bed and into the darkness until I awoke on the floor with my ankle chain holding me back at full stretch. Someone was out there.

Stumbling to my feet, I headed for the screams but they seemed to come from everywhere, making my head swim. I hit the floor hard; fighting back against the sadness and agony in the recesses of my haunted mind. The shadow world of the Ghosts slipped in and out of my consciousness and I tried to hold onto reality. My fingers reached out tentatively, expecting to feel the hard concrete of the warehouse floor but instead there was grass beneath me, and something warm and wet. Reality slipped into view, flickering and hazy, but I could see Eve standing in front of me clutching Babit, a scream emanating from her tiny mouth. I turned to see what she was looking at.

To my horror, I could make out the giant shadowy form of a Ghost prowling the perimeter fence for a way in – and then it found it. Its sinewy body pushed through the gap as it made a hideous screaming noise like the death cry of all those it had devoured. Closing the distance between myself and Eve, I threw myself into the gap between beast and child. But I wasn't fast enough; as hard as I pushed, I was no match for the giant strides of the Ghost. With one swipe of its claw, it flung me aside as if I were nothing and my body soared through the air. The ground rushed up to greet me with a fresh dose of agony. Blinking away the disorientating haze that filled my vision, I hunted for Eve but she was gone. The Ghost stood in her place, a smear of bright-red blood christening its mouth.

"Eve," I cried out, my voice cracking.

I could hear other people now: the sound of gunfire and light from their torches cut through the night's blackness. The sirens were still wailing. Clambering my feet, I sprinted towards the beast as fast as my broken body allowed. I tried to activate my Mech arm but it wasn't there. I could see it in my mind's eye, sitting on the workbench. Still, I didn't stop. But as the lights drew nearer, the beast turned and fled.

I was the first to reach the spot where Eve had stood; the first to see blood-soaked Babit. I was the first to drop to my knees with my head in my hands, sobbing. Anna was next, then Seb. Their crying surrounded me. I felt her heart breaking in the same way I had felt in Dad's on those nights he came to my room to remember all he'd lost. The thud of guns firing into the night vibrated through the earth but it was pointless: the creature was gone. So was Eve.

Taking a deep breath, I dared to glance over at Anna, raising my head from the ground, and instantly felt Seb's boot on the back of my neck pushing me back into warm blood that still lay in a crimson pool. Closing my eyes, I waited for the beating. It came with all the fury I expected. He kicked me hard in the ribs, knocking the air out of my lungs. Then again in the head, chest, stomach, inducing wails of pain. I felt the hard toe of his boot over and over until my blood mingled with Eve's.

"Stop!" came a cry. "Stop, Seb!"

Don't ask him to stop, Anna, I deserve this. You should have let him kill me when he first tried. Rolling onto my back, I felt the hot barrel of a gun on my forehead. I opened my eyes to look up at my killer and wished I hadn't; I'd never seen so much hate and so much grief in anyone until I looked into Seb's face. I didn't blame him. I'd let the monster in. It was I who murdered Eve; the blood of an innocent four-year-old was on my hands. Turning my face away, I breathed in the metallic, bloody soil, so that I couldn't see the sorrow I had caused.

But the shot never came. After a moment, I opened my eyes once more and Anna was standing over me, her hand outstretched. I hesitated, then took it gratefully and let her help me painfully to my feet. I tasted blood and the world looked blurry from the side of my face that had taken the brunt of Seb's grief. Stood before her, I was ready to take whatever other punishment she saw fit to give me. I was ready to face death should she choose it.

"Just go, Ava," she said, so very quietly, before turning away.

Her dismissal was worse that her wrath. She crumpled into Seb's arms, her body shaking with silent sobs. I wanted to reach out and touch her, just one last time, but he glared at me, full of rage he was barely able to control. Had Anna not been there, I would have been dead – brains splattered across the grass. But once again Anna had saved me. Someone was shouting at Seb about going after the Ghost, but everyone else had seen the amount of blood on the ground; they knew as well as I did that she was gone. I ran away as quickly as I could.

Anna's weeping following me as I headed back to the warehouse. Pushing open the door, I cursed the unused lock and the toppled desk, then gathered the Mech arm, along with everything else I had left in this world, and left. I didn't look back as I stepped out into oblivion.

Chapter 14

The thud of the ground beneath my feet was the only thing that registered; strangely loud, it echoed in my head, blocking out anything else. Though I willed my legs to move, they were heavy and slow. Trudging on, I concentrated on putting one foot in front of the other; my mind was as numb as my body. I didn't know where I was going, or what I was going to do. Inside the Barrier, I knew my way around; not out here. When Dad, Cain and I had squeezed onto that train all those years ago, I had been too young to learn the names of roads and towns that had sped past my window, too excited about going into the city to think about the way home.

Drifting aimlessly past rows of houses, abandoned cars and derelict corner shops, my mind lingered on Dad. The heartbreak was tangible again, bubbling up to the surface with fresh vigour, mixed with a new loss. I shivered despite the mildness of the night. Eventually, the habitation disappeared around me, leaving me alone with the darkness and the wide-open countryside. Here, even the dim streetlights could not penetrate the inky blackness, and I stared out across the empty plateau of nothingness that lay before me, a feeling of dread seeping into my bones. The rest of the world was pinned back only by another perimeter fence: razor wire dappled with dark blood. I lifted a hand to touch the cold metal and a sting of pain made me draw back, the numbness of shock starting to lift. Blood, cold and thick, covered my hands, sprayed up my arms and smeared across my face; I could taste it, smell the metal. Eve's blood and mine mingled together, crusting on my torn skin.

I closed my eyes, hugging my hand to my chest. I had done it; *I* had torn open that fencing. It was the only explanation. The voices in my head had won, drawn me out into the shadows and destroyed so many lives. Eve's face was emblazoned on the back of my eyes; I couldn't shake the heart-stopping terror in her eyes as the Ghost approached her. My stomach lurched in the same way it had when I'd opened the door of flat 625, back on the inside, and seen Dad, dead, his arm hanging from the side of the sofa, vomit pooling on the floor. I sunk to the floor as a heavy sorrow overwhelmed me, pinning me to the ground, unable to move. I cried until my eyes felt like the desert and my throat was raw from the sobs. My chest hurt from the guilt and grief that racked it. The sound of footsteps approaching lifted me from my pit and as the pale light of the dawn broke, I finally opened my eyes. Through a hazy film, I peered up at the approaching figure. Was it Seb, having regretted his mercy? It would be a relief to die and never again feel the things that tore me up inside, still as sharp in my memory as they had been last night. The morning sun hung low in the sky, covering the figure in shadow but I could make out the curve of a woman and, for a moment, my heart skipped a beat. Anna? Yet I knew she would be too consumed by the loss of her precious baby to care what I did or where I went – and I didn't blame her. Our bond was severed once and for all.

As she blotted out the sun, her face became clear. It was DiDi. Her cheeks were flushed, and she rested her hands on her knees, while her unruly dark ringlets tried to escape from a bandana that she had hurriedly wrapped around her head. My jaw went slack, words I should have said rolling back into my chest. She smiled down at me, then knelt at my side and took my wounded hand in hers.

She examined it and slipped off her backpack. Wordlessly, she pulled out a pack of bandages and wipes, and cleaned my hand before wrapping it tightly. I stared at her while she worked, unsure what to say, worried I might be imagining things.

"DiDi?" I finally managed. It was more of a croak than a word. She pinned the last part of the bandage and looked up at me.

"What are you doing?" I asked.

"I'm about to clean your face," she said, reaching for the wipes once more and cleaning me up like I was a child. I didn't miss the shifting of her eyes as she focused on the job at hand, avoiding my stare.

"I'm coming with you," she said with her usual cheeriness, repacking her bag and straightening up. "Come on!"

She reached out and took my forearm, pulling me to my feet. I groaned as everything span; an ache throbbed through my chest and drummed in my skull. One eye was still bleary. DiDi plunged her hand into her pocket and pulled out a key, lifting it up for me to see.

"There's a gate a bit further along," she said, turning and starting to walk.

I followed her in a state of numb disbelief. *Why on earth would she want to go with me?* I was a dangerous killer; throwing her lot in with me was like suicide. As I grabbed her arm, she span around to face me again, a look of annoyance on her face. It was the first time I'd seen her anything but happy.

"What are you doing?" I asked her again, reaching for her arm.

She shrugged my hand away and put her hands on her hips like she was telling off a child, and I shrunk back.

"It wasn't your fault," she said.

I made to argue but her look silenced me.

"They made you do it…but you fought back, Ava. I couldn't let you go on your own. No one deserves to be alone."

"You saw what I did. I can't keep you safe. Not from them and not from me," I said.

She didn't understand; I was as likely to harm her as the Ghosts were, yet she just shook her head.

"I don't need your protection, believe me."

"But you're just a nurse," I said.

"And you're *just* a woman with a metal arm. I was an A&E nurse and I served in the army for a short stint. I can handle myself," DiDi retorted.

I looked at her, taken back. I didn't have a comeback; she wasn't going to back down. DiDi was as stubborn as me. I shrugged: it was her choice – she knew what was out there better than I did.

"OK," I said quietly. Any strength I had to argue had been sapped. All I could see was Eve's face and a blood-soaked Babit.

"OK," she echoed.

She turned once more and continued along the fence until we came to a wire-framed door. She pushed the key into the padlock and it swung open with a whine. She gestured for me to go through and then followed, turning to lock the door once more. The air on this side of the fence felt different. It was cold and sharp, even though it was the same air we were breathing inside the compound. I shuddered. My body was still wracked with pain from Seb's beating but I tried not to let it show, pushing it down inside until it became lost along with my fear. My thoughts turned to Jackson: where would we even begin to look for him?

"There's another compound about two days' walk away. We could start there," said DiDi, as if she had read my mind.

I nodded. "Sounds like as good a place as any."

We walked side by side, sticking to the main roads in the day and keeping to the surrounding woodland at night. The pace was slow – my bruised body held us back. DiDi had packed a few supplies with her; she was more prepared than I was for this strange, abandoned world. The roads we trudged were long and deserted, often dotted with cars forgotten left in a colourful patina of rust and dirt. Peering into the windows, I saw possessions cast aside; suitcases still jammed full on the back seats, books with their pages spread open for all the world to see, food hard and dried in freezer bags.

The houses were much the same; abandoned in a hurry, now home to wild animals. The worst thing was the children's toys – teddies lying face down in the road, fur worn off their backs from love, and dolls half-naked, their eyes wide and staring. There were games consoles and MP3 players with headphones still plugged in, tiny pairs of shoes. I paused in front of a pair of dirty, cream ballet pumps. They were just like the ones that were tucked away in the cupboard in the flat. There was no one to take them out and look at them anymore, or touch their soft fabric. They would gather dust until MTech registered us as dead: a whole family gone. All the things that had been so precious to me would be thrown into a skip. The Scotts were gone: Ava, Cain, Dad, and Mum, all gone. And now Anna was lost to me too.

The thought hung over me, twisting in my gut, a reminder of what I had done. Eve's blood still stained my clothes and matted my cropped hair. All of a sudden my skin began to burn. Frantically I pulled at my clothes, letting out a cry that stopped DiDi in her tracks a little way ahead. She turned with her hands clenched into fists, her eyes scanning for the threat. But after a moment I felt the warmth of her body at my side. I collapsed into her arms, burying my head in her shoulder. My body shook as she held me tight. I focused on the smell of her warmth and the steady drum of her heart.

"Tell me," she said, her voice hushed and gentle.
Pulling back from her arms, I peered up at her through red eyes.

"I've lost everything, DiDi. I made everything worse by being here. I should have stayed on the inside, been content with my nine-to-five." I murmured.

"It would've killed you."

"But I killed her! I came and I destroyed the few good things that Anna had!"

I pushed DiDi away, catching a look of surprise on her face.

"I told you before, Ava: it's not you, it's them. They're a plague…an evil that we're going to stop. You're going to help us do it!"

"What if I can't? What if we don't find him?"
I felt the tears swell.

"Jackson?"

I nodded.

"We will, I know it!"

DiDi gave me confident smile before glancing up at the sky; the sun was dying, the sky blood-red, and the air was starting to cool.

204

"Let's stop for today. I think I saw a corner shop up ahead. We might be able to find some tinned food. You still got some wood left over?" she asked, turning towards a building ahead of us.

I followed her slowly. The windows of the shop were shattered and glass littered the ground in shards that crunched under our feet. There was the distinct smell of rot and mould but the empty shelves harboured a few tins of peaches and potatoes which we scavenged before leaving the town behind and disappearing into the shelter of the trees. As I fought with the tins, DiDi tipped out the wood we had collected and built a base for the fire. She took a moment to cultivate a few sparks before flames began to devour the dry kindling. I opened the tins and she plunged her fingers into the can of soft potatoes, eating hungrily. The guilt in my stomach still made it hard to swallow.

"You need to eat," she told me.

Begrudgingly, I took a potato, biting into the salty flesh. We sat shoulder to shoulder watching the fire for a while, as night descended and the light of the flames danced off the trees around us, creating long shadows. I could hear the Ghosts around us – feel them drawing nearer. I knew they could taste us on the air. Something inside me called to them, and they came, skirting around the fire, fearful of its brightness. Their icy breath touched the back of my neck even though they kept their distance. And still I felt something else from them, something that called to me for help.

"You should try and sleep," I told DiDi as she stifled a yawn.

"You first, I'm not tired."

I shook my head. "Don't lie to me!"

"OK, OK," she raised her hands in surrender. "Let me get the cable ties."

She took out the ties and bound us together: she would keep me safe, grounding me if the Ghosts were too strong for me to fight. With one last reassuring smile, she shoved her bag under her head and curled up into a ball. Within a moment she was asleep and I was alone.

Sleep was cruel: the minute DiDi's breathing softened, I felt its tempting fingers curling around me, weighing down my eyelids. I poked the fire with a stick and dumped another handful of wood onto it. The smell of smoke hung in the air, hot and acrid, as the flames twisted around each other, burning a brilliant orange. Alone, I tried to remember the good things about life before the Barrier, before the Ghosts and MTech. I remembered throwing sticks in the river near our house, long muddy walks with Mum and Dad. I smiled at Cain's Goth phase: dark ringed eyes and jet-black hair. There were birthdays and family dinners, laughter and friends. It seemed so long ago now, so many things had happened.

"Ava!"

My body twitched awake. DIDi's face was inches from mine, her hand clasped over my mouth. We were surrounded by darkness. Pale shadows moved amongst the trees.

"You fell asleep and the fire's gone out," she murmured. "They're here!"

She released me from her grip and we watched as the Ghosts drifted past.

"Why haven't they attacked?" I whispered.

DiDi shrugged beside me; her hand reached for mine in the silvery blackness. Gripping her hand in return, I closed my eyes listening to the Ghosts' voices as they whispered to me from the night. We were nothing to them; I was damaged already. They were more interested in the compound, with its many voices and heartbeats.

"Just keep still!" I whispered.

Neither of us slept again until the hazy light of the dawn finally broke. I woke with the sun on my face to find DiDi's warm, strong, arms around me, protecting me like no one had ever done before. She was my rock; she reminded me of Mum. Mum had been the hugger; I could still smell her perfume if I thought about it hard enough. Dad hadn't known what to do with me when I'd cried as a child – he'd simply punch me on the shoulder and tell me to keep my chin up. Growing up, I'd longed for the affection he hadn't known how to give. But now DiDi's friendship filled that ache inside me; she saw me for me.

The next morning, I was ready to face what had happened two nights ago.

"How did it happen?" I asked DiDi as she swigged the last of her water.

Her eyes flicked away from mine and she busied herself with packing her bag and gathering a few unburnt bits of wood.

"DiDi, please," I murmured to her back.
Before she turned, she hurriedly wiped her face.

"Why beat yourself up with it? It wasn't your fault – I've already told you that."

"It wasn't Eve's fault though, was it?"

Anger and guilt scratched at my throat.

"No," DiDi breathed.

"Tell me! I have to know."

"You don't need…"

I cut her off with my artificial hand on her arm; her eyes widened.

"Ava, you're hurting me."

I withdrew immediately, turning away. My head slumped forwards. After a moment, the warmth of her hand radiated through my shoulder.

"Eve was in awe of you. I heard the way she pleaded with Anna to let her go and see you. She'd even scratched the black paint off her window so she could peer out and see the light of the warehouse." DiDi told me, as I turned to listen. "They found the lock on the fire escape was broken. Eve climbed out looking for you that night when the sirens had sounded – she was worried that you weren't safe in the school."

DiDi crumbled, pressing the back of her hand to her mouth. I could barely shoulder the guilt. DiDi had been right; it was best if the hurt remained unspoken. A lingering silence accompanied us for the rest of the day as we followed the dusty roads towards the next compound. As we walked, we passed deep craters that seemed to hum from within, calling to me. Some of the holes had sucked in houses and roads, and broken fronds of steel wrapped in concrete dangled over the edge like fingers. The Ghosts had been indiscriminate in their attack.

"What's down there?" I asked DiDi as we walked past a particularly large hole.

"Buried ships," she murmured, pulling me away and steering us towards an abandoned petrol station. "The light is starting to fade, let's camp out in there, it'll be dry and safer than being outside so closer to *that*."

Her eyes darted over to the crater.

"We'll reach the compound tomorrow – I remember this petrol station," DiDi informed me, "right now I'm hungry."

I let DiDi eat the last of the food as we sat huddled inside the staffroom of the petrol station. We slept fitfully in shifts until the morning light slipped in through a small, frosted glass window. The early sun was warm and bright, hovering like an egg yolk in the sky as we walked, yet my skin puckered; I was nervous about who we would meet at the compound – there would be people who didn't accept me like DiDi did. There would be judgement and questions. Before I had the chance to tell DiDi how I felt, the tell-tale glimmer of metal fences soared into the sky on the horizon and I swallowed my anxiety.

We were treated with caution at the compound, ushered hurriedly through the perimeter fence while anxious looks inspected us. People stopped to stare as we walked the main path through the camp. Their voices batted back and forth, low and hushed, filled with apprehension. People rarely left the safety of their compound, so two women wandering around alone and unarmed was an irregular sight – and my metal arm a further intrigue. The things that lurked beyond the tall, razor-wire topped fences were dangerous, and I felt the fear in the people's stares.

Two men with large guns slung over their backs and knives wedged into their belts escorted us through, steering us towards a large supermarket with shuttered windows and sliding doors. Inside, the lights were low and the hum of fridges and freezers buzzed in the air. People milled around, sorting and organising food, dispensing it to others who waited with bags in their hands. A tall woman with thick ginger hair twisted into a tight bun turned from the group as we approached. I felt her eyes on me, taking in the blood, the filth, and my arm. Her arms crossed tightly over her chest and suspicion creased her face.

"And you are?" she questioned.

I shifted uncomfortably under her stare; under its pierce, I simply wanted to get some food and go.

"No one," replied DiDi, "we're just passing through from the southern compound. Looking for a friend."

"No one *just* passes through," she said with a sarcastic laugh.

DiDi took a deep breath. Her hands landed on her hips and she stepped forward menacingly.

"We lost someone, and we have to find him. He's can help us end the Ghosts, end the Barrier and get our lives back. We just need some food and water and then we'll be out of your hair. We don't want any trouble," I interjected, putting a hand on DiDi's arm. Her face softened. The tall lady didn't speak. Her piecing blue eyes made me want to flinch but I fixed my eyes on hers and waited; the seconds passed like hours.

"Who're you looking for?" came a voice from over her shoulder.

A man with a shaved head and a long, dark beard limped out from the crowd, placing a hand on the woman's back. His eyes were kind but wary. I stepped forward, a surge of confidence rising in me at the sight of a fellow amputee.

"Jackson Quinn. Tall, black, quiet, lots of tattoos," I told him.

"Yeah, I spoke to him. He was just as keen as you are to restock and get on his way again. Tell me about him," the man ordered.

210

"We need him to help us find a way to back into the inside, so we can bring this all to an end. Please – we just need some food and then we'll be on our way. Please!"

The woman next to him rolled her eyes and turned away with a shrug of her shoulders. My tension drained away as her slim back disappeared back into the crowd of people that had gathered, although my hands still trembled at my side. DiDi's hand rested on mine, warm and still, and I allowed myself to let out a long breath.

"Maria tells me there'll be no food left for us if I keep feeding strays," he chuckled, "but if you're telling the truth then we have nothing to lose. The food won't last forever – we all know that."

His eyes wandered briefly to my Mech arm.

"This way," he said, leading us towards the back of the shop. He grabbed a few tins of food for us – dried fruit and packets of instant meals – as questions poured out of him, answered in exchange for each packet or tin. Deep down, I longed for silence; my body itched and I struggled to keep still. The longer we stood answering questions the further Jackson got from us. I could still feel eyes on us from the others at the front of the store, judging me, scrutinising me. There was a pause in the conversation and I took my chance.

"Thank you so much for all your help, but we have to find Jackson," I interjected.

The man's face fell and I felt a pang of guilt. He wanted to know more about our mission; to feel that soaring buzz of hope we had brought with us – but it would never come if we didn't find Quinn.

"Of course, of course," he bustled. "Fill your water bottles first, OK?"

"Thank you," I repeated.

"We'll find a way." DiDi reiterated. "Don't lose hope – be ready. The southern compound will take the lead but we need everyone we can get. Keep an ear to the ground."

Outside the supermarket we shook hands, thanking him before we were escorted by armed men once more, back across the compound and out into the unguarded wilderness. Standing on the edge of another world, full of death and danger, I could feel DiDi's exhaustion; it matched my own. How I wished we could lay on soft beds, under a solid roof, protected by fences and locks. I wanted a bath, to wash the memories away in scalding hot water.

"I'm sorry," I murmured.

DiDi's smile was as bright as ever.

"I know," she replied. "It's OK."

She knew we had no choice but to keep going: the danger I posed was too great. We must take our chances with the night rather than be surrounded by strangers.

Chapter 15

Long, plodding days were followed by nights as black as pitch; no longer lit by busy houses and twenty-four-hour supermarkets, our fire was all that accompanied us along the dark streets. There was no traffic, nobody; everything was so still and silent that every breath of wind carried the whispering voices of the Ghosts and every falling leaf on the edge of my vision was their elongated form. It was another two days of walking before we stumbled on a small village: a 'one-road-in, one-road-out' kind of place nestled at the bottom of a hill. The houses had broken windows and open doors, like missing teeth. The dark doorways spewed out rubbish and broken possessions, and nature had begun reclaiming the brick. Plants weaved in and out of the cement. Front gardens spread over the crumbling brick walls and out onto the pavements, creeping towards the road or into the open front doors of neighbouring houses. Splashes of colour dotted the fronts of the houses as flower beds, once well-tended, still bloomed with life. There was something reassuring about the fact that life had still carried on; the Ghosts hadn't destroyed everything.

As the sun stained the sky pink, we stood amongst the houses. DiDi's hand slipped into mine.

"I don't like it," she said.

I shook my hand free.

"There's no one here, DiDi. Come on!"

"I don't like it!" she repeated, shaking her head.

Her gaze seemed to be fixed on something in the distance. I put my hands on her shoulders and her eyes, dark and frightened, finally met mine. I'd never seen that look on her face before – not even when she'd spoken about the night the Ghosts arrived and took her mother and father. This was different. I peered over my shoulder down the road. It seemed ordinary enough – desolate and sad but nothing unusual, nothing we hadn't seen before.

"If you really don't want to…" I began, but she seemed to snap out of her trance and smiled at me.

"No, I'm just being silly. We'll be fine. I've got you and you've got me, right?"

She laughed, all teeth, but her shoulders were still stiff and her hands were clenched. Her eyes darted from me to the houses and back again and I gestured for her to follow me. Together, we wandered down a narrow village road, making a beeline for the first house with a front door. DiDi relaxed slightly.

"Let's see what we've got here," she said, giving the door a shove.

It swung open – in their hurry to escape no-one had locked their doors – and I followed DiDi in. There were three bedrooms upstairs with several old beds which were dusty but dry. I threw the covers on the floor leaving the untouched mattresses bare, wondering who had slept there fourteen years ago. DiDi stood watching with her hands on her hips.

"It'll do," she smiled. "I'll pop downstairs and see what's left in the kitchen."

Her footsteps disappeared down the stairs and I heard her pottering around below me, opening kitchen cupboards and drawers. I guessed we would end up lying shoulder to shoulder, despite the spare beds: my Mech arm on the bedside table and a knife under DiDi's pillow. I slung my bag on the bed and the mustiness of abandonment wafted from it. Coughing, I turned away and noticed that the window had remained intact. The world

214

outside seemed quiet, street lamps flickering in the growing darkness. A sharp itch under the Mech arm stole my attention and I glanced down at it, pushing my finger between skin and metal in an attempt to relieve the perpetual niggle. As I scratched, I caught sight of something out of the corner of my eye. Pressing my forehead against the cold window pane, I scanned the street desperately, my heart racing. It was empty. Rain had started to fall. Shaking my head, I wiped my foggy breath from the window and decided that it was the half-light playing tricks on me. All was peaceful, except for the gentle drum of the rain. We were alone here.

Something hit the floor downstairs, sending my heart into overdrive once more. I tore myself away from the window and bolted for the door, taking the stairs two at a time and landing at the bottom with the thud that travelled up my legs. I turned into the kitchen. There was a Ghost standing between DiDi and I. Its head turned towards me as I stood in the doorway, trying not to breathe, and I was struck by the horror of the thing that stood before me, pale and hunched over on all fours, sniffing at the ground. DiDi's eyes widened. She shook her head silently, her eyes leading me back to the Ghost, which had turned back to the half-opened tin of processed ham whose contents were splayed across the floor. It rooted around in the pink mush, distracted by the meaty smell. DiDi shook her head at the hand I reached out silently to her. Fear had stopped her like cement. I had a vision of Lucy, her eyes red from crying, a look of terror on her pretty face. Not again: I wouldn't let this happen again! Slowly, I lifted my Mech arm; if I aimed well, I might be able to give DiDi enough time to escape. I gestured for her to come towards me and she nodded, gently lifting one foot and placing it closer to the door. She edged towards me with her back to the wall.

Holding my breath, I watched as her fingertips appeared around the door frame, just inches from my own. Then her foot made contact with a discarded spoon, which clattered across the wooden floor. The Ghost looked up and wailed. Grabbing DiDi, I pulled her out of the way and fired wildly at the Ghost's head. It slumped against the kitchen cupboard, momentarily stunned.

"Run!" I shouted, pushing her away and reaching to slam the kitchen door shut.

I didn't wait to see if I had killed it or not; I ran after DiDi, out into the driving rain and descending night. We didn't know where we were going; our only thought was to put as much distance between ourselves and the Ghost as we could. The sound of splintering wood and brick hitting the street rang out behind us but we didn't dare look back. The creature's limbs pounded the ground behind.

My legs ached and my body was still weak from the beatings it had taken. Leaving the village, we darted into the surrounding trees for cover, weaving our way through the trunks, knowing the beast's size would hinder it in the dense woodland. A tree root caught my foot and I put my hand out to stop myself, landing with a thud on the damp ground. Pain shot through my wrist as I tried to push myself up. Then the creature was on me. I rolled onto my back to face the demon. Black soil and leaves clung to my clothes and hair; the heat of its sour breath made me tremble as it breathed in my scent. It lingered over me, savouring the moment before the kill, like a cat with a mouse. I reached across my body, holding its eyeless gaze as it lowered its foul face towards mine: maybe it sensed the presence of its kind within me? But the pause was all I needed, I flicked on the high-powered light on my Mech arm and thrust it into the creature's eye socket. It shrieked and flailed, trying to get away from the light penetrating its skull. With my free hand, I punched it over and over, gripping it tightly with my metal hand. Then, suddenly, the weight of it was lifted from me. Streams of black blood spurted from the eye I had been bludgeoning and its large gruesome head contorted at an unearthly angle before it was ripped from the beast's body.

I scrabbled to my feet. Breathing hard, I searched for my saviour in the torchlight. The beam fell over the twitching body of the Ghost and there, soaked to the skin, clutching a bloody machete, was Jackson Quinn. He held his hand up to his eyes, shielding them from the light.

"What the hell are you doing here?" he questioned.

"We were trying to find you!" I shouted. "DiDi and I."

I stopped. DiDi! I threw the torchlight over the surrounding trees but couldn't see her. The Mech arm faltered and the torchlight died.

"DiDi!" I bellowed.

The cry that greeted me turned my stomach. I sprinted in the direction it came from, dodging trees and ducking under low branches until I came to a small clearing. In the darkness, DiDi was struggling to get to her feet in the middle of the trees, her hands searching for her knife, which was just out of reach. Another Ghost was circling her. As I approached, it locked me in its sights before rounding on DiDi and gathering her up into its arms. Lifting my Mech arm, I tried to fire the gun but it hung dormant and useless. DiDi's terrified cries filled the woods as with a screech the Ghost bared its teeth at me and then disappeared into the trees. Only Jackson's strong arms wrapped around my waist prevented me from running after it.

"DiDi!" I called her name into the darkness. "DiDi!"

My words were lost in the vast expanse of night. Spinning around, I pushed hard against Jackson's chest, trying to break free, but he simply held me as the pouring rain soaked us both to the skin.

"No!" I shouted, thrashing around.

My feet were slipping in the mud. My body was weary and my anger was fading into something else; there was heat in the back of my eyes. DiDi was so nice, so happy – and I was so hateful, full of anger and bitterness; yet they took her and left me. *Me,* the one who deserved whatever foul purpose they used us for.

"No, DiDi!" I repeated.

But the words were barely a murmur as I sunk into Jackson's chest. What would I do now? My rock – my steady ground – was gone. I took a step back from Jackson.

"I just wanted someone to see me," I cried into the space between us.

My skin prickled painfully in the freezing rain and I began to shiver. I dug my teeth into my lip to stop it from trembling.

"I just wanted to be me. And DiDi seemed to know who that was," I told him. "They took her!"

Jackson reached out and brushed away the hair that was plastered to my forehead. I knew I was being selfish, but I needed her. The unexpected, gentle warmth of his touch took me by surprise and I stood there, staring at him. His hand lingered on my cheek and I closed my eyes. I stood in the rain just feeling him, not knowing what else to do. It was a caress so different from anything I had felt before, not like the rough molestation of my brother or the

218

healing hands of DiDi. My legs crumbled beneath me and he held me up. I could feel him drawing closer, the air between us heating up with my apprehensive breath. I swallowed hard.

No, I can't. No! The last thought becoming an utterance that threw wide the hair's breadth between us. With the rain drumming on my face, I opened my eyes but he was not where I thought he was. I was no longer stood before him. He had lifted me up, carried me out of the rain and back into the trees away from DiDi. The warmth I had felt was the sweating skin of his tattooed neck.

Chapter 16

Jackson's voice filtered through to my dreamless sleep that night. Exhausted, sleep had overcome me as he cradled me to his chest like a child, but now morning brought a sense of urgency, pulling roughly me from my erratic sleep. As I unscrewed my eyes and wiped the sweat from my face, it all came flooding back to me: the rain, the Ghost, Jackson – and DiDi.

"DiDi," I murmured, pushing myself up off the thin mat I had been lying on.

The cool morning air rushed over my bare legs. My feet were dressed in nothing but socks, my boots gone. There was a smell of damp plastic, and the light was pale and yellow through the canvas of the grubby tent I found myself in. Jackson was nowhere to be seen. There was movement outside: the squelch of wet grass under heavy boots. Arming my Mech gun, I pushed back the tent door cautiously. A bird that was picking through the undergrowth took flight as I emerged, but there was no-one else around. I stood in unfamiliar woodland, the early morning sun mottling the ground around me and the smell of last night's rain pervading the air. Everything was peaceful as if nothing had happened the previous night. There was a shuffle of earth underfoot behind me and I spun around with my Mech gun raised.

"Woah!" said Jackson, raising his hands in surrender. I relaxed my arm and the gun sunk back into its slot.

"Where are my clothes?" I asked.

He gestured to a tree branch on which my trousers were draped.

"You were soaked, didn't want you to get ill," he said with a shrug.

"I don't get ill," I snapped at him, grabbing the trousers and pulling them on.

They were still a little damp and stuck to my skin as I tugged at them. I felt Jackson watching me and sensed a smirk on his face. Doing up the zip on my trousers, I turned, fighting the tightness in my throat and the urgency that made me want to run. I had come for him yet *he* had found *me*. Now we needed to get DiDi back.

"What are you doing here?" I asked him.

"Looking for someone who lived near here. What are you doing looking for me?"

"Your son?" I said before I could stop myself.

He looked away from me into the distance, leaving my question unanswered.

"Quinn, I'm going to square with you," I said.

"Oh, Quinn is it now?" Jackson said.

My face burnt; I was still a child to him, the one he had adapted an implant for all those years ago. I clenched my fists – one metal, one flesh.

"Cut the bull! I came here looking for you, to bring you back to the edge of the compound. They need you. But things have changed now – they have DiDi," I explained.

"Why? After what you said to me, I didn't think I'd ever see you again," Jackson said.

My finger nails bit into my palm. Every minute we stood here talking was another minute wasted in the hunt for DiDi.

"I'm sorry," I managed. "I didn't know."

"You didn't want to know," said Jackson.

I looked away. He had helped me escape and I hadn't given him the chance to explain why he had done the things he had. The fire that had blazed in my gut fizzled out; the words I'd wanted to spit at him melted away. He waited for me silently, arms folded across his chest. My fists unclenched. I wasn't proud of who I was; back on the inside I lived for me, for Ava, under the guise of wanting to help others. And look where that had got the people I called my friends – death followed me like a bad smell.

"I was angry," I said, at last.

"You let it consume you, Ava," he told me.

I let myself look up at him. Our eyes met but guilt still choked me and I shook my head, my eyes searching for the way we had come the previous night instead. A thinner line of trees to the left seemed familiar and I started walking, urgency rising in my stomach.

"I don't have time for this," I murmured, pushing past Jackson.

"Where are you going?" he called after me.

"To get DiDi back!" I shouted without stopping. "She was still alive when it took her."

Within moments he was next to me, his hand on my arm. I tried to shake him off but he held on tightly. I reached over and prised his fingers off with my Mech arm.

"Listen to me!" he shouted. "For God's sake, Ava, just listen for once!"

"What, Jackson? Going to kill me if I don't? Finish the job you started?" I argued but the fight was gone from my words, the sound of my heartbeat raging noisily in my head. *DiDi,* it pounded. *DiDi.*

He let go and pushed me away, muttering something under his breath and shaking his head. He took a breath before speaking again.

"I won't have to if you carry on like this. Look, Ava, we've all done some crap that we're not proud of…" he began, his voice level and calm again.

He ran his hand over his head, where a thin layer of dark hair was starting to grow.

"Like shooting a man by the kebab shop? Or assassinating me?" I interrupted.

He was wasting my time.

"You don't know what you're talking about, Ava. This is just what I was talking about…all this hate, this anger. I never had any intention of killing you. I'd heard about you and your little group. I wanted in, but I needed to know you were legit. I recognised your surname – I remembered your Dad and I wanted to get out as much as you did, but everyone else was too bloody frightened of their own shadows to do anything about it. And as for that man you *thought* I shot – that was one of those half-Mech, half-man things. MTech like to keep tabs on me as a disgruntled ex-employee – as someone who knows how the Barrier works. They think they've got me under their thumb, feeding them information, but it's a load of bull. I make myself useful to them to save my own skin. That's how my path crossed with Cain's," explained Jackson.

"Cain," I murmured; the thought of him still made my blood run cold. Jackson must have read something in my face, because I saw his hand move at his side.

"That thing was not your brother, never was. It just wore his skin. I guess MTech saw an opportunity to get close to you and took it. If they just killed you, they got nothing and someone else was bound to take your place. I guess you didn't tell him much?" said Jackson.

I thought back to my relationship with Cain. It was a necessity; what I thought was brotherly protection was

223

nothing more than an unwanted burden on Cain's part – a promise to Dad. I never really knew him and he never knew me. Maybe that was why I never noticed when they replaced him? I'd always been alone really.

"But he knew things. He knew who I was," I said.

"Yeah, they used Cain's mind, too. They added to it, saved him from death, reprogrammed his brain and in return he fed them information. They knew you were Ava, not Alec," he told me.

"But they never came for me. And it was you that stole the memory stick."

"They obviously didn't have what they wanted from you yet. No point rocking the boat until they had all the information. Believe it or not, some people are happy in there. Some people like the lie and MTech wants to be seen as doing a good job. Maybe they were going to make an example of you," Jackson said. "As for the memory stick, well, once I realised how close you were, once I'd made the connection between you and Cain, I didn't think it was safe to leave it behind."

"Why on earth would it have been safer with you?" I placed my hands on my hips, but he just shrugged. "They sent you to kill me."

Like I said, that came from your brother, I don't know all the ins and outs of it," he said with a shrug. "I guess it worked…you let Cain in."

"How much of him was left in there?" I asked. The thought of his fingers running up and down my skin forced its way into my head.

"I don't know. It was him and it wasn't; I couldn't tell you how much of him was left. Some of the programmers are twisted though. They want to scare people, keep them submissive – they love to play God. I hated everything they stood for in the end."

I ran my hand through my hair. All the fear, the hurt and the anger hit me again as I relived those last moments with the man I had thought was still Cain. Yet now there was a sadness that hadn't been there before. It only took a moment to pinpoint the day I had lost the real Cain. I knew the week that he had disappeared, and when he eventually unlocked the door of our flat one day he was a different man. What awful thing had happened to my brother for him to be so close to death that he needed MTech to save him? Thinking about it would destroy me – there was so much in my head; I couldn't keep this hurt too.

"I need to find DiDi," I said, pushing the thought away and bringing her back into focus.

Jackson nodded, "I think I can help you with that."

He collected his things and I followed him back down to the town, a feeling of foreboding creeping over me as we drew closer. DiDi's things were still in that house waiting for me – the only pieces of her I had left. All I could think about was getting DiDi back, getting back to the compound and shutting that Barrier down. I wanted to burn the skin off those Ghosts, to watch them writhe as their flesh disintegrated; I finally had a chance to do something good in this quagmire of hate.

Leading Jackson to the house where DiDi and I had set up camp, I found her bag still in the kitchen, the tin of processed ham gone. The sight of it was like a knife in my side. Jackson stepped forward, reaching for it.

"No!" I cried.

He couldn't have it; it was DiDi's. He looked up at me, frowning.

"I'll take it – you see if there is anything in here we can make use of," I told him, gathering the bag into my arms like a lost child. It smelt like her. With the contents of both my bag and DiDi's, we left the house. The warmth of the sun greeted us on the street beyond but I pulled my jacket tighter around myself.

"We'll eat as we go," Jackson told me. "We've got about a day's walk ahead of us."

"To where?" I asked.

"The Hive," he replied.

Chapter 17

We trekked for most of the day, along empty roads. All around us, the scars of the day the Ghosts came were still unhealed. Great craters scattered over the face of the earth like pockmarked skin, a reminder of how the Ghosts had come blasting holes into the ground to make their underground homes, destroying anything that got in their way. The eerie stillness of once-busy roads and towns felt heavier now DiDi was gone; I hadn't realised how much her presence had lightened the air. The weight of our task pressed down on me. The human race was fighting a losing battle against a stronger, more formidable enemy here to devour us and use us as fuel. There were so few of us left now.

"Jackson," I said as we came to a stop, "did you find who you were looking for?"

He shook his head and changed the subject.

"Just over that hill," he said pointing, "that's where they are."

Peering in the direction he was indicating there was nothing much to see; a grassy hill rose up to meet the cloudless sky.

"Come on then," I said taking a step forward, but Jackson stopped me.

"The light is starting to fade, we need to wait here. Get prepared…" he smiled, "…we're going to catch a Ghost!"

I stood knee-deep in a large hole, the palm of my hand burning as I slung spade after spade full of gritty dirt to the side. Wiping the sweat off my forehead, I tossed the spade at Jackson's feet and stretched my arm across my body.

"Your turn," I called breathlessly up to Quinn, who stood fiddling with a can of processed ham.

He glanced up from the meat and gave me a nod before jumping down into the hole. His feet made a satisfying thud on the loose earth next to me. He, too, smelt like dirt and sweat.

"Where did you find the spade?" I asked, reaching for my water and taking a long gulp.

"Garden shed," he said casually, flinging more earth out of the hole. "The machete was there too."

I couldn't think of anything else to say as I watched him dig. I wanted to ask about his son, about the family he had lost but the words stuck in my throat. As the last of the light disappeared, Jackson stood, pressing his fingers into his back while I sat leaning against the damp mound of earth that had piled up on the side of the hole.

"That should be enough," he said, snatching the tin of meat from the ground and emptying it into the pit. "Grab the other one, would you?"

"And then what?"

"They'll be here soon, they'll smell us. You distract the Ghost with the light on that," he gestured at my arm. "I'll kill it."

With the trap set, we lay in wait as the night descended, our bodies pressed into the damp earth. The smell of ham and rain yet to fall hung in the air as I tried not to give in to sleep; my brain cried out for it. I focused on Jackson's steady breathing and the solidness of his body next to mine.

Then I heard it: the sound of heavy footfall on the ground, slowly drawing closer, and of breathing as the Ghost recognised our scent. Jackson moved next to me. His machete glistened in the moonlight. I swallowed hard as the creature approached, luminous in the silver light. It breathed in deeply, as if drawing all the oxygen from the air, as it hunted for the ham in front of us. I twitched and Jackson put a hand on mine, signalling to me to wait: not yet.

The creature gave a rumble of glee as it buried its fingers in the pink, sloppy meat. It bent down to eat, exposing its sinewy, blanched neck to us and Jackson leapt from his hiding place in the dirt, the machete raised above his head. I flicked on my torch, shining it square in the Ghost's face. It writhed in the burning light – but only for a moment. As a burning sensation pierced my skull, Jackson's machete hit the creature on the neck, slicing clean through like butter. The creature dropped to the ground, its body twitching and spewing blood. Its head rolled in the hole. The thick, black liquid that flowed from the Ghost's neck filled the damp air with a faintly metallic tang, not unlike human blood, and I watched as Jackson hurriedly emptied his water bottle and began to fill it with the blood.

"Quick, find something to catch it in!" he instructed.

I emptied out my water and pushed the neck of the bottle into the pulsating artery. As the blood spilt over onto my hands, I fought the urge to retch. To my relief, after a minute or two, the flow of blood slowed and finally stopped. Placing the bottle on the floor, I sat back. I ran my trembling hand through my hair, ungluing it from my forehead.

"What now?" I asked quietly.

"Cover yourself in it. Make sure you keep some for DiDi," Jackson told me. I screwed my nose up, then stared at Jackson wide-eyed.

"Just do it!" he growled. "It will mask our scent when we go in to find her. They rely on their sense of smell, remember."

Tipping the blood onto my hands, I held my breath and began to rub it onto my skin. It was still warm but as I spread it over my skin, I thought about DiDi – and Eve; for them, I could do anything. Then I emptied my bag, leaving only the bottle of blood inside, and faced Jackson, who carried nothing but his machete.

"Why are we going in now? I thought they only came out at night – won't they be asleep in the day?" I asked.

"Those things never sleep," he told me. "When I found my home empty, I spent time here watching them, trying to understand them. If we go in now, there will be fewer of them."

I rubbed my face with my hand; I needed a moment to just breathe and take on board what we were about to do. Eyes closed, I took a deep breath, and then another. The terrible unknown was worse than the knowing; I wanted to see what I was facing, but there was only one way to do that. Heart pounding, I nodded at Jackson.

"Okay, let's go," I said.

He nodded and we set off up the hill, walking side by side in silence until we reached the summit. Pausing at the top, toes on the edge of the precipice, I stared down at the vast crater that had swallowed the land around the base of the hill. Dilapidated houses clung to the edge of it, desperately trying to stay above ground like drowning souls. Water and gas pipes poked out of the sides of the hole, entangled with tree roots and long since run dry. The base of the crater was pocked with smaller holes at least two metres in diameter, like open mouths waiting to swallow me up. My gut told me this was the way in; it had

230

to be. My heart sounded so loud in my ears I could hardly hear myself think. The faint smell of earth and blood wafted on the wind. It took me a moment to realise the smell was me.

"Yep," said Jackson as I opened my mouth to speak, "that's the way in."

I exhaled sharply and pushed on, scouting around the edge of the crater until I found a place where the crumbling earth lay at less of a gradient. As I edged my way down sideways, the mud shifted under my weight, eventually hardening up as we reached the lower levels of the pit. At the bottom, it seemed so much bigger – darker and more terrifying. Suddenly, my skin pricked and my vision was blurred. I shook my head to disperse the fog. *No, not now: they will not get to me!* Fighting the shadows that lurked at the edge of my vision, I headed for the nearest hole and peered in. There was no bottom; nothing but black earth.

"Any particular one?" I whispered to Jackson.

He shook his head. "They come out of all of them. This is as good as any."

"OK," I said.

For DiDi and Eve, I thought, stepping over the edge of the hole. It was a short, sharp drop, only a couple of metres or so, then the hole became a tunnel that sloped gently down to the centre of the crater. Jackson landed behind me with a thud and I flicked my torch on but he quickly covered it with his hand, shaking his head.

"Save it for later," he murmured in my ear. "Let your eyes get used to the dark."

We stood for a moment, staring down the tunnel until gradually the texture of the earth became apparent and the path ahead revealed itself. With my Mech arm ready, I led the way down into the hive, while the Ghosts whispered to me in their shadow tongue. The tunnel took us slowly on downwards, deeper and deeper, while the air grew colder. It was hard to breathe and the crumbling earth walls seemed to close in on me – my heart lodged itself in my throat. Just as I thought the tunnel would never end, it began to open up again. There was movement beyond. Grabbing Jackson's arm, I pulled him to a halt protectively. This was not about me anymore. It was about something bigger: the sacrifice of the one for the many. I took another deep breath; even if I didn't get out of here, I made up my mind to get Jackson and DiDi out.

Jackson slid in front of me and emerged out of the tunnel into the chamber beyond. I followed and we found ourselves standing in a vast room which pulsated with hazy sepia light emanating from thick veins embedded in the translucent skin-like walls. Evenly spaced around the room, the veins ran from floor to ceiling, pulsing with a thick amber fluid. There was the smell of blood and rot in the bitter air; it accosted my senses and I tried not to breathe too deeply. We had entered another world, one of fear and terror. I stood, transfixed for a moment by the bizarre sight, which horrified me and fascinated me at the same time. The ship was alive. I looked over at Jackson but he, too, was in awe; touching his arm I brought him back to our mission. The room around us was empty but dozens of tunnels led off it, pulsing in the sepia light. As I gazed around, something about the room felt familiar. It came back to me with sickening clarity: my nightmares were of this labyrinth of tunnels and chambers through the eyes of the Ghosts.

"This way!" I whispered urgently.

Jackson frowned but followed as I headed down one of the tunnels to the right. I knew where I was headed; I had been within these walls of skin before. My shadow world had become flesh. The things I had seen in my nightmares started to make sense to me as, with confident steps, I traversed the maze of tunnels. A living, breathing ship needed fuel. After a long journey through space, they needed a whole race to refuel. Why feed it with their own kind when the whole human race was at their disposal? I shuddered but something still felt out of place – a feeling I couldn't quite put my finger on. Pushing on, I broke into a run along the winding tunnels. I was in the mind of the Ghost again, my feet pounding on the ship's mottled floor, the smell of human flesh and blood filling my nose.

"This way," I said, turning sharply left into another tunnel.

So far, we hadn't met a single Ghost – we were still in the outer tunnels – but I knew we would soon. I headed for where I knew DiDi would be, taking a right before slamming on the brakes and holding my arm out to stop Jackson. My adrenaline was pumping hard but the fear was gone. These demons had tried to corrupt my mind but instead, they had given me a gift; they had laid themselves bare in front of me and now they weren't in me; I was in them.

"Ghosts!" I breathed, pressing my body to the wall.

Jackson did the same and we waited. As we did, a Ghost emerged from the chamber we were about to enter. It slunk past us, pausing momentarily as it did, sniffing the air. It's haunting face, pale and taut, drew closer to us. Closing my eyes, I waited. Jackson went tense next to me and I could feel his body contract. I willed him to be still. After a moment, I opened my eyes to see the Ghost retract its head and move along; fooled by the bloody mess smeared on our skin.

Pressing a finger to my lips to silence Jackson, I beckoned him to follow me once more. The smell of human filth, of death and decomposition, grew stronger; I could taste it. Creeping as silently as possible, we emerged into the room at the end of the tunnel, to be greeted with a sight I hoped had only been a nightmare. My heart sunk at the sight of rows of cages lining the flickering walls. They grew out of the flesh of the ship like boney ribs; each one housing several emancipated men and women, their bones visible beneath papery skin. Three more Ghosts wandered around the room, busy with various tasks. One appeared to be filling dishes of water inside the cages while the other two were gathering something from one of the cages at the far end of the room.

Then I spotted DiDi. She was sitting on the floor, leaning against the bars of the nearest cage with her back to me. Her clothes were torn and filthy and she was smattered with blood, but I knew it was her. A cry rose in my throat – *I'm here, DiDi!* – but I caught myself; instead I signalled to Jackson and we snuck over to the cage.

As we approached, she turned in the direction of our footsteps. I gasped silently as I saw her face. DiDi's eyes were blank: open and staring but not seeing. The colour had drained from her face and her usual smile was gone. She drew her knees to her chest and dropped her head against them. *What had done this to her in one day?* I felt anger churning in the pit of my stomach, but I clenched my fists and swallowed it back down.

"DiDi," I murmured softly, kneeling next to her.

Her head flicked up, blind eyes searched desperately for me, but she could not sense me. She cowered back from the bars of the cage, crawling on the floor like an animal. I hesitated for a moment before reaching in. My fingers barely touched hers.

"DiDi, it's me," I whispered.

Tears welled up in her eyes as she reached out for my hand. Taking hers in mine, I drew her to the edge of the cage. The tears fell softly down her face and I reached in to wipe them away. She pressed her cheek to my hand. Her skin icy against my hand.

"It's really you," she said. "I thought I heard your voice so many times."

"I'm here now, I'm going to get you out," I told her, but she suddenly backed away, shaking her head.

"No," she murmured. "They've done something to me. It's inside me. You have to kill me."

I shook my head, forgetting she couldn't see me.

"I won't leave you, DiDi."

I began running my hand along the bars of the cage. They felt like bones, solid and unmoving. I stood, searching for a way in but there was nothing. It appeared to be a complete structure with no way in or out.

"We need to find a way in," I whispered to Jackson.

There was a scream from the furthest cage and I looked up. Jackson shifted the machete in his hands. DiDi shuffled to the furthest corner of her prison and hugged her knees to her chest once more. On the far side of the room the Ghost with the water raised one hand to the bars of one of the cages and ran a long middle finger gently down it. A moment later, the bars slowly parted to let it out, closing slowly behind it again. I turned to Jackson and he nodded. Raising my hand, I repeated the action and waited. Nothing happened. I tried again but nothing. Gritting my teeth, I kicked the bars as hard as I could. A loud howl made the floor tremble, and I was swamped with a wave of regret. All the prisoners dropped to the floor and the three Ghosts turned their hideous faces towards us.

Flicking on the light, I shone it at them. With an ear-splitting squeal, they threw their arms over their faces – yet still they approached, breathing us in. They covered the ground between us in seconds. There was barely time to react. I fired up the Mech arm, aiming at the Ghosts' heads. They gave an almighty cry as savage spines erupted from their backs and bony spikes protruded from their once-expressionless faces. Rows of sharp teeth dropped into place, ready for the fight. Jackson and I met them head-on. I saw him out of the corner of my eye swinging his machete, hacking off limbs. Giving a cry, I fired into the face of the nearest one. It took one to the eye and one to the throat before it slumped to its knees, blood spurting from the hole in its neck. But behind it was a third. As its comrade fell, it took its place, leaping at me and pinning me to the floor. Teeth bared, it closed in on me. Saliva dripped onto my face as it inhaled my scent. It paused for a moment, confused by the smell of Ghost mixed with my sweat. I pulled out my gun, pushing it into the Ghost's face. Our eyes met – its eyeless sockets and mine full of black rage – and I hesitated. For the briefest of moments, I stopped. I was listening. Theirs was a voice so small, so distant, I could barely hear it. A rush of colours burnt into my eyes and I saw before me all the worlds the Ghosts had seen in the deep fathoms of space, cold and dark and endless. I saw the place they had come from and the places they had devoured. I saw their home star going super nova, and those they left behind. Words, unfamiliar and strange, filled my senses, some loud, some quiet – full of a lingering sadness, of never settling or being still. There was a longing to stop and just *be*. There was fear too: startling, penetrating every inch of me. It was theirs. A fear of what, I couldn't tell – I only knew that it drove them on, propelling them through time and space, onwards and onwards, never stopping, searching for bodies to fuel their ships. They scouted the universe in a hunt for a world of darkness – a planet where they could abandon their living ships, eat its flesh and make a home in its bone: a place they could be free. Earth had only been a stopping point of their journey, but they had decimated it all the same, stripping it bare and leaving us humans on the brink of extinction. Now they were preparing one last hunt – one last massacre – to fuel their ship. They needed every last one of us for their endless search. But there was something else hovering in my senses, something else waiting, controlling everything. It reached into every Ghost, stifling and oppressive. I sensed regret.

Then I was back with my gun still poised – but that was all the creature needed. Pain coursing through me, tearing into my stomach. The foreboding warmth of blood leached into my clothes as I fired my gun into its open mouth. Its brains sprayed from the back of its head, then it slumped down heavily on top of me. Something long and hard retracted from my side and I groaned as I shoved the thing off me. There was a snap as the Ghost's talon broke inside my body. A deep burning sensation spread inside me like fire and I clutched my side, unable to move or speak. Jackson's face appeared beside me, hazy and distant, as he hauled me to my feet. He was shouting something at me but I couldn't hear him. My legs stumbled beneath me, while the room span. Steadying myself against the wall, I gestured to Jackson for his machete. The weapon felt heavy in my hands and I struggled to lift it as I hacked off one of the Ghost's hands. I thrust the machete back at Jackson, lifting the severed hand, and stumbled towards DiDi. Alien blood, still warm, dribbled out of the arm as I brushed its middle finger along the bars of DiDi's cage, which parted with a crack. As Jackson dived in and pulled her out, the whole ship shook, emitting a loud, low drone. There was a drum of feet in the tunnels, all descending on the collection rooms. All coming for us.

"Get out!" I shouted at Jackson. "Take her and get out!"

"But…" he began to argue.

I knelt down painfully and rubbed my hands in the dead creature's blood, wiping it over DiDi's face, arms and legs.

"Just go, I'll follow you – head upwards!"

He gathered DiDi to him, leading her by the hand. Knuckles white, I gripped the cage, while I watched them go. Desperately trying to ignore the excruciating burning in my side, I covered myself in as much blood as possible and headed in the opposite direction, still clutching the dead Ghost's arm. Entering a tunnel on the far side of the collection room, I pushed on deeper into the ship, winding through the maze of tunnels and chambers, which contained more rooms filled with the bone cages. People huddled in corners, blinded and skeletal; they cried out as I ran past, or disappeared further into their prisons in fear. I dodged the Ghosts stalking the ship, pressing my body against the walls as the smell of their own blood masked my presence.

Finally, I came to the place I was looking for: a small room where the light was strongest and the quiet thud, thud, thud of the ship's heartbeat was louder. I had reached the epicentre – the ship's life source. A large, glowing ball of light was encased in a transparent, skin-like sack. Veins branched from it into the floor, walls and ceiling. It was quiet here; there was nothing to be heard but the steady beating of the ship's heart. I reached out to touch it and it shuddered. Without hesitation I armed my gun and fired over and over into the heart.

The ship's life blood began pouring out of the holes in the sack and a deep amber nectar splashed onto the floor. It felt as if an earthquake were tearing up the ground beneath my feet. The ship roared but I carried on, puncturing the heart again and again. A loud cry echoed through the ship as it threw itself from side to side, trying to dislodge the thorn in its heart. I clutched one of the veins to steady myself and pain ripped through me. With all I had left I ran back the way I had come, leaving the bleeding heart to drain out.

None of the Ghosts stopped me as I felt my way along the tunnels; they were too busy trying to get out – rats leaving a sinking ship. Finally, I stumbled back into the last collection room and, taking the severed Ghost arm I was still clinging to, I opened the cages. The smell of death was overwhelming as it suddenly hit me – all of the occupants in this room were dead and rotting. With a small cry of despair, I carried on until I found a room where the skeletons still breathed. Lifting the severed hand, I released them all. The bars of the cages clanged back as a wail of fear filled the air.

"You're free, go!" I cried over the drone of the ship.

Some moved, feeling the bars of the cage until they found the way out, an utterance of amazement on their lips. Others I pulled by the hands, urging them forwards as they wept.

"Please!" I pleaded.

Many of them retreated into the back of their cages, too scared and tortured to leave. My heart fractured as I begged them over and over, their blind eyes staring up at me full of terror. I couldn't save them. Only a handful heard my voice and realised it was not just a trick of the demons, but a real voice calling through the darkness that held them.

Dejected, I tore myself away from the ones I couldn't coax out of their prisons and turning on my torch, I held out my hand to lead the rest. The thin, bony fingers of a woman wrapped around mine and we walked through the trembling tunnels, hand in hand, pressing against the walls to keep our balance. Finally, the ground began to rise up. The air on our faces smelt like rain. I picked up the pace, unsure of how many people I still had with me. I couldn't look back; I had to keep pushing on, knowing that otherwise the pain in my side would overwhelm me and I would drown in the blood I was losing.

As I reached the entrance to the hive, the hazy light of dawn greeted me. I took a deep breath of the warm morning air, which felt soft on my face. But then the ground quaked. The walls of the crater started crumbling as the inside of the hive disintegrated. There was a loud rumble and sheets of earth descended on us. Everything went dark as my lungs were crushed by the weight of the soil. *This was it. This was the end.* And then everything went black.

240

Chapter 18

If this is the moment I die, then I've done something good; I can leave knowing I've saved life, not destroyed it. Everything was quiet and still; there was no pain, just warmth. But something was tugging on my arms. *No, leave me. I'm finished!* It happened again; it made my shoulders burn as the joints stretched. Wrenching open my eyes, I tried to scream but all I could taste was dirt in my nose, mouth, and eyes. It covered my skin, damp and cold, pressing down on me like a truck as I was sucked into the void the dying ship had left. The tugging began again and pain ripped once more through my side as I was pulled clean of the earth. I lay there, gulping lungs full of air, my body crying out for more. Somewhere in the distance there were voices, worrying and arguing. Rough, warm hands pressed against my skin and fingers pushed into my mouth making me gag. Several hands seemed to lift me; they carried me away. Finally, we stopped and I was laid down once more. I prised open my eyes.

I peered up at Jackson through eyes that were stinging and scratching with grit. He brushed the dirt from my face with a damp rag, his face full of concern, brows furrowed.

"Ava?" he murmured, lifting my head and shoulders with one strong arm and pressing water to my lips.

Spluttering, I swallowed, washing away the clawing dirt that clogged my airways. I coughed and spat out the last bits of grit and mud.

"How many survived?" I finally managed.

My voice sounded strange and choked in my ears. Jackson shook his head. There was another hand on mine and I turned my head to see DiDi, her pale, blind eyes looking for me somewhere she would never find me.

"How many survived?" I rasped again.

"Some of the Ghosts made it out," Jackson replied. My stomach dropped like a stone. "That's not what I meant."

"None," said DiDi. "We only found you."

I tried to sit up but a cry of pain escaped my lips and I collapsed back against Jackson's arm. A sob trembled out of my mouth and my body shook as Jackson reached down and pulled back my jacket. There was nothing left inside me anymore; all my fire was gone. Tears squeezed their way out from between my eyelids, betraying me. The faces of those I had tried to free pushed their way into my mind. I couldn't save any of them in the end – the good I had done was lost.

"Bloody hell, Ava," he said, lifting my top, "you've lost a lot of blood."

I glanced down and saw my blood still mingled with Eve's and now the Ghost's in a grimy layer of blood and dirt that covered me from head to foot.

"I think the bleeding has stopped – the weight of the earth probably put pressure on it," I told them, wincing.

Jackson shook his head and leant in closer to get a better look. He cursed under his breath then laid me down and stood up. He rifled through the items we'd collected the night before, returning with DiDi's first aid kit.

"You're going to have to talk me through it, DiDi," he said, clearing his throat.

There was a tightness in his voice. DiDi nodded and clasped my hand a little tighter. "Okay, describe it to me. Describe the wound!"

"Left side, just below the ribs. Wound is about five centimetres long, the bleeding appears to have stopped but the wound itself is full of earth. It's hard to see how deep it is," Jackson explained.

"How did it happen, Ava?" asked DiDi.

"A Ghost," I said, turning to face her.

I needed to see her smile, to feel her reassurance, but she just stared blindly in Jackson's direction, somewhere over his left shoulder. I wondered what she was imagining in her enforced darkness, and if she regretted following me from the compound; but she was so determined my warnings had fallen on deaf ears. Watching her haggard, downturned face, I added this new guilt to the rest, which pricked at me like needles.

"You need to clean the wound carefully and make sure the bleeding has stopped, then we can see if it needs stitching. It probably will," DiDi said. "Use one of the sealed bandages and a sealed eye wash to clean it."

Jackson nodded and reached for the equipment. He began cleaning away the mud carefully from the wound. Eyes fixed on DiDi, I waited, teeth gritted and fists clenched.

"Just breathe," said DiDi, her hand still holding mine.

"Ok," said Jackson straightening up. "Now what?"

"How deep is it? Is there anything in there?" DiDi asked him again.

"Looks deep and it's about two centimetres wide. Can't see anything in there though," he said.

"Good," said DiDi. "How do you feel about stitches?"

There was silence from Jackson. His eyes met mine and I nodded at him.

"Just do it," I murmured. "It's OK."

He nodded, one hand hovering hesitantly over the implements before he grabbed a small package and opened it, pulling out a needle and a length of thread for the sutures. He avoided my eyes, staring down at the wound instead, as I watched sweat gathering on his upper lip. Closing my eyes, I lifted my face to the sky. The coolness of the morning was starting to fade and I could feel the warmth of the sun on my face. Jackson's hands trembled against my skin as DiDi whispered in my ear. The first stitch made me cry out. A nest of thin, scraggy birds flew from their perches with a flurry of squawking. Silent tears rolled down my cheeks and onto the loose earth as I flinched with each stab of the needle, drawing my breath in through my teeth. Jackson's hands were steady now, his breathing uniform, each stitch was quick and fluid. I thought of everything but the pain, letting my mind wander, anywhere and everywhere until it eventually found its way back to Anna. The thought of seeing her after everything that had happened turned me inside out. The look on her face when she told me to go was still burnt into my memory. I was still alive; her little girl was dead. I prayed that the promise of an end to this invasion would be enough to ease her pain. Not enough for her forgiveness, nor for her love – just enough for her to get through it.

"OK," said Jackson eventually. "OK, Ava?"

I barely heard him. Numb and exhausted, eventually I nodded. I turned to DiDi, who was still holding my hand. She looked so small and helpless. My rock.

Pushing to my feet, I clutched my side and gritted my teeth. As I leaned against DiDi, a haze crept into the

244

edges of my vision and my head was spinning. Hurriedly, Jackson dressed the wound and stood back with a taking in his handy work, his brow creased.

"It'll have to do," he murmured to himself.

"It's fine. I'll live," I said to the pair of them, letting go of DiDi as the world came to a standstill once more.

"You need to rest," said DiDi, reaching out for me.

"We don't have time," I told her. "We've started something here – I need to finish it. They're getting ready to attack the Barrier, to take the rest of mankind and move on."

Jackson looked at me, the lines on his forehead even deeper now.

"The nightmares I've had finally make sense. I've seen their plans…I've been inside their heads. We have to act now, before they do," I explained.

I made my way over to the bags and knelt down slowly. I almost cried out as I tried to stand again.

"Help me," I said. "Please?"

Without a word, Jackson rushed over, gathering what was left of the food and water into his own bag, while DiDi shouldered mine. There were a couple of tins of beans and three packets of jerky left, as well as a slightly crushed plastic water bottle that was half full. It was pitiful but it would get us through.

We walked in painful silence, DiDi's hand always in mine. It was all I could do not to cry. She was still there, still walking beside me – but so much of her had been lost. The air that was once filled with her gentle chatter was now cold and empty, just like the streets we walked through. Every building we passed was empty. There were no lights, no noise; just destruction – lives tossed out onto the roads, and left to blow away in the wind. I tried not to stare too long at the schools, once full of laughing children, or the silent parks – swings still and slides covered in leaves and dust. Everything reminded me of Eve, of Anna, and everything that had been lost. The closer we got, the thought of seeing Anna again became heavier and heavier.

I didn't sleep at night, despite Jackson's reassuring presence; the pain in my side kept me awake – a strange heat spreading out from the wound, pushing its way and deep into my body. It was taking root inside of me. The skulking voices of the Ghosts pushed their way into my head, louder and louder with each night that passed.

"Tell me something," said Jackson, as he pushed the fire with a long stick, hot ash wafting into the air. "What is it exactly that you need me for?"

So many things.

"They want to find a way to use the Barrier as a power source and drive the Ghosts out with light. You created the tech, you know how it works. They're running out of car batteries and fuel. Solar panels aren't enough to power the floodlights for long enough," I explained.

"I see," he mused.

"The end is coming, one way or another. If the Ghosts don't kill everyone, then starvation will."

Jackson watched the flickering flames with an intensity that silenced me. The light danced over his dark skin, illuminating the tattoos that were inscribed on his body. I opened my mouth and closed it again. Eventually, I fell into a sleep haunted by shadows and the faces of those I had left behind.

Morning came once more and we made our way along the same roads DiDi and I had trekked days before. We passed the same deep craters and broken houses, the abandoned cars and lost shoes, yet around us the world still buzzed with life. Birds soared in the sky above us, landing in nests made of scraps of lost clothing and twigs, while deer filtered silently through the trees, wandering across the road in front of us, unafraid and bold. The air smelt cleaner than it did inside the Barrier and the rain was cool and refreshing on my sore skin. I let the water wash everything away, refusing to shelter in a doorway with the other two while it fell from the sky in great torrents. The drenching rain made the dusty roads dark and the smell of earth deepen. I shivered, wiping the wet hair from my forehead with one hand. The clothes I'd found inside one of the houses were too big but they were clean of blood: no more reminders.

As the sun rose higher in the sky, the outskirts of the last compound we had passed through appeared in the distance. Suddenly all the energy I had left drained away from me. Calling out to the others, I stopped and collapsed onto the damp grass to rest. My skin prickled and my head felt thick, but I ignored it – I had to get back to Anna, and there was so little time. The Ghosts were drawing nearer, calling to me in my dreams making me wake with a start. Without DiDi's strength, I couldn't face the enemy; I didn't dare sleep, catching snatches of their worlds and glimpses of their plans in the instances I allowed myself to rest. They were coming.

DiDi sat next to me and I placed a hand on hers. She cupped my hand with hers; tears gathered in the corners of her eyes.

"What is it?" I asked.

"I'm not coming with you," she replied, quietly.

"What?"

"They did something to me. It's bad. There was another woman in my cell with me, it happened to her. It

247

was happening to someone else when you came," she told me.

"What did they do?"

Anger bubbled up my throat. Didi turned away. I grabbed her by the shoulders with both hands, twisting her towards me but she pulled away.

"I couldn't see it…I just heard. I just know they did it to me. I can feel it churning inside me."

Her voice had risen an octave and her body trembled. Wrapping my arm around her, I tried to draw her in, to comfort her, the Ghost's talon that twisted in my side forgotten momentarily, but she shrugged me off.

"Please! Leave me here," DiDi pleaded, shuffling away and scrambling to her feet.

"No," I said, rising up to follow her. I wound my fingers into hers but she pushed me away forcefully.

Staggering back, I clutched my side, in a swirl of pain and shock. She, too, crumpled, tearing at her stomach. Sweat was gathering on her face.

"DiDi," I shouted, falling to my knees next to her. My side throbbed and thoughts about my own fate crept into the back of my mind. "Please go," she murmured before curling up in the foetal position and crying out in agony. She whimpered, her arms wrapped tightly around her middle.

"Jackson!" I called, pulling DiDi to me, her head in my lap. I touched her face, wiped the sweat from her lip, and cradled her head while I talked to her, telling her it would be OK. But it was useless. And then I saw it: a last howl of pain escaped from DiDi's lips and blood blossomed from between her legs. She arched her back, her face ripped with

248

agony and torrents of blood poured from her mouth, eyes and ears, soaking her clothes and pooling on the ground beneath her. Then she went limp. Her bloodshot eyes stared up at the sky and into oblivion.

I whispered into her hair, urging her to wake up but she didn't. She lay there, unmoving and lifeless. Jackson's hand pressed heavily on my shoulder and his voice appeared close to my ear.

"Get up," he said.

He was brandishing his machete.

"Get away from her!" he shouted with more urgency, tearing me away from DiDi's body and pulling me back.

I scrambled painfully to my feet and opened my mouth, a torrent of anger about to flood out, but the expression on Jackson's face stopped me in my tracks. DiDi's skin was growing paler, empty, dark veins visible through it as it contracted over her muscles. There was a nauseating crack of breaking bones as her body contorted. Her beautiful dark curls dropped away from her scalp and skin covered over her eyes, which sunk back into her skull.

Arming my Mech gun, I pointed it at the Ghost.

"Damn!" I cried, stepping back, my body shaking.

This was what DiDi was trying to warn me about. The creature before us took a deep breath and I fired round after round into its head. Tears streamed down my face, blurring my vision, and I was glad of them. I couldn't see what DiDi had become; my memory would remember her as she was when she held me safe through the nights.

I stared through the fog of tears at the bloody mess in front of me which was surrounded by DiDi's clothes. Then I walked away, while I still had the resolve. Being on the outside had sparked feelings I had never experienced, feelings which scared me and elated me all in the same breath – a strange, tender mix of love and pain. I headed for the perimeter fence of the compound in the distance. I didn't look back.

Jackson's quick footsteps fell on the ground behind me. He hung back and I was grateful for that; there were no words and every breath was agony. The Barrier waited for me, the Ghosts were pushing closer; they wouldn't wait for my wounds to heal or my heart to mend. As I approached the fence, I expected to see a guard, gun in hand trained on our every move, but the perimeter was empty. Reaching to touch the cold wire mesh, I shook the fence and it rattled noisily. Still no one came.

"Hello?" I called out.

Jackson joined me.

"That's odd," he said. "Where's the guard?"

He still had a smear of my blood on his face. I thought about reaching up to wipe it away.

"Hello?" I tried again, but I was greeted with silence once more.

"This isn't good," said Jackson, pulling his machete around to the front of his body.

I nodded. Something must have gone wrong. Had the Ghosts moved faster than I'd anticipated?

"Come on. Let's find a way in," I said, urgently. "There must be an entrance around here. I…"

Jackson silenced me with his hand. He lifted his machete to waist height and adjusted his grip on the handle. I followed his line of sight to a shadow on the ground cast by something that lurked behind a building to the left of the compound.

"Hey!" I shouted.

"What are you doing?" Jackson hissed at me. "It could be a Ghost!"

I ignored him: Ghosts don't hide in the shadows. There wasn't time to go all the way around the compound – I needed to go through it and tell people that the Ghosts were coming; they were getting ready for the final harvest.

"We're here to help," I tried again and the shadow shuffled.

After a moment, a boy of no more than sixteen emerged and stood facing us. He peered at us down the shaking barrel of his gun.

"Who're you?" he shouted.

"What happened here?" I asked.

"Tell me who you are first!" he demanded.
His fingers trembled against the barrel of the gun. I raised my voice.

"My name is Ava Scott and this is Jackson Quinn. We've come to help."

"You're too late," he said, lowering his gun. "There's no one left to help."

I leant against the fence, pressing my forehead against the metal, and my hand went to my side, which felt hot and tender even through the dressing. My face was cold and clammy, yet my eyes felt as if they were burning in my skull.

The boy in front of us was dishevelled, hair matted to his face with sweat and dirt, and his eyes flitted around, terrified and wild. He shifted from one foot to the next and brushed his dusky hair from his face. His knuckles were bloody. A moment later, he let the gun hang at his side and wandered slowly over. There was death in his eyes; he probably saw the same in me. I took a painful breath through clenched teeth.

251

"What's wrong with you?" he asked, peering at me.

"Nothing," I tried to assure him, attempting to stand up straight, but my legs gave way and my knees hit the ground.

I caught myself on the fence as the world started to spin. The pain came in waves. Glancing up, I saw a look of panic on the boy's face. His gun was pointed at me once more and he was shouting something about me being one of them, but I could barely hear him over the rushing of blood in my ears. As the pain overwhelmed me and the darkness closed in once more, the last thing I saw was Jackson's horrified face.

Chapter 19

My body was trembling. My skin was on fire and my breath stuck in my lungs. Voices were all around me and I tried to focus on them, ignoring the pain filling every sense. In the shadows, I saw the Ghosts gathering, calling to each other telepathically – moving in on the Barrier. I sensed their desire to hunt down what remained of humanity – to harvest them and move on. It was a stirring in them that seemed to fill their whole mind. Yet something else called to me – a cry for help, a deep regret that was pushed down and silenced. Something small wanted to leave, to be free once more, to leave the death and bloodshed behind.

But a stronger voice drowned it out, urging them on towards Anna's compound; the final human harvest had begun. The Barrier was like a beacon for them, blinking in the darkness. Constructed to protect us, it now called out to them, luring them in with a fresh source of food ready for their evacuation of the planet.

I tried to move but my skin lay taut over my muscles, pinning me down. I caught glimpses of faces I knew and some I didn't. Pain, like needles over my body, battered me endlessly, yet I didn't give up. I had come too far – there was too much to do before I left this world. In my oblivion, I strained to hear the voices of those around me.

"I know she can pull through," they said.

I can! I'm still fighting.

"There's no response!"

I'm still here.

"Ava!"

Yes. I'm Ava. I'm not gone!

I willed myself to leave the Ghosts and their shadows; I would find them in the daylight, not stopping until I had destroyed them. I would hunt them on my terms. These creatures had taken too much from me – from humanity.

I am here.

Taking a deep breath, I filled my lungs with oxygen. The air rushed in, deep and sweet, revitalising me. Opening my eyes, I was alone in a dark, bare room. A layer of dust had settled on my clothes from the crumbling plaster walls. The pain still twinged in my side but it was duller than before. I could breathe again. An IV tugged at my arm as I moved and, reaching over with my Mech arm, I yanked it out; the bag was empty, a solitary drip of saline clinging to the clear plastic. I ripped it from its mount, threw it on the floor and swung my legs off of the bed. My tongue stuck to the roof of my mouth and my head pounded as I placed my feet down tentatively. The world was spinning but somehow I stumbled to the door. Reaching for the handle, I froze. The sight of my hand stopped me in my tracks. I stared at it as if seeing it for the first time, taking in the thin black veins that covered it. My metal fingers followed one of the veins up my arm, where it disappeared under the strap of my top. The same small dark veins that had spread like fire across DiDi's skin now tracked over my own. Now, there was something alien in me, too.

Ignoring the panic that whirled around my mind, I finally gave the door a tug. It swung open easily and I stepped out into an empty corridor. The dank smell of abandonment filled the air and the floor was covered in a layer of dirt which suggested no one had walked these corridors for several days.

254

"Hello?" I called out, my voice bouncing off the walls.

My chest tightened as I found my way to a stairwell and out of the building, emerging into the daylight. The sun that should have been warm on my skin felt like hundreds of scratches and I pulled my jumper sleeves down to my wrists. They may have left me for dead but I was not finished. There was more at stake now than just my freedom; I was part of something bigger. The darkness would not win.

I recognised the compound immediately. The ebb and flow of people carrying supplies, washing clothes, or herding children was gone. The big supermarket now stood silent and empty. I stood in the middle of the road and cried out but there was nothing; not even the birds returned my call. Urgency forced my legs to move, to gather speed as I broke into a run. With each footfall I heard my name being called, like a desperate cry rising from the masses: Ava. Ava. Ava! As I searched frantically for signs of life, I wondered if Jackson had watched me while he thought I was dying; if he had stood over me, machete in hand, waiting for me to turn. Had he felt anything at all when I didn't become a monster? Did he just turn and leave? I pictured his hand on mine, his fingers tracing their way to my fingertips. I hoped he'd been relieved when I didn't turn into one of those creatures. I hoped he'd said goodbye.

A distinct smell wafted through the air, and I covered my mouth and nose as I came to an abrupt halt and stood staring in horror at what lay before me. A large tear ran the height of the fence and my eyes came to rest on the bloody bodies of several Ghosts. Surrounding them, like fallen leaves, were twenty or so men and women.

Flies swarmed over the bodies, buzzing in the sun like a sorry anthem of death. The ground was sticky with congealed blood and excrement. Gagging painfully, my throat dry and raw, I stood there unable to move for a moment.

"No," I sobbed, "no!"

It was the only word my lips could form. It poured out of me as if by denying it, maybe it would all change and I wouldn't be too late. If I closed my eyes I could hear their screams. I had to get to Anna. As I picked my way through the bodies carefully, I tried not to look at their dead faces. Out of necessity, I scavenged what I could from my fallen comrades before arming the Mech gun and pushing on into the surrounding countryside. I had about three days' walk before I reached Anna's compound and I was so tired already.

There was more of the same devastation as I went: bodies, both human and alien – a bloody trail leading me back to my old prison, the Barrier. By the time I reached Anna's compound, the sunlight was starting to hurt my eyes and making my skin sting just as it did to the Ghosts. I walked with my hood up and my face down, feeling a strange battle between strength and weakness warring inside me; I couldn't get DiDi's dying moments out of my head. Dusk was falling and on the horizon I could see spots of light cast by the floodlights, criss-crossed by the links of the perimeter fence. Running up to it, I flung my bag onto the ground, and started to rattle the metal wires, not caring who came; it didn't even matter if it was Seb with his gun ready to push against my temple. I needed to see someone: human life – not death! But once again I was greeted with silence, taunting me with its deep emptiness. Gripping the fence with my hands – one metal, one flesh

– I cried out again, my face pushed against the metal, using all the breath I had left in my lungs.

"Anna…Jackson! Please!" I shouted. "Anyone!"

I kicked the fence and it rattled as the links shook. Then I couldn't stop: I kicked again, releasing all the anger that had built up inside me. I knew they were there, inside safe and warm; the ground around me was still clean, fresh, and green – it hadn't yet been soaked in the blood of men, women, and children.

"Anna…" I cried one last time. "Anna!"

Finally, there was the drum of feet on the hard ground, getting steadily louder, and out of the shadows came the familiar bulk of Jackson, his skin like polished ebony in the half-light of the evening. He caught sight of me and his eyes widened. He stood several metres from the fence, one hand on a new gun. I grabbed the fences again, pushing my hand through the small gap so my fingers wriggled inside of the compound. I could almost smell him.

"Jackson," I called to him. "It's me!"

He shook his head and shifted from one foot to the other, moving into a fighting stance. His finger closed around the handle of his gun.

"No, Jackson, please!" I begged.
I had come so far, he had to trust me. *I'm still me!*

"I watched you die," he said in a small voice.

"I know," I said.

"I watched you change," he murmured, his voice betraying the sadness he felt.

"I know!"

He ventured towards me, his gun ready to fire. He came within arm's reach from my fingertips but didn't come any closer. I felt his eyes all over my body; he was taking in the state of my clothes, the hollowness of my eyes, and the lines on my skin. I pushed my fingers a little further through the Barrier and he stepped back. Tears at the back of my eyes felt hot and I fought them, blinking hard. Out of everyone, I thought he would understand – see how hard I'd worked to battle the darkness, day and night.

"I saw you change," he repeated.

"Look at me, Jackson!" I told him. "Here I am. I'm still Ava! Still that ragged, mismatched stray you found."

"You're not a stray," he said gently.

"I am really," I replied, leaning my forehead against the fence; it was cold and smooth against my face.

His gun fell to his side, swinging on its strap. There was a brief warmth from his fingers on my skin as he reached through to me and traced the lines of my face. It was a strange sensation; I could see him touching me, smell his skin, but could hardly feel him. The pressure of his fingers on my cheek felt distant, as if I were wrapped in many layers of clothes. Closing my eyes, I tried desperately to concentrate on his touch but it was no more than a whisper on the wind.

"Ava…" I heard Jackson's voice, "…she's here!"

When I opened my eyes, Jackson was talking on a radio to someone. There was a buzz and the person at the other end came through with a crackle.

"*I thought she was dead,*" I heard them say.

"No, she's here. We need to let her in – she can help us," Jackson told them.

There was a resounding silence on the other end of the radio which seemed to drag on for ages. Then I heard a voice I knew.

"*I'll come down,*" said Anna.

258

Jackson put the radio back in his pocket and leaned against the fence, sliding down to the ground.

"It's at least a twenty-minute walk," he said, "might as well have a seat."

I followed suit, sliding down the fence to sit back-to-back with him, hoping to feel the heat of his body through it but I felt only a vague warmth, like a blanket that was too thin to keep out the cold. We sat there in silence – I didn't want to ask what had happened to me and I guessed he didn't want to tell me. Neither of us knew why I hadn't fully changed into a Ghost. The faces of the dead I'd passed played in front of my eyes, their smell still lingered in my nose but as much as I wanted to share my horror with someone, I was sure he already knew it.

"Did you see the other compound?" I spoke into the falling darkness.

I felt him move a little.

"Yeah," he said.

Silence again.

"Okay?" I asked.

"Yeah," he said. "It's coming to an end, isn't it?"

"One way or another," I told him.

"Hmmm…"

"We can give them a fighting chance though, you and I. I have a plan," I said.

"I thought you probably would," I could hear Jackson smiling.

Picturing his face with those dark eyes and strong nose, I thought about the time I followed him into the tattoo parlour, and all the ink that covered his skin.

"What are the tattoos for?" I asked him.

He was quiet for a moment before he answered.

"To remember."

We didn't speak after that, each lost in our own memories until a torch loomed out of the darkness, tracking across the ground in front of us. I got to my feet unsteadily and Jackson reached through the links to help but I lifted a hand to show him I was OK. He gave me a loud tut but stepped back all the same.

"Jackson?" came Anna's voice from the blackness.

"Anna! Here!" he said.

The torch flicked over to us and I shielded my eyes from the glare. Jackson stepped aside and I tried to look at Anna. She stood before me, staring, and I recognised the same sadness in her eyes that I'd seen when Eve was taken; it had never left. And I had caused it. I fixed my stare at the ground; I couldn't look at her anymore.

"Is it really you, Ava?" she asked, keeping her distance.

"Yeah," I murmured. "It's me."

Anna unlocked the gate cautiously, still staring at me as if I were an apparition. She held one hand to her mouth as she took in my wretched figure while the other remained resting lightly on her gun.

"Anna!" I managed.

I stepped forwards but she moved away. Her rejection of me was justified; I'd expected it, but it still cut deeply. It felt like an eternity stretched between us like a vast cavern I had no way of crossing. Nothing I could do would make it better. I dropped to my knees at her feet, unable to hold her sorrow-filled gaze. I expected her to scream at me, to tear at my clothes and pound her fists into my flesh, but there was nothing but silence – it hurt more than any blow she could have dealt.

When she spoke, I could hear tears clinging to her words.

"At first I hated you, Ava, there was so much grief and anger. I never wanted to see you again – all I could picture was you lying in Eve's blood, and I found myself wishing it had taken you and not her...part of me still wants that."

She took a deep breath as if what she was about to say next was hard to get out. She hesitated.

"But once that fog had lessened, there was nothing but emptiness. I realised that your death wouldn't fill the space that Eve has left. Nothing would. Nothing ever will," she told me.

"I don't understand," I managed to murmur. "I'm so sorry, Anna, you have every right to end this here and now."

My whole body trembled. But, instead of the barrel of her gun, I felt Anna's arms pulling me into her chest. I'd seen her hug Eve the same way. I let the tears fall until there were no more left, and still she held me, strong as ever.

"You're still my sister. I still love you," she told me. Her voice cracked as she looked away. I knew how much it cost her to say those words.

"Too many people I love have been taken from me. I don't want anyone else to die. I just want this all to end, Ava."

"Anna," I murmured, "I don't deserve your forgiveness."

She cupped my chin with her hand, lifted my face to hers and pressed her forehead to mine. Then I realised how child-like I still was compared to her – how much more mature she was, even though she was only ten minutes older. Trapped inside the Barrier, I was as naïve, selfish and underdeveloped as I had been when we had shared a womb. The world outside the Barrier had shown me what really mattered. I placed my hands on hers. Her eyes flickered towards the Mech hand and then back to my face.

"I love you," I said.

It was the first true thing I'd ever said: the first real utterance that had escaped my lips. I lowered her hands from my face, letting mine linger over hers for a moment, but she pulled away quickly; I was forgiven but it would never be forgotten. Once this was over, I would make sure she never had to see me again.

"What now?" she said.

"I think I have a way to end it," I breathed.

Chapter 20

As we walked through the compound, my stomach churned and my legs felt heavy as I tried to keep up with Anna and Jackson. A feeling of dread sat deep in my gut and I remembered Seb's face after Eve had been taken. If I closed my eyes, I could still feel his boot against the back of my head. I noticed Anna glance over as we passed the place where Eve had died. A small patch of withered grass was all that remained of such a soul-destroying moment. I couldn't bear to look, focusing instead on the bulk of the school that loomed ahead of us, lit only by the glow of the floodlights. The closer we got, the slower my legs moved; I wasn't ready to face all the people I'd hurt. Even though I was here to make it right, I knew they wouldn't see it that way; a child had died.

Before I knew it, Anna was drumming on the door, turning to Jackson and I, and saying something, but I could hardly hear her. Seb's face appeared at the door and instantly his gaze locked onto me. He threw himself out of the door, avoiding Anna's clutches and thrashing wildly at me. In one stride, Jackson stepped between Seb and me, hauling him up against the wall.

"Get off me," he growled at Jackson. "That bitch killed Eve!"

"Stop," said Jackson, pushing Seb hard, making his face scrape against the rough brick.

"Not until she's dead," he spat.

More faces appeared at the door, all eyes fixed on me. Seb breathed heavily as Jackson spoke quietly to him; the rise and fall of his chest slowed and the fire in his eyes calmed. He shook off Jackson's grip and swung his gun into his hand before pushing his way inside. Anna dashed

263

after him, catching him by the sleeve just inside the doorway.

"Seb," I heard her say. "Please!"

"How can you look at her and not see the blood of our baby all over her?" he said, his voice booming.

Anna opened and closed her mouth unable, or unwilling, to stand up for me.

"You should have let me shoot her when she was first linked – I told you she would be trouble, Anna, and now Eve is dead. She's dead, and she's not coming back!" Grief clutched at his words, his voice uneven and tight.

Anna reached out to him but he shrugged her off.

"I don't care if she's your sister: she's a stranger. I'm your partner, Eve was your daughter…yet you put *her* above both of us."

"Don't you dare say those terrible things, Seb," Anna said, her voice shaking.

"The moment she's alone, I'll kill her, Anna. Just watch me!" shouted Seb.

I slunk back from the door, unable to watch the hurt I was causing. I stood with my back to it all, letting the evening air wash over my skin; just in case this was the last time, I wanted to take it all in. Heavy footsteps disappeared inside the school and heard Anna calling after Seb, her voice small and desperate. A door inside banged and the crowd scattered as I turned to see Anna emerging alone from the building. Jackson scratched his head awkwardly as Anna walked over to me.

"I'm sorry," I told her, but she shook her head and gestured for me to follow her.

Nothing I could say would be enough. No one wanted me here. I didn't blame them. Keeping close to Jackson, I stood in the sports hall in front of a small group of people who were in charge of the southern compound. Every gun was pointed at me, keeping watch in case I turned feral and killed them where they stood. Their voices bounced off the high ceilings, painfully loud, amplified as they argued as though I wasn't there, like a naughty child whose punishment they were deciding. Glancing at Anna, I willed her to say something – yet she remained unnervingly silent. She stood, twiddling with the hair that had fallen from her ponytail in the absent-minded way she always did. My eyes flicked from her to Seb, who slunk about at the edge of the room, pacing back and forth, and then back again to Anna until I could take it no longer and sort comfort in the familiarity of my boots.

"Enough!" I heard Anna shout over the melee of voices. "Enough! I'm with Ava. If anyone has reason to have a problem with her then it's me…it's my pain to deal with, not yours!"

Seb's eyes widened, his knuckles turning white on the grip of his gun, and his mouth went slack as rage ripped across his face. He started to speak but Anna stilled him with a single glance. She jumped to her feet, sending her chair crashing to the ground and slammed her fist on the table.

"I've had enough of this life – of living this pathetic existence, encased in a bloody fence. I'm done. It's now or never! Either we kill them or they kill us, simple as that. What else have we got to live for?" said Anna.

I winced at her words, knowing I had taken her reason for living. There was a recklessness in her that I saw in myself; she was my other half, after all. Her hand pounded the table, strong and determined; although I could still hear the drum of her heartbeat and the quickness of her breathing.

"Ava," she turned to me, "what do you need us to do?"

Everyone's faces turned to me, some angry, some worried but most were lined with exhaustion; they were tired of fighting and not knowing if this day would be their last. It was a life of pure existence – one just like the one I tried to escape. I took a deep breath, the weight of what we were about to do making it hard to breathe.

Jackson stood up, took my hand, and pulled me to the table to join the others. Sitting shoulder to shoulder with him I was grateful for his presence, yet still unable to feel the heat of his body next to mine. I was numb. Getting to my feet, I pulled my shirt around myself and began: "I know most of you hate me, that you think I'm one of the aliens…" there were murmurings of agreement from the group and my heart sank, "but don't take any notice of my skin. I'm sorry for everything that's happened since I arrived, truly I am. I have no way of making that right, and once we've got rid of the Ghosts then I will go far away – you'll never have to see me again. But for now, please listen to me!"

I paused, then carried on. "Look, they tried to take me and they failed. Now I'm in their heads – prey become predator! I see their inner workings. I know their plans. They're preparing to leave but they want more of us to feed their ships. They're headed for the Barrier. I've seen their vessels and they're gathering at a hive nearby: a mother ship. If we take that one out then the others will die. Like bees without a queen."

I stole a breath as the hall fell silent. They were listening but it was hard to read anything but hate on their faces.

266

"I say we let them take those on the inside, and then they will leave us alone," called Seb from the end of the table where he was standing with a crazed look in his eyes.

There was a hum of agreement. Anna's face fell.

"What are you saying, Seb?" she placed her hands on her hips. "That our lives are worth more than theirs?"

"What have they done for us? MTech shut us out and left us to die, Anna. Why shouldn't we extend the same courtesy?"

A cheer filled the room but it was half-hearted, petering out as quickly as it had started.

"You don't know that. Ava had no idea that we even existed out here. She found a way out to find me; she hadn't given up on us and what's to say there aren't others like her?" Anna retorted.

"You're basing your argument on her?" Seb laughed, and as I gazed down at the table, I lowered myself into my seat; I wanted to shrink away beneath his hatred.

Anna sat down again, pushing her head into her hands. Her shoulders shook, silently. Seb's face softened and he stepped towards her but his eyes fell on me and he stopped.

"I'm so tired of all this, Seb," came Anna's voice from behind her hands.

The hall fell silent, her grief making the atmosphere awkward. No one spoke.

"We need an end," said a man with dark hair tied back and a dark beard, "we have nothing to lose anymore. I vote we hear Ava out."

He lifted a hand, staring down the others as he did. His eyes eventually met mine. I gave him a nod as other hands rose into the air slowly – all except Seb's.

"Go ahead, Ava," said the man softly.

267

I stood once more and cleared my throat, worried the words would get stuck there.

"Jackson is the key really. He knows the tech, he helped me get out and he can help us get in again. Jackson, can you find us a way into the Barrier? I still have the virus for the Mechs, and we have a couple of dead ones in the warehouse. Can you work with that?"

Jackson gave an encouraging nod and the buzz of talk began to liven up the room. I recognised the sound of hope; I'd had it once, too.

"Maybe there's an old laptop somewhere?" I asked, and a small man with a shock of white hair raised his hand in response.

"I can get you one," he said.

"Thank you," I replied.

"And the Ghosts?" asked Anna.

"We need to locate the mothership first…it's close."

"I'll find it," said Seb quietly, his eyes fixed on Anna. Her fingers moved towards him across the table but he ignored her.

"We know they don't like light or noise, so we use that to our advantage," I continued. "We take everything we've got, everything from the other compound, all the floodlights and speakers, and surround the mothership. They're living ships and anything that's alive can be killed! We use the power from the Barrier's generation terminal, throw everything we have at them. We flush out the darkness with light!" I explained.

My breath stuck in my lungs from the effort and I coughed a little.

"But that will leave us vulnerable," said an older man.

"Yes, but, as Anna said, they're coming whether we like it or not. And it's not just one or two like before, they're coming like a swarm. We have to strike first, before it's too late," interjected Jackson.

"I'm not prepared to wait for death to come to me," rallied Anna.

"How long have we got?" asked a woman with fair hair and skin.

"Days. Four at most. They're coming. The last compound…"

My voice trailed off and Jackson stood up, his large figure commanding attention.

"The last compound gave their lives to delay the Ghosts," he said. "They took out some but there will be more coming. We have to act now! Ava's plan makes sense, she has insight that we need to take advantage of."

Heads began to nod as I looked around the room, yet out of the corner of my eye, I saw the sports hall double door swinging on its hinges. Anna, too, was staring at the doors. Seb was gone.

"He doesn't even want me anymore," she murmured, turning to look at me. Her eyes were filled with sadness, her body seemed smaller and her skin paler.

I opened my mouth to answer with whatever small wisdom I could muster when the sound of gunfire ricocheted around the room. The blare of the sirens drowned out any talking and everyone scrambled out of their seats, dashing out of the room towards one of the large store cupboards along the hall.

One of the men threw back the cupboard doors, revealing an array of guns and knives, and those who didn't already have a weapon began lining up to get one. As the firearms were handed out, others emerged from the stairs, rubbing their eyes and throwing on clothes. I looked at each face as it passed me: there was nothing but fear. A small boy appeared in the hallway, alone and shivering. He clutched a small, pink bear to his chest, his little eyes so wide with fear they seemed to swallow me whole. No one heard me cry out over the stampede as I ventured over to him. He looked up at me as if I were some kind of apparition, with my veined skin and robot arm. He cowered. I was about to reach out when I heard a voice behind me.

"Get away from him!" called a middle-aged woman, pushing me out of the way and gathering him into her arms. She clutched him to her chest, stroking his head, her eyes fixed on me.

"Don't come near him, I know what you did to Eve! I won't let you get him," she continued, her eyes flitting between me and the gun cupboard.

As she walked away, the boy's face peered at me over his mother's shoulder. Her words were like a knife and my energy crumbled away again. People pushed past me, their elbows in my back and shoulders shoving me out of the way. I stared at the spot where the boy had stood until I felt a gentle hand on my shoulder.

"Come on, Ava, we need to go!"

Jackson ushered me towards the front door, pushing a knife into my hands. I steeled myself, my eyes on the front door, which was being manned by a man about my age. He had dark hair and nice eyes but he didn't look at me as I approached; instead, he spoke to the others who were rushing out with me. He unlocked the door and hurried us through. I felt his bitter stare as I passed, when he thought I could no longer see him. There was a look of disgust on his face.

Pushing my way through the crowd, I emerged into the night. Guns were firing all around me; the only thing louder were the sirens blaring at an intolerable pitch. I covered my ears, my head spinning with the pain. The floodlights scorched my eyes and my skin was on fire – but I pushed on. Devastation lay before me. Ghosts breached the perimeter fence and were lurking on the outskirts of the floodlights, clamouring to get to us. The odd creature howled and writhed on the floor, pinned to the ground by the pitch of the sirens. Others edged closer, their mouths open and teeth bared, but keeping their distance. The ground was already awash with alien and human blood alike. I readied my gun and ran into the fray, firing shot after shot at any Ghost that dared put a foot into the light.

I could see them in the darkness, circling, waiting for their moment. What were they waiting for? Their thoughts were all around me, but they were jumbled. Standing still in the midst of the chaos, I tried to make sense of it but the sound of the siren was too loud, it penetrated every aspect of my mind. I cried out in anger, firing into the darkness wildly.

"What are you waiting for?" I cried.

Covering my head, I crouched on the floor, blocking as much of the noise out as possible, retreating into the world of shadows: a world that filled me with dread. Finally, in the darkness I saw a plethora of Ghosts, hiding in the blackness on the outskirts of the compound. There must have been at least a hundred of them waiting. *But for what?* I probed further. Then I saw them: three Ghosts had strayed from the group and were heading for the generators that powered the floodlights around the school.

"No!" I cried.

Then darkness. I was transported back to the moment the bombs hit, trembling in the oblivion, but there was no warmth from Dad's chest, no smell of his aftershave. Just the sparks of gunfire in the moonlight, the screams of the dying and the spray of warm blood.

"No!" I murmured, turning on my torch and illuminating the darkness. I instantly wished I hadn't. In front of me, a Ghost leered over a woman. Blood smattered its face; it dripped from its mouth in great salivary globs. The woman was splayed on the floor, wailing as the creature pinned her to the ground with a large, clawed foot. I recognised the mother who had snatched her son away from me. I took a step back but it was too late: the Ghost turned its head in my direction, its wide nostrils sniffing deeply as it inhaled my scent. It flinched in the light of the torch but wasn't deterred. I felt its adrenaline as if it were my own.

Leaving the woman, it came towards me slowly, its teeth bared, growling softly as it approached. I could sense its confusion – my clothes were still covered in DiDi's blood – the blood of whatever she had become – and, as much as I denied it, my body was changing. It came close enough that I could feel its breath, hot and sour with blood, on my face. I remained as still as I could, whilst raising my Mech arm slowly. As I brought my arm to head height, the thing launched at me and I fired into its open mouth. Its brains splattered wetly across the grass behind it and it landed heavily on top of me, crushing the air out of my lungs.

"Get to the school!" I heard someone cry as I lay there, motionless under the weight of the beast, trying to get my breath back.

"No!" I coughed.

Footsteps approached and heaved my Mech arm out from underneath the creature, flicking the torch above me. It was Seb. He stood over me with his gun in his hand, covered in blood. Two blue eyes peered down at me. I knew then he would fulfil his promise. My gaze met his and I waited.

"Go on then," I shouted at him over the noise of the attack, "just do it!"

He stared down at me as if I were something vile on the ground, his gun pointed at my head. Finally, he walked away into the darkness once more. With difficulty, I heaved the Ghost off and dragged myself back to my feet. Everywhere, the beam of my torch illuminated deathly struggles between Ghost and human, whilst the cries of those already snatched away echoed through the night. I ran at the closest enemy, firing as I went. The Ghost fell with a howl and I moved onto the next, and then the next, and the next.

I fought my way back to the school as the blackness started to fade, making way for the burning light of the dawn. I didn't want to see what was left; I couldn't bear to look. At the school, three Ghosts were still prowling around, hammering at the doors and windows, looking for a way in. Hanging back in the shadows of a building, I watched as one of them pulled down the floodlight and used it to ram the front door. I grimaced at the irony: the thing that kept the Ghosts out was now letting them in. Taking a deep breath, I fought back an urge to cough that rose in my aching chest; I had to be silent. Then the glass shattered and knew I couldn't wait any longer. I forced myself around the corner to face them.

"Hey!" I cried. "Over here!"

There was no one else any more, just me and the Ghosts. The one carrying the floodlight turned to face me, its hollow eye sockets somehow fixing on me. Its nostrils flared and I heard its voice inside my head, calling to the others. One by one they turned to face me until I had the attention of all three. Stepping forwards, through the blood and the excrement and the bodies, I focused on putting one foot in front of the other, while my head screamed 'run'. Edging nearer, I powered up the Mech arm and held my own. Closer and closer they came, their voices getting louder and louder.

"Come on!" I cried.

My fear escaped through my lips as I cursed them, shouting at them until I was blue in the face. There were faces at the windows as the Ghosts left the school and came at me. The Ghosts' anger and confusion prickled along my spine; I was like them, yet I wasn't. I was incomplete: a defect to be destroyed. Most of all, I'd interrupted them. Pushing myself into a run, with my gun raised, I fired over and over. The first Ghost fell quickly with a shot to the eye socket. The second took several shots to the chest and face before it came to a thrashing halt at my feet.

As it fell, the third was upon me, pinning me to the ground, its spikes covering its body in the same way they had when I was rescuing DiDi. It clawed at me, slicing into my flesh. I cried in agony and it seemed to laugh. Then it stopped. Gunfire echoed through the street and the creature collapsed onto the ground next to me.

Clutching at my bleeding face, I closed my eyes. My body was tired now; I just wanted to lie here, surrounded by the dead, and not move. But I had to keep going. This wasn't the end, not yet. There was a hand on my shoulder and I opened my eyes.

"Get up," said Jackson, helping me to my feet and pulling my arm over his broad shoulders.

We walked back to the school together in silence, our eyes fixed on the battered front door, trying to ignore the devastation that lay around us.

Chapter 21

Jackson hammered on the door and waited. The warmth of fresh blood ran down my cheek and I struggled to see out of my right eye. There was the clunk of a lock being opened and Jackson and I were ushered through the door, which had been reinforced. He carefully sat me down on the floor along with a handful of others all nursing injuries, and knelt next to me.

"Ava, can you hear me?" he asked.

I nodded.

"I need to have a look at you. Can you open your eyes?"

I wanted him to go away, so I could sleep but he kept on at me. Anger rose in my chest; an anger like nothing I had ever felt before. Opening my eyes to tell him to leave me alone, I expected to see lots of people, but it was just me and him. The corridor was quiet, except for a plump woman wandering up and down with a mop; the squeak of her shoes was the only sound in the once-packed space.

"What?" I murmured, but my voice stuck in my throat.

"Don't speak! Here," Jackson said, pushing a plastic cup of water into my hand.

Trembling, I managed to get it to my mouth. It was cold and refreshing. I could feel it trickle all the way down to my stomach. I placed the cup on the floor.

"The others?" I asked.

"Safe. Tended to," he replied.

"How many did they take?"

"Not as many as we killed."

Lifting my head to look at him, I felt the vision slipping slowly away from my right eye, and blinked heavily. I could sense him trying to decide what to do with me. The end was close. There was nothing he could do for me anymore.

"How long was I out?" I asked.

"Only an hour or so. They're doing some breakfast in the sports hall. You want to eat?" Jackson asked me. I shook my head.

"There's no time. We have to have something in place by nightfall."

I pushed myself up using the wall but my legs felt heavy and I reached out for Jackson. He took my hand to steady me.

"You really need to rest, Ava," he said.

"There's no time – not for me, not for anyone here," I told him.

Jackson bit his lip and cleared his throat. I could tell he wanted to say more, but he didn't.

"The computer…you need to modify the virus, find a way back in. Never thought I would be asking you to do that," I tried to smile.

Jackson smiled too.

"Go and speak to that guy who had the laptop. I just need a minute. Meet you back here in ten," I said.

I waited for him to disappear around the corner before slumping to the floor again. My breathing was fast and hard, and I couldn't slow it down. Reaching for the water, I took another long drink. I wasn't sure how I wasn't dead already – why I wasn't one of them – but I was still Ava. For now, anyway.

I dragged myself towards the showers, using the wall for support, and gave the changing room door a shove. It swung open before me revealing the neat, white tiles that lined the walls and small, circular drains in a row across the middle of the floor. Heading for the row of mirrors that hung above a small shelf, I peered into the nearest one, and did a double-take. The face that stared back at me was no longer mine. It wasn't Alec and it wasn't Ava. A strange, pale thin face, neither male nor female, stared back at me. Deep, dark veins lined my skin and four deep gashes ran across my face cutting through my right eye, turning it white, rendering it useless. I leaned closer. Dirt and blood were crusted over the cuts and down my clothes. I stared hard at my reflection, hoping it might change and fill out once again into someone I knew. I tried to scratch the dirt from my face but the skin was sore, so I headed for the nearest shower.

A trickle of cold water gurgled from the showerhead and I cupped my hands underneath it until there was enough to wash with, splashing it onto my face and watching the drops of muddy, red water fall onto the floor. I pushed my head under the flow of cold water. It soaked my hair and into the collar of my shirt, but I didn't care. Turning off the water, I took another look in the mirror. With the dirt and blood gone, I could still see a little of the face I had once known; that was good enough.

I patted my face dry before ambling out of the changing room and back to the front door. Jackson was already waiting for me, as well as a woman with a gun on door duty. He had a large, bulky-looking laptop under his arm, which he lifted up for me to see as I approached.

"Now what?" he asked.

"I need to speak to Anna. You go to the warehouse, see if my generator is still there," I said.

Jackson nodded. "How long have I got?"

278

"A day, maybe two…that enough?" I asked.

"It'll have to be."

With that, he turned to the woman, who unlocked the door for him, and disappeared in the pink light of the dawn. I headed for the sports hall. As I entered, heads turned to face me and a flurry of whispers exploded across the room. Ignoring them, I scanned the room for Anna. I finally located her, alone in the kitchen, angrily whisking rehydrated eggs.

"Anna," I said, but she didn't turn.

Her hand whisked faster and faster, flecks of egg flicking out of the bowl and onto the work surface.

"Anna," I said a little louder. "Anna!"

She turned to me and the bowl slipped from her hands, hitting the Lino floor and smashing into a thousand pieces. The slippery egg dripped off of the counter and into a pool on the ground. Immediately she knelt down and started picking up the broken shards of glass. Kneeling next to her, I grabbed her hands.

"Anna, stop. Please!" I said.

Her eyes were red from crying and her face blotchy. I could feel her hands in mine, but they were cold and lifeless to me. There was blood blossoming from a small cut on her finger.

"It's Seb," she said, sitting back heavily onto the floor. "The idiot's gone off alone."

"What do you mean 'gone'?" I asked her.

"Gone. To find the mothership. To try and find Eve!"

Wiping the hair from her face, I took the broken glass from her. I went into the store cupboard and found a dustpan and brush, and a mop, and began clearing up the mess. Once I'd finished, I sat down on the floor next to

279

her. She was watching the blood drip from her finger. I wanted to put my arm around her and pull her into me like she would've done to me, but it felt strange and uncomfortable. I put my hand on hers and she looked up at me, her eyes wet with tears again.

"He'll be back, Anna. I know he will," I told her.

She blinked heavily and turned her face away again. I shuffled, trying to get my sore body comfortable on the hard floor.

"He can't bear to look at me anymore, Ava – because I look like you," she told me.

There was an anger in her words that she couldn't hide.

"Anna," I murmured, as she pulled her hands out of mine.

"Seb's just angry, it's me he hates not you," I told her. "Let him do what he needs to do and we'll be ready when he gets back. We need to gather as many generators and lights as we can – sirens too. And send someone to the next compound. We need everything we can get," I said.

Anna looked at me, her eyes burning into mine, then she sighed and started to stand up. I stood too, and she went over to the tap and ran her finger underneath the cold water.

"And the bodies of the Ghosts…take whatever blood you can from them. Paint the doors, the windows, the building, yourselves even! It confuses them," I explained.

"Okay," she said, still with her back to me. "We'll be ready. You go and do what you need to do, you and Jackson."

She glanced over her shoulder at me, her eyes still red but determined once more. One hand on the kitchen door, I paused.

280

"Ava," Anna called after me. "Go get some more clothes from the staffroom!"

I tried a smile but she didn't acknowledge it, facing the sink once more. In the staffroom, I changed my clothes into a comfortable hoodie and jeans, throwing away the bloody ones. I sat down for a few moments, letting my body be still, gearing myself up for what was to come. A mix of apprehension and excitement churned in my stomach as I made my way over to the warehouse to find Jackson.

The people who were left had begun clearing the bodies from the streets. The morning light, revealed a horrific scene as it stung my skin and eyes. I walked quickly, avoiding eye contact with anyone who passed me by, but they didn't care about me – they were all caught up in their own grief. They all looked greyer, older, and slower as they went about their harrowing work. I heard Anna's voice as I reached the edge of the industrial sector, ordering people to gather the things we needed. Then the warehouse came into view.

The door was open when I reached it, but I knocked. Jackson was sitting at my old workbench hunched over the bulky laptop, a generator chugging away next to him. The smell of petrol filled the space. He looked up and beckoned me over.

"Going to need that arm of yours," he said.

I glanced down at the rows of numbers and letters on the screen. It meant very little to me; I knew something from what Dad had shown me, but this kind of programming was another language. I reached up and felt the back of my neck. The implant was still there – a little reminder of everything I once was, and all those I left behind. As my fingers stroked the back of my neck, the realisation struck me: the implant – that was why I was still me. Whatever the Ghosts had put in me was being confused by the tech in the implant, which was attached to my DNA. The tech Dad had made was saving my life once again – but I wasn't sure how long for; slowly, I was changing. I couldn't deny the dark veins or my paper-white skin anymore. They were winning. Removing the Mech arm, I placed it on the table in front of Jackson.

"It's you I need, not the arm. I thought the virus chip was in the arm," he said, getting up and pulling another chair up to the workbench.

I sat down and lay my arm out for him to see. He thought for a moment, his eyes flicking from the computer screen to my arm and back again.

"Alright?" I asked.

He leaned back and ran his large hands over his head. Over a week's worth of dark hair bristled under his fingers; I preferred it short.

"This is going to be harder than I thought. I can't just plug you in," he smiled.

"Take it out," I said.

Jackson sat forward.

"But what about you?"

"I've got another arm," I said with a smile.

"But…" he began.

"Really, I don't need it anymore!"

He nodded, rubbing his chin with one hand. There was something he wanted to say but he changed his mind.

"Spit it out," I said, nudging his shoulder.

"If I do this – if I modify the chip, connect it to the implant – it will probably fry the implant. I don't know what'll happen to you, Ava," he told me, unable to look me in the eyes.

282

I ran a finger over the implant on my neck: the thing that had kept me hidden – my little reminder of Dad and of his love for me. It was time. I was ready to let go of it all; it wasn't about me anymore.

"It's okay," I said, quietly. "I'm ready."

He looked at me, a sadness in his dark eyes. He knew as well as I did that I didn't have long left, that whatever virus the Ghosts had put inside me was taking over; it was all over my skin and without the implant would only consume me faster. He gave me a soft smile and then turned back to the laptop, punching in numbers while the screen changed with each command. Eventually, he needed the chip and the virus. I watched the blade pierce my skin as he cut the chip out of my arm but barely felt it. The wound hardly bled; it oozed a thick reddish-brown liquid instead. Jackson said nothing, carrying on doggedly with his work.

At last, exhausted, I headed for bed. I hadn't eaten or slept in what felt like days. I wasn't even sure how long I'd been presumed dead. As I lay staring at the ceiling, the world became gradually darker and darker until it was gone.

"Ava," came a voice, rousing me from sleep. "Ava, wake up. I'm done."

Jackson was hovering over me, a triumphant look on his face. He straightened up and went back over to the workbench. I swung my legs off the bed and tried to get up but they gave way under my weight and I sat back down heavily.

"You okay?" said Jackson, reaching out a hand to me.

"Yeah, yeah, I'm fine," I said, ignoring his hand and trying again.

This time my legs held me – just. The change was happening faster. I could feel my bones stretching and my skin thinning. My blood felt thick in my veins.

"Show me," I said, shuffling over to the workbench.

My Mech arm had been altered and others were laying dissembled beside it. Jackson had made adjusted them so the guns emitted a range of electrical pulses that would interrupt the frequency of the Barrier for just long enough for one of us to get inside and re-route the power to our generators.

"The Barrier will have to reset – that's our window; that's when we redirect its power," he told me.

"How?" I asked.

"The control panel we used has an external terminal. We plug in; I can do a manual override and divert the power to it."

"Like a giant plug?"

"Exactly," he said, with a grin.

I liked his smile.

"And the cabling?" I asked.

"There's tons here, just look around," he said.

"And it's really going to work, just plugging our generators in?" I replied.

"Never underestimate the simple things," replied Jackson.

He turned away and gathered up the Mech arm, then reached out for my stub of an arm. I frowned, but he smiled and pushed it on to me. There was a scratch as something dug into my arm.

"I made some adjustments. It works a little differently – no implants under your skin. I took the one in your neck and made it talk to your arm," he looked proud of himself. "Let's go out with a bang."

"How did you do it without me noticing?" I asked, baffled.

Jackson shrugged.

"You just didn't wake up."

His words worried me but I pushed the fear down. It was nearly time. We were almost ready.

Chapter 22

As we walked back to the school the sun was high in the sky, its warmth singeing my skin. Pulling my jacket hood over my head, I forced myself to carry on, staying close to Jackson as we wandered through the now empty streets, nothing left of the previous night but a selection of dark stains. A few sections of perimeter fence still stood like solitary guards. My eyes shifted over to the end of the street, where the school appeared in the distance, and I could just make out a row of floodlights. Not long now.

I straightened up. Somehow, knowing this would all be over soon, I could walk a little taller. The new Mech arm felt heavy, dragging me towards the ground, and there was a strange tingling running from my neck down to my arm, but it was good to feel something other than pain.

"Ava," Jackson said as we came to a stop outside the school.

He lifted his hand and drummed loudly on the door, which was scarred with pockmarks and dents where it had been battered by the Ghosts. Fragments of glass still littered the floor.

"Yeah?" I said.

"After all this is done, let's…" he began.

But the door in front of us swung open, halting our conversation. Jackson hesitated for a moment and then stepped inside. When I didn't follow, he turned back to look at me; I waited, hoping he would finish what he was about to say but he smiled sadly at me and carried on inside. I had no choice but to follow, never knowing what he wanted to tell me.

Inside, generators lined the hallway and people milled about, arranging and organising, checking wires and

286

topping up the fuel tanks with what fuel was left. There was a murmur as Jackson and I entered, so subtle that if you had blinked you would have missed it. Quickly, the voices in the echoing hall resumed and I started looking for Anna. I found her on the floor tinkering with the faulty generator. Her face was streaked with black, oily smudges.

"How's it going?" I asked.

She wiped the hair from her face with the back of her hand.

"Yeah, it's okay. Just waiting for Nicolas and his lot to get back from the next compound with some more generators. They took the truck – there was one battery left."

I nodded.

"We're done," said Jackson, tapping my Mech arm. "What can I do to help here?"

A couple of generators needed some attention at the end of the hallway and he disappeared in the direction that she pointed. A man with a bald head and large teeth came over, asking Anna about lunch. After a moment the flow of people died down and the corridor was quiet.

"Seb?" I asked.

Anna shook her head.

"He'll be back," I said. "I…"

I was interrupted by a loud banging on the front door. The sound exploded inside my head and I thrust my hands over my ears instinctively. Anna put her hand on my shoulder.

"It's okay," I told her.

Seb came barrelling in, his gun still in his hand and his face bloody and fierce, but triumphant. There was a mix of red blood and black on his clothes. His hair was dirty and I could smell the sweat on his body. He thrust his gun into the air along with his clenched fist. Anna stepped forward to face him.

"I found the buggers," he told her.

"Seb!" she began, but he wasn't listening.

He turned to the crowd that was gathering in the corridor, curious about the commotion.

"I found them – now we kill them!" he shouted.

More faces appeared.

"They've tormented us long enough. I'm going to slaughter them with a smile on my face! Who's with me?"

There was a cheer from the crowd, and Seb joined in. There was a madness in his eyes that scared me. As he turned to face Anna and me, my eyes met with Jackson's, who stood motionless at the back of the crowd.

"Starting with her!" Seb said, pointing his gun at me.

Every eye turned on me, burning like searing needles. No one moved at first; then one or two stepped forward, until the whole crowd was surging towards me. Anna moved in front of me but Seb pushed her away, sending her reeling to the floor.

"What the hell, Seb!" she shouted, but her voice was drowned out by the roaring of the crowd as they descended on me.

Seb grabbed me by the arm and hauled me into the middle of them. They surrounded me like flies on a corpse, pushing and pulling at me, and dragging me down to the ground. I curled up in the foetal position and prayed for a quick death. Fists and shoes struck all over my body, bringing more agony.

Suddenly it stopped and I was alone. Gingerly, I opened my eyes. Jackson stood over me protectively, and Seb was sprawled on the floor at his feet nursing a bleeding lip. He scrambled to his feet and took a swing at Jackson, but he was too full of unbridled rage; Jackson dodged his fist and caught hold of him, pulling his arms behind his back so he couldn't move.

"Enough!" I heard Jackson say to him. "She's not the enemy."

"Look at her," Seb spat, breathing hard, "she's one of them!"

"Ava's your way out of this mess," said Jackson as Seb struggled, futile against Jackson's bulk. "We need her."

He let go of Seb, who dived towards me. As I braced myself, Jackson stopped him once again, hauling him away and shoving him into the surrounding crowd. Seb looked like he was going to attack me again but Anna stepped forward, reaching her small arms around him and pulling her husband into her, like she used to do with Eve. That small gesture was enough to break him: his knees gave way as she cradled him, his whole body shaking with sobs as his grief, unspoken, poured out for everyone to see.

I knew where he'd been, what he'd seen: where Eve had been. To see the place where your child had seen the last moments of their life, alone, was enough to destroy any father or mother. And it was all because of me. I struggled to my feet and headed for the door; the crowd parted before me as if I was contagious. In the commotion, the front door had been left unlocked and I slipped out quietly. I would never enter that building again. Too many people there were hurting because of me; I was better off alone. The weight of Eve's death, Seb's anger and Anna's grief were so heavy that it was a struggle to breathe. I forced my legs to move and my feet to walk. To my relief, the late afternoon sun was cooler on my skin than earlier in the day as I headed slowly for the warehouse. Seb's words echoed in my head, his face burning with hate stuck in my mind. I had to get away from everyone until we were ready to strike; I didn't have the strength to fight them anymore. The change in me was growing stronger with every minute that passed. The Ghosts' blood flowed through my veins and I could hear them calling to me. I had one chance to destroy the Ghosts; I couldn't let them get to me first.

The darkness of the warehouse was pleasant, its damp coolness safe. I waited, lying prone on the camp-bed, listening to the sound of people in the distance moving things and voices calling to each other, rallying each other. There was the grind of tyres on the dirt as the floodlights were wheeled away on carts but as the dusk fell, the world outside of the warehouse became silent again. Heaving myself off the bed, I wandered slowly over to the window. The moon was just visible in the twilight, bathing everything in a strange, haunting light.

The street beyond my window was empty: nothing moved, not even the leaves on the trees. It was as if nature itself was holding its breath. I leant on the windowsill, pressing my head against the cool pane of glass. I, too, was waiting. As darkness fell, I took a breath and exhaled hard on the window. A cloudy circle formed, proof I was still alive, and I drew my initials in it: *AS*. Through the clear line of the 'A' I saw the Ghosts approach. My skin crawled as my head filled with their thoughts. They were here to hunt those who were left. They sensed our vulnerability. Dashing for the door, I swung it open but they ignored me, not even glancing in my direction; I wasn't worth their time. I thought about running out in front of them but they were twice my size and double my strength. I had nothing left inside anymore. Watching them heading for the unlit school, helpless to stop them, I let out a cry of frustration.

290

I wanted to run and tell the others to hide, but I wouldn't get there in time. Standing in the darkness as their tall, thin figures drifted away from me, I felt like a child again: helpless and small.

I waited for the screaming, the gunfire and the wailing but it didn't come. I held my breath until I could take it no longer; I walked as fast as I could towards the school. I would face Seb and Anna, all of them if it meant knowing they were safe. As I took my next step, there was an explosion and the night's sky turned red. Clouds of smoke billowed from the direction of the school.

"No!" I cried.

I pushed myself into a run but after only a minute I collapsed to my knees. Debris was falling from the sky, illuminated by the flames of the burning school. With a wail, I dropped my head to my knees. I stayed there, unable to move.

Chapter 23

As the fires began to die down and the sun began to rise once more, I crawled back to the warehouse. Stripped of hope, I curled up on the hard concrete and closed my tired eyes. Eve found me as I slept. I saw her face: soft, round and laughing, but I couldn't catch up with her. I saw the Ghost that killed her, that bloody Babit and the place where she had once stood. She was screaming, crying out for me: "Ava, Ava, Ava!" Her screaming became louder until it made my ears bleed; it was all I could hear. There was no longer the sound of the wind in the trees, the birds in the sky or the sound of feet pounding the ground.

I woke up to find the screaming was my own: a strange, inhuman noise that felt like it projected from my chest as if my body was crying out without my mouth knowing it. Reaching out a hand in the hazy light of the warehouse, I felt walls on either side of me; I was huddled in a corner, my arm around my knees. I shivered, despite the burning fever that had taken hold of me. Pushing myself up using the walls for support, I waited for the nauseating spinning to pass. Then I remembered: the school, the explosion, the fire. Sinking back to the floor, my hand brushed against something soft on the ground next to me. Handfuls of hair covered the floor. I touched my head, felt nothing but naked skin: another part of my humanity gone. I let out a small laugh and curled back up again. What was the point? I might as well wait for death to find me here, as I knew it inevitably would.

A loud banging on the door jolted me from sleep. It seemed louder than normal, disrupting the stillness inside. There was no power left in my muscles as I pushed against the wall, attempting to stand. I tried to call out but my words were nothing but dry breath. Light flooded in as the door swung open, tearing at my skin like thousands of razor-sharp needles. Strong hands lifted me up, taking hold of my chin, and I dared to look into the eyes of the person who had interrupted my death.

"Ava," said Jackson, his low voice finally reaching me. "Get up, we're ready!"

I stared into his face, reaching up to touch his skin. *He wasn't there; he wasn't real.* It was just my dying mind playing tricks. Closing my eyes again, I let my hand fall to my side once more. But the hands around me held on.

"Ava," said Jackson again with urgency.

I could hear the panic in his voice.

"Ava!"

His hand brushed over my face like the faintest of breezes. I forced my heavy eyes open and took another look at him. His eyes were wide, his lips parted as he called my name.

"Jackson? You're OK?" I managed.

"Thank God!" he said, his hands still supporting my weight. "I'm fine. It's you I'm worried about. Can you stand?"

I blinked slowly, took a deep breath, and nodded.

"But the explosion?"

"Don't worry about that now, we're all OK. No one was in there," Jackson explained, pulling my arm over his shoulders. He led me to the camping-bed where he sat down heavily next to me and swung his bag onto the floor.

He handed me a bottle of water and some jerky. The water slipped easily down my throat, cool and refreshing, cushioning the salty-sweet jerky that followed it. Thirst gripped me and I finished the bottle in a few gulps. Life filled my body once more and death retracted its claws, drawing back, yet still lurking nearby for its moment. I mustered a small smile at Jackson. His eyes wandered to my bald scalp, but he said nothing. I wanted to say something but couldn't find the words.

"Let's go then, get this over with," I said instead.

I pulled the hood of my jumper back over my head, drawing the cuffs over my hands as we left the warehouse. It must have been late afternoon; the sun was starting to lose height amongst the pale, grey clouds. The smell of rain hung in the air, mingled with fire and blood. Instead of leading me to the school, Jackson led me in the opposite direction from the destruction of the explosion and towards the gaping hole in the perimeter fence. A small, solar power buggy was parked just outside and he ushered me into it.

"It's slow, but faster than walking," he said, climbing in next to me.

The vehicle was cramped with the two of us in there but all the same it whirred into life and we powered off into the distance, following a road away from the compound. The world flew past; piles of rubble that were once homes were visible in every direction. But the destruction seemed normal to me now; instead, I thought of a world without it and the lives the survivors would make for themselves once the Barrier was gone and the invaders had left. I thought of the life I might have had. Glancing over at Jackson, I wondered what he would be doing in five years' time, or even in two years. I wondered what he would be doing tomorrow.

****

I heard the familiar drone of the Barrier before I saw it: the tell-tale hum of my old prison. My stomach sank and

294

a cold feeling of dread crept over my skin. Here it was: the end. The place I'd wanted desperately to escape from would be what saved us all in the end. Rows of floodlights and generators had been set up, ready and waiting like an army. They all pointed towards a large crater, a matter of metres from the Barrier, much like the one Jackson had pulled me from a week ago, except this one was much bigger. We climbed out of the buggy and wandered over to the edge as people milled around looking busy. Apprehension was tangible in the air; some of them stopped to stare at us but we carried on.

The crater was vast and deep; it felt as if I were peering down into the centre of the Earth. My toes were dangerously close to the edge. I shifted my foot and a trickle of earth came away and ran down into the hole. The urge to jump in and end it all right here was overwhelming. It would be so easy. I leant further over the precipice.

"Ava," came a voice.

I turned to see Anna and retreated from the edge. She looked older than when I had seen her only a day ago: paler and thinner. Grief exuded from her like a smell; it changed her face and her body, even the hair on her head had lost its lustre.

"Looks like you're ready," I said.

She gave me a smile but it was hollow and empty.

"Yes, all we need now is you," she said.

I nodded.

"Lead the way."

The three of us walked across the site to the Barrier; I swallowed down the nausea that crept up my throat. I let them talk, barely able to stay steady on my feet.

"We just need to lay out the last few metres of cabling. You got a location?" Anna asked.

"I know where they need to go," interjected Jackson.

Anna nodded.

"Okay, sure," she said.

"You go get them sorted. I'll be over soon to show you where," he explained.

Anna shrugged and joined the others. Seb was among them. I didn't look over; I could barely tolerate Jackson and Anna seeing me like this, never mind Seb. Closing my eyes, I could hear the Ghosts deep in the earth waiting for the darkness, preparing for their departure. They churned, shifting and writhing in the dark tunnels of their living ships. They wanted an end, I felt it. But, again, something made my hate soften. The small voice called to me one last time before it was squashed by the roar of their collective minds.

"I'm coming in with you," said Jackson quietly, his words shaking me from my daze.

I opened my mouth to argue but he cut me off.

"Don't argue with me, Ava, you can barely walk! There's no way you can haul a hundred metres of cable to the generation terminal."

He was right. I could feel my strength draining away again as I settled down against the tree.

"How long until sun down?" I asked.

"About four hours but I reckon they will come out sooner, at dusk probably. They can smell us," Jackson said, "we're too tempting."

All I had to do now was wait. Jackson left, joining the others. They followed him to a point two hundred or so metres away from where I sat and stared up at the Barrier as Jackson explained something to them that I couldn't hear. I glanced around at the sparse woodland that had survived the mothership's landing and breathed in the smell of the damp, earthy ground. The grass was soft beneath me and I savoured the feel of it, compared to the roughness of the twigs and dead leaves. A caterpillar crawled slowly through the layers of grass and leaves and earth on a journey to somewhere awfully important; I envied him.

Jackson returned a little while later with more food and water as I waited, slipping in and out of the shadowy Ghost world. I let him make a fuss of me, in a way that reminded me of Lucy, and as I rested, the thought of all the people I had lost along the way crossed my mind. I tried to remember something good about each of them, a happy memory we had together, and to forget all the terrible things that had happened. In my desperation, I started to pray. I spoke to the God I had forgotten about, whom I had ignored since I was a child – the heavenly Father my mother used to tell me about. As I prayed, the sorrow I carried lifted from me, and the heaviness that sucked me down, dissipated. As the dusk fell, energy returned to my limbs. I may be dying but I was not dead yet. I was no longer full of hate; instead, another emotion was taking its place. My love for Anna, for Jackson, for Eve, even for Seb, propelled me forwards. The end was in sight and I was ready for it.

Chapter 24

Following close behind Jackson, we made our way to the entry point on the Barrier. Even from this side, it reflected back a woodland scene; a clever mirage that changed with the seasons and altered for day and night. I dropped my hood to feel the coolness of the evening, refreshing on my paper-white skin, ignoring the stares of the others. Before me lay a maze of cables running from the floodlights to the bundle Jackson hugged close to his chest; others were plugged into solar generators, ready to give them a much-needed boost. It was everything we had; I prayed it would be enough. Standing in front of the Barrier, I pushed the charge button on the Mech arm. A strange tingling ran down the back of my neck and into my spine, and red light illuminated on the Mech arm. Adrenaline ripped through me, pounding my heart against my ribs as the dark blood in my veins rushed around my body.

"When it turns blue, Ava, it's ready," said Jackson, his arms full of cable, and even more of it bundled in his bag.

We waited in the silence above ground; I could feel the Ghosts surging up from the depths of the earth.

"They're coming," I said to Jackson.
As I spoke, the earth beneath our feet began to shift and a deep rumbling filled the air. I turned to Jackson in panic.

"The button, Ava –push the button!" he shouted over the roaring of the earth.
I slammed the button with my hand as they emerged from the depths like a great swarm of pale insects. They knocked over floodlights and threw the generators as they came. There was screaming and guns firing. A jolt of electricity

ran through my body and my flesh shook as the Mech arm drew power from the implant in my neck. The sound of slaughter behind me faded away as I dropped to my knees, a pulse emitting from the arm, firing over and over in rapid succession. My muscles twitched and my skin crawled with agonising pins and needles. I vomited up the small amount that was in my stomach before Jackson reached around my waist and hauled me up once more.

"Just hang on!" he said. "Look!"

Through the blur of pain, I could see the Barrier flickering before my eyes. It was fading away, revealing a single row of Mechs waiting for us. There was a final jolt and a searing pain in the back of my neck while blood seeped out and soaked into my jumper, warm and thick. With quivering fingers, I felt the metal of the implant once buried in my neck, now exposed.

"Go hide!" shouted Jackson, pushing past me, but I ignored him.

This is what I was meant to do; I had been restored for this final task. Lifting my arm, I fired into the wall of Mechs. They fell left and right as I approached, their shots flying past me until one struck me on the cheek, streaking my face with a deep line of blackish-red. Wiping the blood away, I carried on; there was no pain anymore. Without the implant, my body was changing. I was already dead. By my side, Jackson pounded rounds into Mechs as we crossed over the Barrier, back into our old prison. As the last one fell, he gathered up his coils of wire and we ran. My last reserves of energy and adrenaline propelled me forward. My eyes were fixed on the generation terminal. Coils of cable thudded behind us as we got near, but still more Mechs poured out.

"Go!" I shouted.

Jackson nodded and I watched him weaving through them as I took their fire. For a moment, I thought I was going to drown in bullets, then there was a cry from behind me and a fresh round of shots fired over my head. Several of the Mechs dropped to the floor as I turned to see Seb and a few of his men running towards me, their guns blazing and their eyes wide with anger as they bellowed a war cry for all those they had lost.

They pushed past me and silently I thanked them. Hunting through the chaos of metal and bullets for Jackson, I spotted him as he disappeared inside the terminal, his bag discarded on the floor and the thick, yellow cable plugged into the outside. A wave of relief washed over me; he was inside – this was the end. Yet to my horror, a Ghost leapt out of the trees, its long, sinewy legs carrying it in bounds towards him.

"No!" I breathed. "Not now, not after all of this!" Forcing one leg in front of the other, I charged through the woodland, a roar escaping my lips that I never knew I had inside of me. As the night grew deeper, I felt alive. My body changed as I ran, blood seeping from my eyes, my ears, my nose. My legs grew longer and thinner, and my arms elongated. The bones in my skull cracked and broke, re-joining in a strange, inhuman form. The colours of the day evaporated and I entered the shadowy world of the Ghosts. I heard everything, smelt the scent of humans, and other Ghosts; my teeth were sharp as knives and my claws were vicious. Voices rang clear inside me like a rushing wind. *Gather, gather, gather!* Then barely a whisper: *let us go…*

Barrelling into the Ghost, I sent it flying. It landed several metres from the terminal and lay there unmoving, but still, I went for it. Like a wild animal, I ripped through its skin and tore at its flesh until I smelt the stench of its

300

blood on the ground, and felt the warmth of it pooling around my feet. I laughed as I forgot who I was; as all I had been – Ava and Alec – slipped away.

****

The darkness was so deep that it suffocated the men and women who fought inside the crater, battling yet outnumbered and overpowered. Then there was light. As deep and terrifying as the dark had been, the light was stronger and more powerful; its brilliance drove out the darkness and brought a ripple of hope among the fighters. A cry of joy carried on the wind across the battlefield as the odds levelled.

The light was so bright and blinding that, as Jackson Quinn stepped out of the generation terminal with his gun raised, he had to shield his eyes with his free hand; it reached into the far corners of the crater, leaving no shadows to hide in, burning the pale flesh of the Ghosts. The smell of seared flesh followed him as he left the generation terminal; their terrible screams followed him as they died, and he prayed that their agony was long and terrible. He prayed for human survivors. Shifting his gun, he wandered towards the floodlights. Something twitched on the periphery of his vision and he dropped his hand from his eyes, squinting against the brightness of the lights. From the shadows, a large Ghost charged at him, its teeth bared, spikes along the contours of its face and down its spine. Without hesitation, Jackson took aim and fired the last two rounds he had left. The beast hit the ground, coming to a grinding halt a few metres from where he stood. The force of its giant body showered him with blood and earth. Lifting his arm to his face, Jackson wiped away the thick, dark, blood before wandering over to the Ghost. He gave it a hard kick and the creature rolled over onto its back, its blood already seeping into the ground around it. A smile formed on his lips as he surveyed his adversary. Then he saw the Mech arm clinging to one of the creature's half-formed limbs.

He fell to his knees at the Ghost's side, bile rising in his throat, a single word on his parted lips.

"Ava!"

Epilogue

I couldn't see Anna and Jackson, but I could sense them; their shapes in the darkness, pulsing and warm. Their voices vibrated inside my head, joined by the thousands of other screaming ones.

I am still here. Anna! Jackson!

But all that spewed from my lips was a torrent of clicks and grunts. Pain splintered through my side, a bleak darkness pulling at my consciousness. Trying to breathe through the agony, I slumped back on the ground while a worrying coldness crept over my skin.

I could wait. They would come back for me eventually, when all the fighting was over. They would help me then, after everything I had sacrificed, I wouldn't be forgotten.

Yet the alien voices kept me from the sleep I so desperately craved. The wailing and sadness filled every part of me. Though it wasn't just pain, but relief. A letting go of something that clawed at the Ghost's very being; at me. Freedom filled my mind as consciousness slipped from my grasp.

Then hands lifted me, warm on my paper-white skin; a small pinprick of hope. My breathing eased as the small bit of humanity left inside of me pushed back against the alien DNA, and I allowed myself to wonder if I would find a way out of this? Would I ever be Ava again?

I wasn't done fighting.

About the Author

Lydia Baker is an author of science-fiction and fantasy, she loves to write novels you can escape into.

Her novel 'The Return of the Queen' won the Pink Heart Society Reviewers Choice Award for Best Paranormal/Fantasy Romance in 2019 and 'Ava' was Shortlisted for the Agora Books - Work in Progress Prize in 2019.

When she's not writing she loves to read, to run and crochet (not all at the same time though!). She lives in Crawley with her husband and four children.

Printed in Great Britain
by Amazon